DESTINY OF A FABLE

ALLY MARIE

Destiny of a Fable

THE FABLE SAVIOR TRILOGY

BOOK ONE

Ebook ISBN: 979-8-9877068-0-0

Paperback ISBN: 979-8-9877068-4-8

Hardcover ISBN: 979-8-9877068-3-1

Audiobook ISBN: 979-8-9877068-2-4

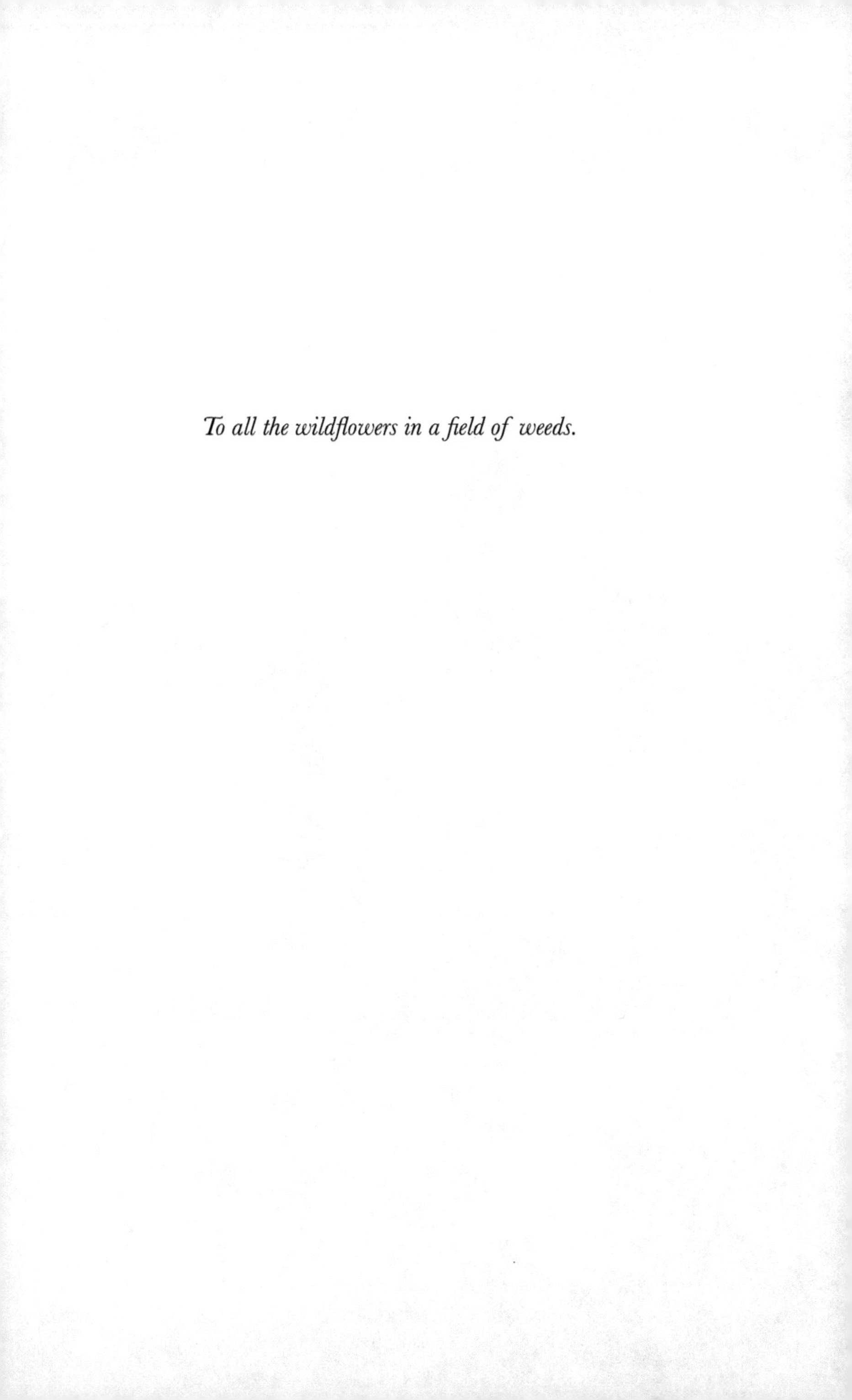

To all the wildflowers in a field of weeds.

I

At the end of the day, I only wanted someone to be here when I needed them. To be wanted. But what I understood now, at three forty-seven on a Monday afternoon, was that I wasn't enough for either of my parents to remember to pick me up from school. But it had been this way since the day I was born. If it hadn't been for Grandma Ana, I didn't know how I would have survived this long.

In thinking of her, the bells chimed from the dark-brown brick cathedral across the street from the school. The school I shouldn't have gone to, but my grandmother made sure I did. Saying that I deserved to go. I held my knees to my chest, pulling down my pinstriped skirt, thinking of my grandmother holding my hand as a child while taking me into that church and reminding me that my parents would be back. That they loved me.

I groaned. This sour mood wasn't only because of my parents. I hadn't been able to sleep well in weeks. Those visions wouldn't go away, and they were all the same. I'd had visions since I was ten, so they weren't anything new, but with each one came an uneasy feeling in the pit of my stomach because they never led to anything good. I couldn't understand what they were trying to tell me. I hated them. It also didn't help that my mom told me to think of them as warnings. What were they warning me of? As I inhaled the humid Canada air, I tried to recall the visions again.

"Another late game, Miss Jenkins?"

That deep baritone voice belonged to Principal Walmudder. Dressed in an elegant golden dress jacket, gray dress pants, and black dress shoes, he was the kind of principal who was the first to arrive, last to leave.

"Yeah, you never know with those." I prayed he wouldn't ask any more about it. I didn't need anyone prying into my life. "But my mom just called." I held up my phone as if it were proof. "She'll be here soon." Of course, I was lying.

He stepped out into the crosswalk to head to the parking garage, but not before turning and giving me a warm smile.

"Well all right then. You have a great evening, Miss Jenkins."

"You too." I waved to him as he walked away.

Principal Walmudder hadn't even made it to the garage when I heard the sound of clinking against tin. I groaned again. Reaching past the protection of the awning, one, then two drops of water splashed across my fingertips.

I hadn't even thought to bring an umbrella. Guess I would have to walk home in the rain. My parents were lucky we only lived fifteen minutes from the school. And with that thought, I trudged out into the rain.

Most people would be glad to live in a town where there were millions of things happening. Like free concerts and movie screenings. Even the population of over a million people was something short of amazing. The weather wasn't bad either. It was August now with temperatures in the eighties. The rain helped bring the heat down, but I couldn't find joy in those things like everyone else could. I had friends —well, maybe acquaintances. But it was better in my own little world.

The bustling noise was finally out of earshot, meaning I could breathe. Think. My school was on the edge of town, but I enjoyed living just outside the city. It was peaceful. Miles and miles of fields passed down through families stole away the noise that made it difficult to think. In my neighborhood, our homes were sold to make bigger ones. But at least we still had ours.

Nearly halfway home, the rain had turned into a downpour. Leaving me no choice but to find cover. I knew what was nearby that would keep me warm until the rain settle down. So I crawled under the fence and ran toward the barn.

Once inside, the wet, woody scent melted away the tension in my muscles and body. I'd found this barn four years ago to this day. I'd been running from a downpour much like this one. Something about the warmth and smell of it calmed me. So a few days later, my parents and I came back to fix it up. I wanted a place to call my own. A place to come to when the world felt like it was falling apart. Which was exactly what was going on now.

With the rain still pinging on the tin roof, I pulled out my phone, hoping one of my parents would have called. But the only thing staring back at me was a picture of me, my mom, and Damian, my adopted brother, around last year's Christmas tree. And a bow on my mom's stomach. Even looking at the picture now, I couldn't understand why my dad got so angry when my mom asked him to be in the picture.

I let my back slide down the side of the banister my parents had built together. God, how they hated to do it. I couldn't understand why they disliked each other so much.

Could I have been the reason they were so unhappy? My chin trembled at the thought of it. But it made sense. My dad spent all his time at work. My mom went on trips for months at a time. What else would they stay away from? It couldn't be each other, because I was the only one at home. I held my knees to my chest as my body shook with uncontrollable sobs. Even now, neither of them came to pick me up. Easily forgotten, it may be easier for them to forget me entirely. I *was* the reason they were so unhappy.

"Rylee! Rylee!" It was my mom, her singsong voice clear even through the rain picking up again. "Rylee!" Her light red hair glistened through the transparent purple curtain draped across the doorframe.

"I'm right here, Mom." Standing, I wiped at my eyes before she saw me.

Her heavy boots stomped on the hardwood as she made her way to me. What I wanted was for her to run to me and hug me. What I got was her arms folded across her small chest and a frown on her dark thin lips.

"Why weren't you at school?" She shook her head, rearranging her features to soften like moms were supposed to do when their children were missing. "We were worried."

Sure she was. That's why she'd called.

"I got tired of waiting. So, I thought I would just walk home," I snapped. "Not like it's my first time doing it." I brushed past her, out of the barn, and toward the van. I wasn't going to give her the satisfaction of knowing how hurt she made me feel.

Opening the door to get into the van, Damian was asleep. I ran my hand through his red hair. My finger grazed the scar he got from a baseball accident a few weeks ago on his left eye. And as always, when it came to my mom and her moods, my dad stayed quiet as he sat in the passenger side. And then, the driver-side door slammed, rattling the van and waking up poor little Damian. I met my mom's dagger glare in the mirror, and I couldn't look away. More now because I was giving her one of my own. I wasn't the one in trouble here. She was.

"If you must know why we couldn't pick you up"—she cut her eyes to my dad now—"your father locked his keys in his car again, so I had to go pick him up."

It was a valid excuse—I could give her that—but she should have called. She always acted like I was just supposed to understand and accept her actions. Like everything she did was right, and that was just the way it was because she was the adult. Sometimes I just wished she would listen to herself talk and pay attention to what she did. Then she would see she's not as right as she thought she was.

"How was school?" My dad always had a deep raspy voice that, when I was younger, kind of scared me. Like a monster wanting to eat me. I knew my dad's question now was more to break the tension as my mom pulled out onto the main road.

But before I could give him a half answer, Damian screamed, "I want juice!" Damian had been the only saving grace in this whole family, but honestly, I pitied him. He was only five and didn't know how big of a disappointment his parents would be.

"We don't have any juice, sweetie." My mom gave my dad a look I knew all too well. The one that said, *You should have remembered.*

As Damian continued to complain, I reached into my backpack, pulled out the Capri Sun I had left over from lunch, poked the straw in, and handed it to his tiny, outstretched hands. His blue eyes grew wide as saucers. "Here you go, bud." I tousled his red hair. It was so weird how Damian looked like me. I figured my mom wanted a kid close enough to look like me so people wouldn't ask questions, but I couldn't imagine they gave her an adopt-a-kid catalogue.

My dad turned to Damian but directed his comment to me. I swear, it was like he couldn't even stand to look at me sometimes. "Thank you, hun."

"Someone has to watch after the kid since it doesn't seem like his parents will," I huffed, turning back to the window.

"Rylee Cornelia Jenkins, last time I checked, you aren't perfect either," my mom scorned.

"I never said I was," I muttered.

My mom sighed, and I couldn't help but glance in the rearview mirror, because *that* sigh meant that she was sorry about something. Maybe she was going to say she was sorry for not calling. Or maybe she was going to say that she was sorry that she hadn't really been around that much and that she wanted to be now.

"I know you and I don't see each other much, but everything I do—"

No, just more excuses.

"You do it because you love me." I rolled my eyes and groaned. "Which makes no sense to me. I mean how can you barely being around me prove in any way that you love me?"

Her eyes pulled away from the mirror. She knew I was right. The van remained ear-ringingly silent. And honestly, it was better this way. The less we spoke, the less it would hurt me when they made another excuse as to why they were doing whatever they were doing. So, I rested my head against the window, watching rain slither down it like a snake. The vibration of the van was like a rocking chair, lulling me to sleep.

"Bridge!" Damian screamed, waking me.

In my daze, I drew in deep, labored breaths, trying to remember where I was. My head swung around until I saw Damian. I was in the van. Damian was talking about the bridge, but his voice drew on a memory he'd never shed. I still couldn't believe it when we'd met with the social worker about Damian. His birth parents died on the bridge and he'd been there.

"It's okay, bud. Just close your eyes and hold my hand, okay?" He took my hand quickly and closed his eyes even though we were miles away from the bridge, even further away from danger.

"Rylee." My mom's eyes met mine again in the rearview mirror. But in them wasn't her usually venomous glare. Now they contained something different. Something pained. "There's something I need to tell you."

And there it was. The words she would always say when she was leaving again.

"How long is it this time?" I couldn't bring myself to meet her gaze. To see that look in her eyes. The look that said, *I'm sorry I have to go, but they mean more to me than you guys do.*

"Ouch, sissy! Too tight," Damian cried, trying to pull away.

"Sorry, little man." He laughed as I kissed each of his tiny knuckles.

I normally would love the sound of his little hiccupping giggles, but right now, they couldn't stop me from thinking of my mom leaving us again. She'd missed so much already. She hadn't been there when the principal told me that I was able to graduate early. She hadn't been there when Damian hit his first home run at Little League. She hadn't been there when I finished reading all the historical fiction books at our small library and they put my picture on the wall. And even made me a medal. They weren't a big deal, small things really, but she'd been there for none of it.

My mom stole a glance at my dad, and though I couldn't see her expression now, his mirrored hers from just seconds ago. So, I asked my question again, with worry of my own. "Mom, please. How long?"

She let out a sigh so agonizing that it hurt *me*. Did it hurt her that much to have to say it? She'd told me plenty of times she was going out of town. What made this one any different?

"Rylee, they need me in London for . . ." She took in a deep breath. "For the next nine months."

My mom hadn't been gone for more than a few months at a time. I didn't want her gone that long then, and I didn't want it now. We didn't see eye to eye a lot, but as strange as it was, I looked up to her. It was like everything I couldn't stand about her, I admired. I admired how bullheaded she was. I admired her don't-take-nothing-from-no-one attitude. But the one thing I could never understand about her was how she could be so kind and loving to all the people she helped, but not to her own family. But my mouth didn't want to say any of that.

"So, you're okay with missing my eighteenth birthday?" I bit down on the inside of my cheek to hide my true pain.

"You make it sound so black and white, Rylee."

"That's because it is, Mother," I snapped, drawing out the name I'd call her when she'd piss me off.

We were coming closer to the bridge, and even from here, the bright red tape caught my eye as a tattered piece swayed in the wind. Bright red tape. I'd seen that before today. But where? It wasn't here yesterday when my mom drove us home. I let my eyes follow the river under the bridge. The water was clear. I closed my eyes, trying to remember. My first vision had exposed a piece of the tape flapping in the wind. As it was right now. My other vision displayed the clear water, but something had disturbed its current.

Looking to it now, the water continued to sway like grass in the wind. What did it mean?

My mom's voice broke my concentration. "Not everything is about you."

Was she seriously still on this? If she wanted a fight, then I would give her one. "You're right. Because if it was for once, it would mean you gave a damn about someone other than yourself," I barked back with all the bite I had. I couldn't sit here and take this anymore. If she was going to leave, I wanted her to know exactly how I felt. "You run off everywhere to help people you've never even heard of, but yet you can't even think to stay where *your family* needs you. For crying out loud, you're about to be a mother again to twins. But you know what"—I threw up my hands—"if you want to go to London, then go. But I never want to see you again."

With my last words hanging in the bitter-tasting air, the van accelerated.

"Liliana, what are you doing?" my dad asked, fear coding every word. But my mom's only answer was steering the van into a sharp right turn, veering toward the side of the bridge. "You're going to run us off into the water!"

But my mom didn't stop. She looked at me in the mirror, but those devilish, crimson eyes didn't belong to my mom. I glanced away from her as the hood of the van clawed through the guardrail. Then came the loud crunch of glass, and a crack spread across the windshield. With nothing else to destroy, we plummeted into the rocky water.

"Sissy help me!"

Air stole into my lungs as water spewed out of my mouth. After it was over, I tried to figure out the images in front of me. Blurred shades of cream and green motioned passed me.

"Rylee, Rylee, can you hear me?" It was my dad. The knowledge of it helped me focus on my vision, and the image sharpened until I made out the water beads on his head.

"Dad?" I croaked. "Where's Mom and Damian?" My dad turned his gaze back to the water, its current disturbed like I had seen it in my vision. I stared to the water, too, as if it would give me the answer to my unspoken question. But they couldn't be dead.

"You have to"—another cough ripped through me— "save them!"

The color and life drained from his eyes, but he didn't speak. And he didn't need to. My mom and Damian were dead.

"Rylee," he'd finally managed to say, "I have to go get us help, but I need you to stay here. Will you do that?"

I couldn't give him a verbal answer, so I just shook my head as he stood and walked farther out onto the road.

I leaned against the guardrail as I watched my dad stand in the middle of the road waiting for someone to stop. The sun lay just below the tree line, which meant no one would be down this way for hours.

Tears stung my eyes. My mom tried to kill us. Though my words had literally drove her to it, *she'd* been the one to swerve the car. But why? Why would she try to kill her family? She was upset with me, but it didn't make sense to kill us.

A car honk drew me from my thoughts. A gold Mini Cooper made its way toward my dad, but it wasn't slowing down. The car continued down the road. Why wasn't my dad moving? My throat was too raw to form even a single word let alone scream for him to get out of the way. So, I would run. But in doing so, my ankle caught a piece of the guardrail, twisting it sideways with a loud *pop* and sending a searing pain through my ankle. And then came the sound of metal against bone. My focus turned toward the sound. The Mini Cooper had careened into my dad's body, which flew in the air and bent as if he were made of rubber. His body crashed behind the car, his left and right leg both turned at the knees at ninety-degree angles.

"No!" I screamed, trying to stand only to fall back again after forgetting about my ankle.

The red of the taillights dimmed out, followed by someone opening and closing the door. A lanky, brown-haired, light-skinned man exited, his face unreadable. Maybe he was coming to make sure my dad was all right. But as the man kneeled to him, something told me that wasn't the case. The man grinned and sat up on his back legs. What the hell was this man planning to do? The lanky man drew up the sleeve of my dad's jacket as he continued to smile. Panic rose in my throat. My dad lay there motionless. Was he dead? Was this man trying to hurt him more? I couldn't sit here and wait for it to happen.

I went to stand again, remembering my ankle this time. I slowed my pace and winced when I finally reached my feet.

"Leave him alone!" I managed in a raw voice as I hobbled on one foot.

The lanky man glared at me, laughing. "Let me work. You'll get your chance."

My chance? My chance to what, die? If my dad wasn't already.

"I said leave him alone!" Something settled in the pit of my stomach then. It was as if every nerve in my body buzzed with this almost unbearable electricity. And I liked it. It made me feel like I could do something. "We don't want your help."

The man glared at me, but then he didn't. He was gone.

In one second, he was back again, only now he stood in front of me, causing me to fall at the unexpected sight of him. His brown eyes shifted into an illuminating white. White light clawed up his body like spiderwebs. I shook my head as if that would erase what I was seeing, but it didn't, and he now towered over me.

"Paraseum!" Every muscle in my body, even my eyelids, went rigid. How had he been able to do this? "You're going to be a lot of fun." He stared back at my dad. "But *he's* on today's agenda." And with another blink, the man reappeared beside my dad.

The man drew up his own sleeve. I couldn't tell if what I was seeing was even real, but on his right wrist was a skull tattoo. The eye sockets deep and soulless as the man in front of me.

His mouth moved, but all I heard was a buzzing sound. In seconds white illuminating smoke drifted in the air. As if all of this couldn't be any more out of the ordinary, the smoke made its way to the man's skull tattoo and into its mouth, looking as if it were freezing from the inside. My dad's body twitched as the lanky man did whatever he was doing to him. In a matter of seconds, my dad was beginning to disintegrate, his body falling to dust at his feet.

I sat frozen. I had to do something. I wouldn't lose anyone else today. I wanted to live. And then came the electric sensation in my nerves again. But something felt different about it. As if it were trying to come out of my body. With that thought, a spark of light came from somewhere near me. I stared down to my fingers, and sparks of electricity wove around them. This couldn't be happening. I had to be seeing things. I stared at the unexplainable sparks around my fingers for a good minute before realizing they weren't going away.

I needed the sparks to do something. I needed to throw

them at the man and make him stop before he killed my dad. And without me doing anything, sparks flew from my fingers and toward the man.

He screamed, jumping back while the smoke faded away. And my body unfroze. "You little brat! You'll pay for that!" His eyes were like daggers tearing into my soul as he stalked over to me. I had to stop him. I didn't want to die.

I noticed the water puddle and trail from last night's rain. I needed the electricity strong enough to knock him out even if it would do the same to me. Electricity sparked to life as if to answer my plea. My dad still wasn't moving. I placed my hand into the water puddle, praying one of us would make it out of here alive.

2

Two months passed, and I hadn't even realized it. I'd watched the world around me change, but I stayed still. Stuck in that day. Those moments. Those thoughts. The things I couldn't explain. Nothing about that day made sense to me. But at least my dad and I had both survived. There'd been a service for my mom at a food bank. Home for the Help of Dundas. She spent a lot of time there when she was home. I couldn't bring myself to go. To see her family. To see her smile or her eyes or her nose in every person's face serving food. I just couldn't.

In the months following my mom's and Damian's deaths, darkness and solitude had become my companions. My dad used this as a reason not to bother me. But dammit, I wanted that. For him to want to check on me every five seconds. I thought he might when he realized I didn't want to be around anyone else.

After a few days of staring at my bedroom door in hopes that he would come but never did, I stopped waiting. Then one warm mid-October morning, my dad suggested I talk to someone. And now, here I slouched in the passenger seat of my dad's old Odyssey to see an out-of-town therapist who'd received a five-star review on Yelp.

Like all other times when my dad didn't know how to help me, off he sent me to someone who could fix me. But in part, this, too, was my fault. I couldn't talk about that day or anything after it. So many things didn't make sense about it. I saw things that shouldn't have been normal. I *felt* things that shouldn't have been normal. I tried to tell myself that it had all been a dream. That the lanky man, whose name I found out was Nikolas, hadn't hit my dad and paralyzed him from the waist down. But it was useless.

Most of all, though, I didn't want to talk about that day because of my mom. What I'd said to her had killed her. It had killed my only brother. I still woke up in the middle of the night hearing him scream. That helpless plea in his innocent blue eyes.

My head now rested on the window, eyes closed, cooling my feverish headache. The slashing rain was the perfect atmosphere for my current state. Lightning attempted to brighten the ominous sky. As the lightning hit again and again, I found myself counting how long until the thunder rolled. A game Damian and I played when he'd sneaked into my room one night. I could still hear his chipmunk voice as he counted with me.

. . . Eight . . . Nine . . . Ten.

When opening my eyes seconds later, lightning struck near my window as if trying to kiss me. As close as it had been on that day.

That low hum of electricity tickling the tips of my fingers. That unbearable surge of a bolt pulsating through my body as my hand landed in the puddle of water. I shook my head. I couldn't think about this again. I drew my hand from the window now as if I'd been subconsciously trying to stop the lightning from getting to me. Laying my head back to clear my mind, my eyes grew heavy. The harsh rain died away with every beat of my heart. It was all in my head.

"Liliana's birthday is today. She would have . . ." But my dad trailed off as if he wanted to say something nice, but he just couldn't bring himself to do it.

My dad had been hurt by my mom's death; it'd been one of the reasons why he'd closed himself off to me. When he would try to nicely talk about her, it always seemed forced. I wasn't in the mood for his small talk, so I turned back to the window.

"She would have been thirty-five." He chuckled then. "She would have probably told us not to do anything, but really she would want something."

I thought of the last thing my mom told me before she died. "No, she wouldn't have been here, remember?"

The van fell silent again as I stared out the window, trying to think of anything but today. Or the last two months, for that matter.

"I think Farrah can help you." My dad focused on the road.

I turned to him now. "Are you going to see her too?"

He reached with a bit of difficulty to turn down the radio as he answered. "No."

"But don't you think it would help you too?" I bit down on my lip, picking my next words carefully. "I mean you kind of seem like you're . . . you're closing yourself off too."

His brow furrowed in thought. "Rylee, you don't . . ." He ran his fingers through his hair. "You don't understand how hard this has been for me."

I laughed hysterically. "Are you freaking kidding me?" My first thought went to the day of their funeral when I'd tried to drown myself in my bathtub. "I saw the glass lodged into Mom's head. I watched Damian suffer. I watched helplessly as a man ran you over and then . . ." But I couldn't tell him anymore because then he would ask more questions. Heat rose in my cheeks as the tears rolled down them. "And you never asked me if I was okay. You never told me I shouldn't have to deal with it alone. Don't tell me it's been hard on *you*, Dad."

I hadn't cried since the day they'd died. So I let them fall. My shoulders shook uncontrollably, and I couldn't get a handle on myself.

"Hun, I'm so sorry. I . . . I . . . I never knew any of that." I tried to stop the sobs quickly, but it only settled to slow heaving sounds.

If he would have asked, then he would have known. But what was the point in repeating that? To start a fight? To get us where?

"I don't know how to do this, Dad." I reached for his free hand and squeezed it, exhaling slowly. "I don't know how to wake up every morning and not hear Damian running in my room and jumping on my bed. I don't know how to deal with knowing that Mom isn't going to call and tell me that her plane's late. But I do know we have to do this together. So, I'm going to try and be better. But I can't do that alone."

He took a small moment to gaze down at our hands. Then his shoulders fell as he released his hand from mine. He opened his mouth to speak, closed it, then opened it again.

"What you're asking for me to do is something I don't know if I can do." His chin trembled. "I'm not the best father, I know, but I don't . . ."

"All you have to do is try."

The setting sun reflected like an ocean in his brown eyes.

"I'm just not . . . I don't know." He couldn't even look at me now.

"Why is it so hard for you?"

His shoulders tensed again. "You *can* move on, hun."

"I know. I just told you I would."

He shook his head. "You can move on but you're not. If I'm being honest, I . . . I feel like you don't want to try. You can't even talk about that day."

How could he say that? Every day I forced myself to get out of bed. To try my damnedest to make it through a school day without punching a wall. "I said I would try and *move on*. Not stay in the past," I snapped. Even though I couldn't get out of it.

He hesitated. "Maybe if you talk about it, it might . . ." He trailed off again. "It could help you understand things that happened."

"*I* know what happened. *You're* the one who doesn't remember." He flinched. A twinge of guilt toyed with me. It wasn't his fault he lost his memory of that day after Nikolas hit him. "I'm sorry." I fidgeted with the end of my hoodie, hoping that it would calm the butterflies in my stomach.

"I wish I remembered." His voice was as raw as the gravel road we were riding on, and as I gazed at him, darkness cast a veil over his face. "I wake up sometimes at night screaming, and I have no idea why."

I bit so hard on my lip, the tang of metal coded my tongue. I knew why, but I couldn't tell him. I could never tell him. Because then it would mean that it was all real. I needed him talking about something else before it was too late.

I didn't look at him as I spoke. "I don't understand how it's so easy for you to talk about it? It's like the day you came home from the hospital, you were just over it."

The back-and-forth motion from the windshield wipers created the only ambiance as he pondered my question.

"I know this might sound weird, but it's like something took the pain away," he said, turning down a long dirt road that carried off into the mountains. "There are times I still think I see her sitting on the edge of the bed. It's gotten better in the last few weeks, though."

I wished that could happen to me.

Since their death, it was as if I was carrying everyone else's pain, I cried at the drop of a hat when someone mentioned my mom. Or when Alvin and Jessie, Damian's best friends, played across the street, I would envision Damian sword fighting with them. How odd it seemed that Cassie, my mom's best friend, already prone to being over-emotional because of her pregnancy, hadn't even cried for her best friend.

"Rylee, it's your time to start healing."

"Everyone deals with loss in their own way. Why is my way wrong?"

"I'm not saying that it is. I just feel like there's something you're not telling me." He turned in to a parking lot with a white stone building. Enough parking spaces for four staff members and three patients. "Something's making this more painful for you. Making it harder to move on. So, I was hoping by seeing Farrah, you might open up a bit."

Why couldn't he just accept that I wasn't ready for this? That I couldn't talk to him about any of this anyway because if he knew the truth, he would never forgive me. And in looking over to tell him to let it go, a tear trickled down his cheek. He didn't wipe it away. As if subconsciously he wanted me to see it. Maybe talking to this doctor could help fix this or maybe not, but there was only one way to know for sure.

"I'll try, Dad."

The aroma of candles filled the air of the claustrophobic, lime green-painted office of Farrah Alastair. Knots twisted like boa constrictors in my stomach. The paper-thin walls carried my dad's and Farrah's voices from the waiting room. Most likely talking about how messed up I was. Strolling around the office, I could have sworn the eyes of the dozens of owl figurines followed my every movement. As if already judging me.

More than a dozen times in the past five minutes, I considered running. Farrah could be a nice person, but that didn't mean I could trust her and tell her my life story. My fingers twirled my oval locket on its chain sending an unexpected calmness through me. My dad had found it a few days after the funeral, saying that it was a birthday gift from my mom. And she'd said it'd been very special, and I was to keep it close to my heart.

Moments passed, and I chose to make my way toward Farrah's gray couch. Something caught my eyes not far from where her owl figurines stood. A picture of what I assumed were her parents. And everything they did in this picture told me all I needed to know about them. The way their eyes wrinkled at the corners as they smiled. The way they held their daughter close to them as if they never wanted to let her go. They were proud of her as she showed off a high school diploma.

My parents loved me. I knew that. But nothing I did was enough. Every time I saw a photo of us together, it was like they had to pretend they were happy. Always tight-lipped smiles. Even on the day they brought home Damian.

"That's one of my favorites."

Turning around, an attractive woman who I could only assume was Farrah smiled back at me. Her raven hair twisted into a bun atop her head, making it almost impossible not to see her sharp, high cheekbones and deep-blue eyes.

"I'm sorry. I wasn't trying to snoop." I turned to the couch.

Farrah sat in the chair across from me and adjusted her navy pinstriped skirt. "It's okay. I put these things out so people can see them." Her voice was airy and soothing. "To let them know that I'm not so different from them." Quickly her eyes darkened. "But like everything, things aren't always as they seem."

What was she expecting me to say? Did she think one comment would bring me some sort of comfort and then I would tell her everything? Because it would take a bit more than that.

"Talking to someone you don't know can be scary." Her features changed to soften. "It can also be hard. Especially if you aren't ready."

She didn't know the half of it.

The scratching of the pen to paper echoed in our silence, twisting my knots tighter.

I only had to be here for one hour.

She spoke to me now as if I were a wounded animal. "Let's start with why you're here."

My eyes darted to the exit. I could still leave. She wasn't holding me against my will. I considered it for a few milliseconds. Then I turned to Farrah. Seeing the comforting gaze in her eyes. Her softening features. Though she didn't know me, she wanted to help me.

I closed my eyes, took a deep, calming breath, and spoke. "I'm not taking my mom's death well."

"And why do you think that is?"

Was this question written in some sort of psychiatrist handbook saying it had to be one of the first questions to ask? Swallowing, my throat felt like the sandpaper my mom would use to smooth wood. I didn't want to think of why. I didn't want to talk about why. Because then I would see it all again.

Flashes of images I didn't even know I'd seen ran through my mind. I shook my head as if that could stop them, but they kept coming. A piece of the bridge breaking off and crashing into the car, sending us further into the water. The pressure of the windshield shattering. Me covering Damian but feeling like we'd all die anyway.

"Rylee." It was like my body shook and I couldn't stop it. "Rylee, are you okay?" It was Farrah's soothing voice.

Heat rose in my cheeks as I gazed at the thoughtfulness in her eyes.

"I'm . . . I'm sorry. But I can't . . . can't do this."

My breaths came out ragged as the room spun like a merry-go-round. Heat rose inside me as if Farrah had turned the thermostat up to ninety. Why was it so hot? I'd felt flushed before, but this was different. And again came the unexplainable tingling in my fingers. Like that day. I gripped the prickly arms of the couch just in case. What the hell was happening to me?

"I need you to look at me. Breathe in your nose and out your mouth."

The images of that day burst into my subconscious. My mom's crimson eyes staring at me one last time. My dad's body flying over the car like a rag doll and landing in an unnatural position. The earsplitting sound of metal from the bridge.

"Come on, Rylee, deep breaths." But it wasn't Farrah who spoke. That melancholy voice belonged to my mom. Her cute little freckles lining the bridge of her nose. "You can do it, sunflower. Deep breath in. Deep breath out." She continued to smile as my heartbeat slowed. I didn't want her to go.

"Mom, I'm so sorry. I didn't mean any of it." But my pleas went unheard as she faded away.

Farrah's office stood still now as I found her eyes questioning me as she handed me a bottle of water. "Do you see her often?"

Realizing what she'd heard, I sucked in a breath and shuddered. "A few times." The water soothed the rawness of my throat. "I'm not ready to talk about my mom. If that's okay."

She nodded, taking the bottle from me and throwing it into her recycling bin. "When you're ready, I'm here. But could I get to know you a bit?"

"How does that help with my mom?"

"Before I can get to the root of the problem, I need to understand. To understand why you are the way you are." Other than coming back to me, she went to where she kept her odd owl figurines. Then she reached below, taking down the picture of herself and her parents.

"I also know that if I want you to trust me, I have to be willing to share myself with you first." She handed me the picture as she went on. "When I lived in Sweden, my—"

"I didn't know you were born in Sweden." I looked away from the picture then to her again as if I might have missed something. But everything about her gave me the opposite impression.

"I moved to Miami about twenty years ago to go to university. And honestly, I didn't care for the blonde mess of hair I had."

Odd choice of words. Though my hair at times was a bit high maintenance, I still liked it. I studied the picture of the happy family. She moved halfway across the world to go to school and didn't like the way she looked. But she was pretty.

I looked up from the picture. "Did something happen back home?"

Her blue eyes dulled. "People just change over time."

All too well, this pain had been mine, and I wouldn't force her to say more. Though she would tell me if I asked. "Like my dad?" I said, seeing a grateful gleam in her eyes.

"He does care for you."

I gritted my teeth, nearly hissing the words. "He cares for me so much that he throws me off to someone to fix me." Farrah wrote something down in her notebook.

"He's done this before then?"

I didn't want to talk about this. But at least this wouldn't cause another mental breakdown.

"When my dad couldn't handle my mom being gone, he'd go to work or whatever and leave me with Grandma Ana. And I loved her with all my heart, but she wasn't the sanest woman."

My pulse drummed when I thought of all the times my dad would leave without even telling me. "And I think what hurt the most was I felt like sometimes it was like my dad literally couldn't look at me."

Farrah eyed me, then wrote something in her notebook. "Let me ask you, what did you and your grandmother do when your parents were gone?"

"What does that matter?"

"Well, you believe that your dad is trying to throw you off on someone else, but I see it as he's sending you to someone who can help you because he doesn't know what he can do for you. And I think your grandmother was one of those people. So, think back, will you? What did you guys do?"

I thought back because it'd been at least six years since she'd died and seven since she'd been able to watch me. "She read to me and then sometimes she'd let me pick things to read. That's where I'd found my love for historical fiction.

She'd told me once about how her grandpa had been in a war or something."

Farrah spent at least five minutes writing, and not even an eyebrow twitch gave away what she was thinking. Seconds later, she looked up from her notebook and asked, "Did you enjoy reading with your grandmother?"

"Yes, but what does that have to do with my parents?"

"Most of the time, when things aren't what we want them to be, we want to get away. Whether that be in books, writing, video games, or TV. Could it be you enjoy reading because it let you see what other lives look like?"

Every word was as true as if I spoke it myself. So many nights I would find myself wide awake, reading story after story of fairytales. Or happily-ever-afters. Praying one day I could have that. Or finding solace in stories worse than mine.

"You know what's sad?" I leaned against the couch, clasping my hands together as if I were going to tell her a secret. "I used to write stories to create a life better than mine."

She wrote something down on her paper again. "Are you saying that you didn't have a good childhood?"

"My parents didn't let me starve or live in a broom closet if that's what you're thinking. They just weren't . . ." I hesitated. My anxiety constricted my thoughts again. How heartbroken Grandma Ana's face had been every time she told me my mom or dad wouldn't be home. "I was just lonely sometimes. And books made me feel better."

After writing something down in her notebook, she placed it in her lap.

"Rylee, I want to say I'm proud of you. Therapy isn't an overnight fix." She chuckled. "If it were, I wouldn't be here. It's clear that you want this, but you have to let your heart want it too."

What she was saying could never happen. I could never

live a life where my mistakes didn't taunt me. And that was that.

"Thank you, Farrah, for trying. But just because you want something, doesn't always mean you should be able to have it."

3

After my session with Farrah, I half expected things to change now between my dad and me. But he didn't ask about my session. He didn't even look at me. He wanted me to move on and be happy, yet he couldn't do the same. And this had nothing to do with my mom's and Damian's deaths. As he drove, I wanted to scream to break the silence between us. Because then, and maybe then, he would see me. But I knew it would be useless.

Fifteen minutes passed, and we made it to the old grain field and the barn, and I asked my dad to stop. He didn't ask why. But dammit, I wanted him to. And why didn't he? Why didn't he care enough about me to want to try? I held the door to the van wide open, taking one last look at my dad. Gray peppered his dark hair. He was still holding out on me, and here I was trying to give my all.

I hadn't been back to the barn since the day of the accident. And standing here now, only memories of what once happened here plagued me. My gaze wandered toward the entrance's top frame. An unfinished wooden sign my mom had been working on hung there. *Home Sweet Home.* The last word was still a stencil because my mom and I had gotten into a fight. She'd said that she couldn't take me to the mother-daughter dance, and she'd stormed off. I shook off the memory. How stupid was it now? How could something so meaningless upset me? I'd known there would have been other dances, but I didn't care. I wanted her here with me. The misty rain had become a light pelt, so I took myself inside, bracing myself for heartache.

Hay and wood varnish welcomed me, as it had every time I'd come here, but now I didn't smile. I crumbled. Images of laughter and voices echoed through the silence of my thoughts. The sound of Damian making *choo-choo* noises on the hardwood when my mom bought him a new train for his birthday that had been a few weeks prior. My mom singing along to the radio as she painted the upstairs loft.

The pain burrowed deeper inside me the more I stared. But it was no longer anguish as the blood pounded in my ears. I didn't want to remember what happened here. I didn't want to see what I'd lost because of *my* mistakes. I hated this place.

"Why, why did you have to leave me!" I screamed, shaking the banister's railing. My knees gave to the floor. My fist banging on it over and over again. Letting all my emotions go. Letting my tears paint the dark wood. Remembering what I'd said to her that day. The hateful words. The things I knew that could have saved her. That could have stopped her from turning the car. I had the answers. My thoughts darkened. But could I have really stopped her? It'd seemed like she wanted us gone when she'd veered the van off the bridge. Why had she done it? Did she hate us, *me*, that much?

"Mom, why weren't we enough for you?" I sobbed. "I just want to understand."

I pressed my head against the floorboard as my breaths came in deep and quick. My tears still fell in on full force. I wasn't sure if I would ever stop. I killed them. They were never coming back. I would have to live with that day's mistakes for the rest of my life. I banged the side of my fist on the floor again and again until it went numb.

The pelting rain echoed on the tin roof as I breathed in and out, taking in the hay-filled air. After a while, my tears turned into sniffles. I had to find peace for myself, but as I stood and gripped the railing for support, I knew that day wouldn't be today.

I walked to the top step of the loft. Nothing had changed. Not the midnight-painted walls. Or the shelves full of books and knickknacks. Only everything had changed. Now I saw Damian sitting on the floor trying to draw what he thought a lion looked like. Or my mom standing on a small ladder to fix the flickering light that was still broken.

I couldn't do this.

I bit back the bile burning and wrestling in my stomach. It was too much too soon. My legs gave to the floor. My fingers clawed the carpet, which looked as if it were a black hole. And if I held onto it long enough, it would pull me under. My head spun.

And then darkness.

The purple haze edged my vision again as it had countless times. The lulling scent of lilies drifted around me in the air. But now Nikolas's scent of licorice staled it.

My eyes opened to floating lights. Like they were blurring out of vision. A popcorn stand sat in front of me as if offering itself to me. My body froze as footsteps crunched behind me. I wasn't terrified by them; I was literally paralyzed. Something or someone was there.

As he came closer, every emotion gradually left me, then Nikolas spoke.

"I'm sorry it had to end this way."

He kneeled next to me and spoke something. But all I could make out was a buzzing noise as my thoughts and feelings faded, but then it stopped.

"Rylee!" The voice came from somewhere around me, but I only saw Nikolas.

A hacking cough ripped from my chest. Hot smoke nearly burned the hair in my nostrils. Where was I? But as my fingers trailed along the soft fabric of the carpet, I remembered. The barn. But something wasn't right about it. Why did it feel so warm? Sweat trickled into my eyes, stinging them. Wiping it away, blurred shades of bright orange danced in my daze of sleep. I reached out to touch it, to pull it out of my eyes, but the bright blur sent a deep searing pain through my finger.

I shrieked and drew my hand away, taking the finger to my mouth. Then I screamed as my vision returned. I had to be seeing things. Flames danced around my fingers like a ballerina, and no matter how much I swiped at them, they wouldn't extinguish. Another deep burning cough ripped from my throat. It was just like that lightning on the bridge. But this couldn't be real.

My head shot up to a snapping noise. The flames consumed the bottom banister, breaking it away from its support because of the fire. My eyes fell to my hands in disbelief. As if I'd been in my own world for the past five minutes. I heard the sizzling hiss of the fire. The flames stretched high like a cage to trap me as I stood, finally seeing it all.

I stared down to my fingers again. Had I somehow done this?

I shook my head. I had to stay focused and get out of here. Through the flames, the moon reflected off one of my broken mirrors. But that didn't make any sense. I shouldn't have been able to see the moon. Jagged edges of wood hung from the ceiling of the barn's roof, teetering and ready to fall. I prayed it wouldn't do that until I was out of here. But the full moon had been the only thing I could see as the flames covered nearly every inch of my vision.

How was I going to get out of here? All I knew was not to panic. I took a deep breath, which made me cough violently, and told myself I would get out of here alive.

I had to scope out the area the best I could for anything I could maybe jump onto. The loft's height gave me a bit of an advantage to see below. Most of the lower-level flames rose with the help of falling wood that continued to fuel it. It had the do-not-try-at-home look to it. But I had to do something. I didn't want to die. Beads of sweat dripped down the back of my neck. The fire stalked closer as my throat grew drier, my eyes burning with the smoke clouding the space around me. There had to be a way out of here. Then I remembered the ladder my mom had put in just in case. My eyes darted to the right side of the loft, but the fire, which I saw through the cracks of the wood beneath me, had reached it, leaving only the nubbed end where she'd connected the top of the ladder to the loft's base.

The window across from where the ladder had once been pulled smoke through it as if leading me to my last hope of escape. A small square window just big enough for me to climb out of. But I had to think of something that could protect me from the fire. Stepping back, I nearly tripped on my answer—my black rug! It would cover at least from my head to my waist, and that was good enough. I stared at my fingers again. Flames still danced around them. I wanted them gone. And just like that, the flames disappeared. More flames clawed up the walls like spiderwebs. I had to get out of here, and fast. With the heat rising and my breaths ragged, I threw the rug around me.

I could make it to that window. I could live.

The heat beneath the wood did all but melt my shoes as I eased in the direction of the window, the rug tight around my neck. This was it. I would get to the window, get out of here, and figure out how, if what I'd woken to was real, I'd caused this.

With another groaning creak, I gazed up to where one of the beams had finally chosen to collapse. I screamed and threw down the rug, tripping and falling until my head bounced off the warm floor. My ringing ears drowned out the flames as everything spun. And then came the beam.

I barely moved out of the way before it crushed me. There was nowhere to go now. The beam buried the rug in flames, which now crept toward me. Even with my eyes closed, I could feel the heat nearly blistering my skin. But I couldn't go out like this. I hadn't survived that car crash just to die now. I rose with caution, my head swimming for countless reasons. My throat felt so raw and dry, I wouldn't be able to talk for weeks if I ever stopped hacking and coughing.

As I rose, a beam that held up one side of the loft snapped. The platform leaned backward, attempting to take me down. I tried to move, but the flames toyed with me. Close but not close enough to burn me alive. Not yet. My skin tingled with heat as the flames drew closer. Sweat dripped down my body like a waterfall. I couldn't even take a breath to calm myself, as the fire had taken most of the air.

The final beam collapsed. I nearly lost my balance as the platform swayed with my weight. When the final beam crashed into the ground, it took my hope with it. I was going to die. And with that truth came one last sound ringing through the raging fire as the platform gave way.

My body met the ashen wood with a sickening crunch, stealing what air I had left. The fall should have killed me. My back should have snapped in half. But instead, I gasped for air. Even the smothering smoked air would be enough. Almost as if my rib cage cracked, and the bones splintered into my lungs. The ringing in my ears still didn't block the loud pop and crackle of the flames. They circled me now as if they'd been waiting so long to consume me. In not being able to find that breath, I knew I would die. My lungs burned as I tried one last time to breathe, but it was hopeless as my eyelids fluttered in exhaustion as the flames drew closer, tantalizing my skin. With it, came peace.

"This is not your end, Rylee Jenkins." The voice belonged to an angel, surely. So hypnotic. Like he was taking me somewhere better than this place. But where he was taking me wasn't what I had in mind as the heat that had nearly consumed me faded. Was this a dream? Heaven? Hell? My eyes grew heavy, and my brain felt foggy.

"Do you have this under control?" It was his voice again. But who was he talking to?

I tried desperately to open my eyes in hopes to see whoever it was the boy had been talking to, but they wouldn't obey.

"Don't I always." Her voice sounded deep and raspy like a rattlesnake.

Once I opened my eyes, I wished I hadn't, because what rested in her cream-colored hands must have been a hallucination from all the smoke I inhaled. Two clear bubbles rested in the palms of her hands. With ease, she threw them to the farthest corner of the barn, extinguishing a large portion of the flames. My eyes grew heavy again.

"You need to take her home," the mysterious girl said, her voice a bit pinched.

My body lifted in the air then. Though I had no idea

who this boy was, I knew one thing for sure. These arms belonged to someone who knew how to protect something. Strong and never wavering. I prayed wherever this boy was taking me, he could help me figure out what the hell just happened.

4

The irritating fabric of my ratty couch prickled against my bare skin. How did I get here? How long had I been out? A deep cough rattled in my rib cage, making me almost keel over. Gripping the side of the couch, I tried to sit back up. In doing so, my hair brushed in front of my face and the smell nearly burned my nostrils. Why did my hair smell like smoke? Smoke. Smoke . . . my bruised ribs. I remembered now. I'd set my barn on fire. That couldn't be, could it? But hadn't I seen that girl with bubbles in her hands?

"You are awake."

The boy. That angelic voice. Now that I'd had some rest, I realized he had a thick British accent. He'd been the one who'd saved me. My vision shifted in and out of focus as I attempted to ease my body up from the couch. But one wrong twist of my back and a spasming pain shot down the lower half of my body.

"You fell," he said. "It is amazing it did not kill you."

It sure as hell was. Knowing any movement right now was pointless, I let my body ease back onto the couch. I couldn't understand that. I should have died from that fall. Wood was poking out from everywhere. But I shook my head. There was nothing I could do about it now. At least I was alive.

The boy pushed a lock of straight black hair from his long tan face as he stared at me. I could have told myself the reason I was staring at him now was because of his sharp cheekbones, a five o'clock shadow I couldn't understand a boy his age having, and slick back hair. Or said that it was his plump red lips and deep ocean eyes. But honestly, it was what he *wasn't* showing me that had my attention. His brow didn't furrow with worry. He didn't glare at me with annoyance. He didn't twitch, bounce his leg, or even bite his lip. He didn't react to me waking or do anything at all. Why?

"I have provided you with water."

He pointed to a chilled glass sitting on a green coffee table my mom had painted a few years back out of a door. He'd even used a magazine as a coaster. Taking the water and drinking it down, felt like when my mom would put aloe vera on my sunburned skin.

"Thanks for pulling . . ." I coughed while setting the glass down. My ribs screamed again, but not enough for a repeat of earlier.

"It is best to stay hydrated."

"Thank you for getting me out," I managed. Still, he wasn't asking how I was. Only giving me aftercare instructions like a robotic nurse. I rubbed the back of my neck because, one, it felt good after falling and living. And two, because this boy, who still hadn't told me his name, was making me very nervous.

"So, can I know the name of my hero?" I chuckled.

His lack of a facial expression sent an unsettling chill down my spine. "My name is Drake Sullivan."

Okay, we were getting somewhere.

"Well, I'm Rylee. Rylee Jenkins." I chuckled nervously. "But you already knew that."

"I should be going now." He stood. "I would not prefer your father to wake."

"No, you can't go. You just got here."

I rose to stop him, nearly throwing out my back again. My only hope of figuring out what happened tonight was leaving, and I couldn't let that happen. He saw what that strange girl could do. What *I* could do. So, he had to know something.

I let my body ease back down on the couch as I said, "I *need* to know what happened out there tonight. I need to know who you and that girl are. Because you knew my name, and I've never met you before in my life."

Nothing about his body language or facial features gave me any indication of what he was thinking as he sat in my dad's recliner. "Her name is Mara. And the reason that I know of your name is that Mara does."

"Okay," I huffed. "So how does Mara know my name?"

"Because of your mother, Liliana. Mara thought of her as if she were a mother. As she tells it."

No, this couldn't be right. My mom and I may have not seen eye to eye, but she would tell me things about her trips. About people and places. She never said anything about a girl named Mara. But if I truly believed that my mom told me everything, then why did I question myself? Like how she'd gone behind my dad's back about Damian. And if Mara had been that close to my mom, wouldn't my mom tell me? Maybe she thought if she did, it would hurt my feelings because of how bad our relationship already was. Nevertheless, I needed more information.

"My mom never said anything about her." I tried to readjust myself.

"I cannot tell you why your mother never spoke of my sister."

A sister? At least something was finally starting to make sense around here.

"But if you're her brother, you have to know my mom, too."

"Not necessarily."

I waited for him to elaborate, but nothing. Between his lack of expressions and him sidestepping me, I was going mad. Mad because I didn't know why. I didn't know why my mom wouldn't have told me about some girl I never met who pretty much helped save my life. Who seemed to do something that I couldn't have seen. But I did. And I did something, too. Somehow. I hated not knowing why.

"Drake, none of this makes sense to me." I hoped he could hear the pleading in my next words. "I *need* answers."

As Drake left me for the window, I felt a flutter of panic. "Many people believe fear is the world's greatest weakness. But *I* believe it to be the unknown." He turned back to me. "I must go now."

"Wait! Why are you in such a rush to leave?" I tried to stand, only to fall back again.

He stopped, his back turned to me.

"I cannot provide the answers you seek."

"I find that hard to believe being that your sister held water in her hands right in front of you." I waited, but after a few seconds of silence, I went on. "You know more than what you're telling me. I'm not asking you to give up some secret or whatever if that's what this is. I just want some answers about me."

His body didn't even twitch. It was beyond infuriating. But as the room remained silent, I remembered something Farrah had said. If I wanted Drake to trust me, I had to be willing to share more about myself.

So, with a deep, long sigh, that's exactly what I would do. "A few times now, I've had this weird feeling inside me. One time I saw lightning around my fingers. I mean, at the time, I thought I was seeing things because of what just happened. And then, tonight, the fire." I waited to see if anything changed, but he never turned around. Never spoke. "Please, help me understand." Moisture built in the corners of my eyes, but I blinked it away. He couldn't see me this way.

He finally turned around but his face remained unreadable. "Many things we perceive are not what they seem."

I gritted my teeth. "Are you telling me I'm seeing things?"

"No, I am providing you with another explanation," he said matter-of-factly.

His cryptic answers were giving me a headache. "Look, just be straightforward. Black and white. Do you know what's going on with me or not?"

"Yes, but my sister is best suited to provide that answer."

As if the heat from the barn scorched my skin again, I glared at him. He wasn't going to sidestep my questions anymore.

"This is my life you're toying with. Why the hell did you even stay here if you weren't going to tell me anything?"

After a moment of silence, Drake took his place at the edge of the coffee table again. "I was told to make sure you were all right."

Was I just some job to him? My blood cooled thinking of how inconvenient I'd become for him. "You can go if you want," I whispered. "I don't want to keep you."

He leaned in closer, the smell of cinnamon refreshing on his skin. "Tell me what you wish to know, and I will do my best to answer."

"Why the change of heart?" I asked.

"You do not seem the type to give up easily."

How had he gotten that observation from knowing me for five seconds? Nevertheless, some answers were better than none at all.

"Can you tell me how Mara made those bubbles come out of her hands?" He shook his head. Testing my nerves again. "Okay then." My breath came out in a huff. "What do you know about my mom?"

"I know not much of Liliana, but my parents have spent time with her over the years. My sister more than them." His eyes were now fixated on my locket. "Your mother saved my stepfather once. Since then, we have vowed to protect you. That is one of the reasons why we are here. But that is all I am told I can share on the matter."

One of the reasons? What was the other one? And protect me? Protect me from what, myself? Because right now *I* was the only real danger if what I did truly happened. The longer this conversation went on, the more I started to think it did.

"Wait a minute. You said stepfather. Where's your real dad?" I asked.

"I do not wish to discuss such things with a stranger."

I thought back to talking with Farrah, how it had made *me* feel to have to talk about my parents. And maybe through that façade of his, he carried pain too.

"Okay, then can you tell me what you guys are protecting me from? Does it have anything to do with what's happening to me?"

"That is all I am told to share," he repeated.

My temples throbbed from his insufferable nature. I was sure my approach now wouldn't even work, given the fact that he didn't show his own emotions, but I had to try.

"Please, Drake, I need to know what's happening to me."

"May I ask what you were doing before the fire?"

I frowned. "What the hell does that have to do with what's going on with me?"

"Your expressive word choice is unnecessary."

He couldn't be much older than me, but he acted like a thirty-year-old British man smoking a pipe in a lavish robe.

"Sorry. It's just frustrating."

"That is why I asked my question."

I didn't know this boy, but he knew more than I did. And if I wanted answers, I had to tell him everything.

"I know this might sound weird." I knotted my fingers, trying to avoid as much eye contact with him as I could. "But then again, it might not with what *you've* seen. I had a vision. I've had them since I was ten."

The room stayed quiet. I drew my gaze up from my fingers to Drake. He didn't look at me like I was crazy. He stared at me as if I were a wall. "May I ask what it was about?"

My mouth dropped. "You actually believe me?"

"As you said, I have seen many things that should not be normal."

"I was in this place where this guy, the one who hit my dad, was. He said he was sorry about something. And then it was like every emotion was just leaving my body."

"Your otherworldly essence is not as strong as I was foretold it to be."

"What do you mean otherworldly essence?"

"I have said too much already. But may I ask, do you know what the vision could have meant?"

I turned away. "I . . . I don't know. I never do. Until after the fact." I gazed up at him then. "What does this have to do with the barn fire?"

He folded his hands in his lap. "Even if dreaming, we do things to protect ourselves."

"So you're saying that whatever was going on in my

vision, I was trying to protect myself and I accidentally started the fire?" He nodded. "Well, if you hadn't saved me, I would have died." I sighed, trying not to show my frustration. "How did you guys know where to find me?"

"My sister has been watching you since the funeral." His eyes shifted to my locket again. Why was he so interested in it? "She preferred to keep a safe distance from you so as not to scare you."

"Why do you keep doing that?" I threw my hand over my locket as if that would do anything.

"Doing what?"

I rolled my eyes. "Why do you keep looking at my locket?"

"It is a rather beautiful piece. Did your mother give it to you?"

I let the locket rest in the palm of my hand. "Yes."

"I need to go," he said, making his way to the door this time.

"Wait, what?" Drake waited as I cautiously rose from the couch and waddled to the front door like a penguin. "Was it something I said?" I asked, using my hands to brace my back for support.

He turned to meet my gaze, his voice still detached. "It is sad your mother never chose to tell you or your father of her nature."

"Nature? What are you talking about?" My heart thudded against my rib cage.

"I cannot answer any more of your questions, Rylee."

In a daze, I hadn't even realized he'd made it to the door. His hand rested on the doorknob.

My voice rose an octave. "You can't leave after telling me something like *that*."

"My sister has invited you and your father to dinner

tomorrow night. If you wish to attend, then all your questions will be answered. Will that suffice for now?"

No, I wanted to know now. I wouldn't be able to sleep without these answers. But from the five minutes we'd spoken, he wouldn't give me answers even if I tortured him. Let alone if I asked him politely.

"What time?" I bit down on the inside of my cheek to keep the disappointment inside.

"How is six?" He opened the door.

"Six sounds fine," I said, unable to look into his expressionless gaze as he eased his way onto my wraparound porch. "Thank you for saving me." My weight rested heavily on the door as if to keep my body from falling.

"You are welcome, Rylee. Good night."

"Good night, Drake."

As if he were a ghost, he disappeared into the fog of the silent night.

5

The next morning, though my eyes were caked with crust and my brain felt like marshmallows, I still went to school. My conversation with Drake, and the barn fire, ran through my head all day. During lunch I sent my dad a text, telling him about the dinner with Mara. Telling him that Mara had been friends with my mom and wanted to meet us. It was true enough. I didn't know how tonight would go, but I hoped that neither Drake nor Mara would say anything about the fire. I wasn't sure if I even wanted to tell my dad about it. After school, I spent the rest of the afternoon at the library reading some of the newest historical fiction novels. Around five thirty, I made my way back home to get ready.

It was five fifty when my dad and I stood on the eerily quiet front porch as I toyed with a frayed sleeve and my dad knocked a second time on Mara's front door.

Maybe she'd changed her mind. But with that thought, the door swung open, the scent of cinnamon greeting me.

"Rylee, I'm glad you came!" A girl with a messy blonde bun poked her head out of the front door. "I wasn't sure my brother would have convinced you."

"More like he left me with questions I needed the answers to."

Mara's violet eyes crinkled as she laughed, opening the door wider to let us in. I would have thought that knowing you were going to have dinner guests Mara would have chosen to wear something a bit nicer than an oversized gray sweater that hung off her right shoulder and ripped black jeans. But in a way, it made all of this a bit less daunting and more comfortable.

"Well let's get this party started then," Mara said, walking more into the house.

My dirt-covered boots echoed on the foyer's white vinyl as I stared up at an ornate chandelier hanging above me. "Wow, I forgot they built this house last year. It's enormous."

"A bit much if you ask me." Mara crinkled her nose. "But beggars can't be choosers. It was meant for Selena and Nathan anyway. My mother"—she frowned—"and her *new* husband." When she rolled her eyes, I felt a certain understanding of how she felt.

"Liliana always wanted a chandelier," my dad said, rolling farther into the foyer. "I offered to go with her to look for one, but life happened, you know."

Hearing my mom's name and knowing that she would have really never taken the time to do anything with my dad saddened me and I had to change the subject. But though I was dying to know why Mara didn't care for her parents, if she was anything like her brother, she wouldn't tell me either way. So, I took a safer approach.

"Why did they want to move here?"

Mara turned away and headed toward the hallway. "Let's have some dinner first." So she was just like her brother.

All three of us could have stood side by side while strolling down the hallway, but I straggled behind. Staring at the walls, one piece reminded me of an abstract painting my mom had done once. I glided my fingers over the glass of the multi- rectangular artwork and frowned. I wished she were here to meet Mara and Drake with me and my dad. She always had a way of breaking the ice. But that was why she was so good at helping people.

"Is your family really into history?" my dad asked, gesturing to a statue.

Mara took a moment to answer. "Selena and I aren't." She stopped in front of a large ornate door that hung open, but without walking forward, I couldn't see inside. Only that its handle was shaped like a feather. "But Drake and Nathan are." She looked at the door. "This is the library. One of Nathan and Drake's favorite rooms. I'm more of the do-it-yourself type of girl than I am just to read about it. But whatever."

At the mention of Drake, he stepped out from behind the open door wearing the boy's version of our school uniform. Long gray dress pants, white button-up shirt, black jacket, and a golden tie. He had a way of making it look much more sophisticated than most boys who wore it.

"Oh how kind of you to grace us with your presence. We are not worthy," Mara mocked, rolling her eyes.

Drake paid no attention to his sister. His vacant gaze remained on me, causing the hair on the back of my neck to prickle. The nervousness I felt now was nothing like attraction, or lust, but confusion. And something else. Like his lack of emotion intimidated me. I didn't know what he thought of me. He heard me last night, yet still I was unsure whether he thought I was a basket case. He drew past Mara and into the kitchen without a word.

"Forgive my brother. He's different." Mara ushered us forward.

Drake Sullivan was different all right. But I wasn't judging him. I just wanted to understand him. Farrah's words of trust flooded back to me. It would take time.

Dinner waited for us in the lavish maroon dining room. Mara had been thoughtful and removed one of the chairs so my dad could pull in his wheelchair. While Mara and Drake brought out a few more things to go with the food, my stomach knotted as if I realized what was about to happen. I would find out what was going on with me. Maybe it was good, or maybe it was bad. Either way, I needed to know. I needed to be told I wasn't seeing things. Mara set down the last bit of food, and I knew I was finally going to get my answers.

But no one said a word as we ate. Every so often, I caught Mara looking at me, but she would either sip her wine or take another bite of food.

Thirty grueling minutes later, everyone had finally finished.

"Mara, I have to say, and I don't say it much, but this food is probably better than mine," my dad said, wiping his mouth.

Mara took a sip of her wine, pressing a napkin against her lips. "Can I let you in on a wee little secret? It's actually your food."

We all laughed, other than Drake. I couldn't put much thought into it as Mara turned her attention to me, a playful glint in her eyes. "I guess I should answer your first question. Liliana always said if anything were to happen to her, Selena and Nathan were to help Lucas watch over you."

Finally. "I don't want to be ungrateful of the fact that you save my life, but why aren't *they* here?"

She chuckled. "You're too nice for your own good." Her eyes darkened. "Nathan and Selena work with an organization known as the Council. Their headquarters are in London. So, due to some new arising problems, they couldn't leave."

I bit my lip thinking of her *too nice* comment.

"Please don't take this the wrong way, but why did they send you and Drake?"

Mara's narrowing gaze wandered to Drake, who stared absentmindedly at his plate. Like she was waiting for *him* to answer the question. And when he still didn't meet her stare, which I wouldn't have wanted to in that moment either, she turned back to me, her pencil-thin lips having a strained look to them as she smiled.

"Selena and Nathan think Drake could get a better education here." They really thought that? It was hard to believe. I'd always heard how well diverse the United Kingdom was. "And as for me," she went on, "because of my diversity in *different* things, they thought I could help you more than they could."

"Like when I tried to ask Drake about those bubbles you had? Or the fire from my fingers."

"Bubbles?" My dad's eyes widened. "I thought I was here to meet some of Liliana's friends. I'm starting to think that's not the case at all."

My heart raced. For a small moment, I'd forgotten that my dad was sitting next to me because he'd barely spoken until now. "Did I say bubbles? I meant—"

Mara placed her hand on mine. It was unnerving because she didn't give me a maternal vibe. "It's okay. Your mum told me if anything were to happen to her, she wanted me to tell you both the truth." She looked at my dad, then back to me. "Before I go into any more of this, you both need to know that Liliana wanted to tell you. She just didn't think it was safe."

All color drained from my dad's face, but he managed to speak. "I never understood Liliana's actions, but I did know that when she kept something, it was for a reason." In his eyes was something like determination. Like Mara's answer to the question he was about to ask would change how he saw my mom forever. "I need to know what she's been hiding."

Knots swam like a school of fish in my stomach. My mom keeping secrets from me didn't surprise me much anymore. But Mara's eyes held this plea for me to understand what she was saying. That sincerity that told me I could trust her. I had to know. Maybe, if I did, I could finally fix the wrong in me. So, I took Mara's hands and smiled.

"I want to know everything."

Mara withdrew her hands and placed them in front of her on the table. "You can see into the future."

I frowned. This was the big secret—something I already knew. "I know about them. My mom even told me that I smell lilies in my visions because she and I are close." By blood, I wanted to say, because we definitely weren't close otherwise.

She frowned. "Was that really what she bloody told you?"

"Yes, why?"

Mara drew in a deep breath, almost as if she knew that I wouldn't like what she was about to say. "You smell lilies in your visions because you, your mum, her mum, and so forth are connected by magical powers."

A lump hung in my throat. This wasn't possible. What, like I was some . . . some . . . What was I? And who would keep a secret like that? I let my eyes wander back to Mara, who patiently waited for me to say something. But where did I start?

My dad was the one who spoke.

"Look, when I'd found out about Rylee's visions when she was little, I thought sure, that's something that people could do. But now you're wanting us to believe that my wife and daughter are magical creatures?"

"Right before Liliana died, she told me that when Rylee started to show that she could do magic, that I was to tell her," Mara clarified. "Because though Liliana had taken precautions, she knew Rylee's magic would still come out."

"What do you mean precautions?" I asked.

"That's not important right now." Mara turned back to my dad. "Lucas, Liliana didn't want you to know about this world because she was afraid if you knew, you would leave her. And in doing that, the Council would wipe your mind of everything you knew and loved. She knew you didn't deserve that."

He couldn't look at her as he asked his question. "But why now?"

"Because she knew how far apart you and Rylee had drifted, and she thought learning about this whole magic thing would bring you guys back together somehow. That you would figure it out together. That, and she knew what secrets did before and she didn't want that between you and Rylee." She chuckled. "Sappy, I know, but that's what she said."

"Mara, how . . . do you . . ." I had to stop her from going on, but I couldn't even make a coherent sentence. "How do you expect me to believe you?" I looked back at my dad.

"I don't. But if you don't, then how can you explain you setting your barn on fire last night?"

My blood went as cold as the water sitting in front of me.

My dad's familiar contorted face told me what his next words would be.

"Fire? What fire?"

As much as I didn't want to tell him, I had to. So, I explained everything that happened last night. From the fire to having Drake over. "I didn't tell you because I thought I was seeing things." My chin trembled. "And things between us . . . You make it so hard to talk to you."

His cool hand nestled against my cheek. For the first time in so many years, my dad gazed deep into my eyes. Like he was looking into my soul. "I'm sorry for what happened to you. And I'm glad you're all right," he said. "I'm sorry I haven't been here for you. I want to be, to ask how you are. I just . . ." He turned away. "I just don't want to be a disappointment to you when you see I'm not the father I should be."

Instinctively, I wanted to feel sorry for how he'd felt. But I couldn't lie and tell him it was okay just to spare his feelings. There'd been too much pain that had burrowed inside me. There was a part of me, a selfish part, that wanted him to feel this way so he could understand *my* pain. But then I thought of what Farrah had said about *why* my dad had sent me to her. That was a start, wasn't it?

"You are the dad I want. I couldn't see you as a disappointment for trying. That's all I ask." I squeezed his hand.

"But what if it's too late?"

I smiled. "It's never too late."

He smiled back, but then his eyes turned serious as he directed his attention back to Mara. "You seem like a nice enough woman, but I don't know if that means we can just trust you."

"I'm not telling you to. You have to decide that on your own. But I won't lie to either one of you." She looked at me, then back to my dad. And then she closed her eyes. Within seconds, a flamed orb rested in the palm of her hand. My dad's eyes nearly fell out of his head. "But can you tell me that this isn't magical? That Rylee's visions aren't something magical?"

Mara extinguished the flamed orb. The oddest thing was, I think I did believe her. How else could I have explained that fire? How could I have caused it if I wasn't something magical? And the lightning.

I tried to gauge a reaction from her that could give me my answer. Nothing. "Mara, I don't understand what this magical power means."

"Think about the water you saw in my hands. Think about the flames on your fingers."

"Or how I spoke of your visions being of an otherworldly essence," Drake added.

Mara went on. "Liliana told me you like to read a lot. What mythical creature can you think of that can control fire and water?"

There was a creature that could control water, fire, and lightning. And Drake had said my visions had an otherworldly essence. So what was the definition for otherworldly? I thought. It had to be something that wasn't of this world. Like an imaginary world. One where I could harness magic. And it all made sense.

"I'm a witch!" I squealed. Just saying it out loud felt so right. Like this weight of confusion was lifted off my shoulders. I. Was. A. Witch. I glanced over to my dad, his face pale. "Are you okay?" I put a hand on his arm.

"That's how I know you." My dad pointed to Mara. "I was trying to figure out why you seemed so familiar when I got here, but I didn't want to seem too forward. Now I remember."

I stared at him. "What do you mean you know her?"

"She'd come and check on Liliana. And one of those times, she told me she was a witch." My dad turned his attention to Mara. "But I don't understand. Aren't humans not supposed to know about magical worlds and witches and stuff?"

"We're called Fables. And I shouldn't have told *you* about me, no. But since Liliana was a witch, it's not technically breaking the rules."

"Why isn't it?"

"If a Fable is married or born into the family, that Fable has the right to choose whether to tell the family of their nature and of our world. She may have chosen not to tell you, but you had the right, so I told you about myself instead."

"I didn't think much of it at the time, I suppose." My dad rubbed the side of his face.

Hadn't Drake said something about that? That he thought it was sad my mom didn't tell us? But *why* didn't she? Did that mean she had visions too?

Mara's attention shifted back to me, but her eyes didn't meet mine. "I know you want to know why she didn't tell you. But I don't know. I won't let you do this alone. I've been where you are. I was ten when I started getting my visions." She stared at Drake but then turned back to me. "But they came in puzzle pieces. Usually three different visions."

Just like the visions I was having before the accident. I didn't know what they meant, even after the fact. But I should have. Mara's voice brought me out of my wallowing.

"There's one more thing I should tell you."

"Telling me my visions are linked with me being a witch isn't enough?" I teased.

"Sadly, no." Suddenly her focus shifted to my locket. "Drake tells me you got that locket from Liliana."

My fingers grazed the locket as I answered. "Yeah. It was

for my eighteenth birthday. But when my mom died, my dad gave it to me early."

"Well I think it's time I tell you its story. I used to work with the Council." She nearly spit out their name. "I took the locket from them because they were using it for the wrong reasons. I didn't want them to know I had it, so I gave it to the one person I trusted the most. Liliana."

I bit down on the inside of my cheek in an attempt to hide my anger. "So you wanted my mom to get caught with it?"

"No, of course not! I cloaked the necklace. Without the caster, a magical signature can't be traced. She was safe."

"What was the Council doing with it that was so bad that you had to take it?"

She waved her hand as if it didn't matter. "All you need to know is that the locket is very special. Now that you are the owner of it, as your magic grows and you learn to control it, so will the power of the locket. Once you see your last initial on the surface, you will be able to use it."

"But why do I need the locket to work or learn magic at all?"

"That locket will help stop a war. That's why I took it and gave it to your mum. I told Liliana what I had planned, but that I didn't have anyone to help carry it out. She told me that she wasn't able to help me. Then one day she told me that she'd seen the locket come to you. Without you even knowing it. And we knew then that *you* were the only one who could possess the locket's powers. So I had an idea. I told Liliana to give you the locket as if it were a birthday gift and then tell you everything." She paused, looking nervously at Drake, then back to me. "Now that you know, I really hate to rush you here, but we only have a few weeks to make this happen, or the Fable world as we know it is over."

My mom had offered me up for something I knew

nothing about. But she had faith that I could do it. If I did it, maybe it would somehow make amends for what I did to her.

"Don't you think this is a lot to ask someone who just found out five seconds ago that she's a witch?" I asked.

"Yes, I do. But I promise you, your mum wouldn't have trusted me if she didn't think I could do something. We can do this. I can help you. But I need to know if *you* want to do this."

I knew nothing about this Fable world or the people in it, but I was part of them now. To add to it all, my mom needed me. I owed her this much. These were her people maybe more than mine. I wouldn't let her or them down.

"Okay, tell me everything."

"I know you have a lot of questions, Rylee, but I think for now you should go home and get some rest."

"Okay, but I have one quick question. Say I wanted to practice some of this magic. How would I do that?"

"Just tell it what you want it to do," she said simply.

I had so many questions. Felt so many emotions. Scared, confused, and even angry. Angry that my mom would keep something so life-changing from me. What was so bad about being a witch that my mom kept it a secret from her family, but yet let a stranger, to me at least, tell me about my origin? Now that I had time to breathe, it was a bit unsettling to hear all of this from a stranger. My pulse throbbed in the back of my head. It was time to go. To think. To wonder.

"Mara, thank you for telling me all this. It *is* a lot and . . . well, I just . . ."

She placed her hand on top of mine. "Take your time. You know where to find me."

6

The next morning's light peeked through the lips of my blinds. The purple butterflies my mom had painted for me blurred between my eyelids. I sprang up from bed, how could I see the butterflies this early in the morning? Turning to check the time, my clock read nine forty-six. I'd never slept this late before. Every morning like clockwork, I would wake just before dawn. Maybe it had something to do with my dad's buttery biscuits and freshly brewed coffee. But as I sat up in bed now, already feeling off from having overslept even for a Saturday, no buttery aroma or hazelnut brew wafted in the air.

It worried me. My dad was anything if not punctual. Had he gone to work? I reached across the bed and to my nightstand for my phone. But no text. I tried to remember how he'd been when we'd come home last night, but with everything that had happened at Mara's, I just couldn't remember.

I made my way out of my room. Maybe he was up and was trying not to wake me.

When stepping out in the hallway, I wasn't expecting the

eerie silence that awaited me. It sent a chill down my spine. If my dad was awake, where was he? I couldn't even make out the light underneath his bedroom door as I glanced down the hallway before heading downstairs. Even his stairlift was still at the top of the stairs.

"Dad? Are you home?" One. Two. Three seconds passed and nothing.

Where the hell was he? My chest tightened and my heart raced. Why was a small part of me feeling like that ten-year-old girl being left alone again?

"Dad! Dad! Are you still here?" I swore I could almost hear that plea, that cry, in her voice again.

Nothing.

I would go to the kitchen next. Before making it halfway down the stairs, the lack of light and banging pans told me he wasn't there. I went anyway. Standing on the threshold of the kitchen, my heart sank. Flies swarmed crusty plates from breakfast the day before, which my dad hated.

Had I done something wrong? Had something Mara said about me last night made him leave everything in such disarray? I would only get that answer by looking out the window. It was childish, but I closed my eyes. My heart pounded in my chest as if it wanted to run away too. If I opened my eyes and his car was gone, it would mean there was no hope for us. But, if I opened my eyes and it was still there, there was hope. I let my eyes flutter open. And there, nestled safe and sound, was our hope.

Going back to the sink, I poured soap in it and let the water run. Once it was full of suds, I grabbed the first item to wash and my heart shattered. In my hand was a rolling pin Grandpa Walter had given my dad. I let my soapy finger trail along the handle, remembering back to when my dad had first shown me how to use it. Him tying my apron because my fingers were too small. Him telling me that he loved me.

More memories continued to invade me. Hearing my giggles in my head as he poked flour on my nose. How they seemed so far and few between. I could never understand why it just stopped. What changed? Had I done something wrong? I shook my head. I would have time to think about it later.

It was ten thirty once the dishes, coffee, and the biscuits in the oven were done. I decided to make my way outside to get the paper. Even with my thick gray jacket, the autumn chill sent goosebumps down my arms.

Too focused on rubbing my arms, something caught my foot, and my body fell forward, but I caught myself on my rocking chair. My eyes met what had caused me to almost break my neck. One of the brightest pumpkins I'd ever seen. Leaning down to place it in a less hazardous place, a tiny piece of paper fluttered on top of the pumpkin.

I do believe every witch should celebrate Halloween.

By the word choice alone, I could make a sure-fire guess that the note and the pumpkin came from Drake. As much as I wanted to be warmed by the gesture, I was more confused. By Drake's actions, and our lack of conversations, him giving me a gift didn't make sense. My eyes wandered to Mara's house, but no cars were in the driveway. Maybe I would see him at school then. I needed to go inside anyway. My dad's light may have not been on, but he was there.

Over the years I'd grown accustomed to light beneath my parent's bedroom door. Still no light. Not a good sign. Opening the door with ease, only the ill-lit lamp on my dad's bedside table filtered in the room. His blue curtains were shut. If it hadn't been for the lamp, I wouldn't have even seen him there, hunched over the side of the bed staring out the window. The air smelled stale, overheated, as if he hadn't come out in days. Even when opening the door wider, which squeaked loudly, he didn't acknowledge me. Just as my mom would, I set both the biscuit and coffee on his dresser.

"Hey, I made you some breakfast." I attempted a laugh, but it came out more like a nervous chuckle.

"Thank you, but I'm . . . I'm not hungry." His voice sounded as if he'd swallowed sandpaper.

I eased myself to the curtains, pulling them slowly so his eyes could adjust to the light in the room. Turning around to sit next to him, my eyes caught his. I stifled a gasp. In a few short hours, his face aged by ten years. Dark bags hung under his brown eyes. His lips were dry and cracked.

"It's going to be all right," I cooed, rubbing his back.

"How many more lies will there be?" He stared into the backyard, his eyes as glassy as the window. "What else has she kept from us?"

I placed my hand on top of his. "I hope nothing else."

"I've stood by her. Through everything."

When his eyes met mine, for a small moment, some deep meaning lay inside them. One I didn't know if I wanted to ask about. I tore myself away and changed the subject before I could.

"I can't understand why Mom didn't want me to know about this other world. Why did she have to die for me to be a part of it?"

"We all make mistakes. But that's not to say that it doesn't hurt that she kept herself . . ." He paused, his haunting eyes boring into me. "And you a secret."

Was I scaring him?

"I don't know why she kept all of this a secret," I said. "But do you think I can do it? Save the other world?"

The room stayed quiet as his face contorted from sadness to confusion. Did he not believe I could do this? Or was there something else?

"Dad, we have to be open with each other."

He didn't meet my gaze as he spoke. "You need to be honest with yourself, hun. Why you're saving this Fable world. I know you feel responsible for Liliana's death. I just don't know why. What happened that day? With your mom and with Nikolas. I remember bits and pieces. But something just isn't right."

Why couldn't he just let this go? I wasn't going to tell him. He thought it would help us, but it would break us apart.

I glanced around the room for anything else to talk about, and a purple envelope caught my eye. My name was written in my mom's handwriting.

"What's that?" I pointed to the envelope.

My dad followed my finger. "I thought about what Mara had said all night. And then it got me thinking. When Liliana told me she'd adopted Damian without telling me, I was angry. She and I got into a fight. And at one point, I thought I saw something fly across the room. At the time I didn't think much of it. It was so long ago, I don't know how I remembered it now." He took the envelope from his bedside and handed it to me. The label was already ripped open. "Sorry." He blushed. "But after last night and the way she went on about making sure you got this on your eighteenth birthday, I had to know what was inside."

"Well then you can wait a few more weeks to give it to me if you want." I tried to hand it back to him.

He shook his head, pushing it back to me. "No, you need to read what's inside."

I took the letter out of the envelope and unfolded it.

Rylee,

I know there are a lot of things in your life right now that are confusing. And you're probably pretty angry at me and I don't blame you. First, you need to know you're a witch. It's crazy I know, but it's true. All the women in our family were witches. I'm amazed even Grandma Ana kept it from you. Then there's the fact you just met some people saying they know me, and I've never told you about them. I met Mara when I went on charity trips to London. And as for her parents, I'd gotten to know them from living in London before meeting your dad.

Mara told me a few weeks ago I was going to die. So, I needed to write you this letter so you would understand what was happening to you. I have a locket that I want you to have. It will help you save our world. I know it's a lot to ask of you. But I know if anyone can do it, it's you.

I want you to understand that I love you. And know I never wanted to lie to you or your dad about you, myself, and the Sullivans. I didn't tell you both about any of it because I was protecting you from the Fable world. Not everyone is as kindhearted as you Rylee. I would be lying to myself though if I told you I also let my past experiences partially reflect on me not telling you. But even with that, I need your help now to save what's left of it. Mara told me what could happen to our world if this madness isn't stopped. I'm sorry I'm not here to help you now. Please let Mara do that. Oh, my sweet girl, this was never supposed to happen.

I'll love you forever and always. Happy Birthday my sweet Sunflower.

Mom

These were her scatterbrained words. Her almost illegible handwriting. Her nickname to me when I was born. It was all true, but the letter didn't tell me *why* she kept it from me. And *for protection* wasn't good enough reasoning. I needed to talk to someone. Someone who could maybe help me understand any of this. I thought of Farrah.

"Dad, do you think you can call Farrah and get me an appointment?"

"Of course, but why?"

"She wants to help me. And I want to understand."

"All right, I'll see what I can do."

I hugged him. "I love you. We're in this together."

"I love you too. And I promise I'm always going to be here for you, hun."

An hour later, my head was still spinning sitting in Farrah's waiting room. Maybe she could help me, maybe she couldn't. But when she called me in, I knew there was only one way to find out.

7

"I didn't see you coming back so soon," Farrah said, grabbing her pen and notebook from her desk. "I hope nothing's wrong."

"Everything is." I sat on her new red leather couch. "Is this new?"

"Yes. I had to bring in my old couch while waiting for this one."

Today Farrah's hair flowed in ringlets down to the collar of a golden turtleneck, with a matching black-and-gold pinstriped skirt. "So, Rylee, what seems to be the problem?"

I couldn't come out and tell her every magical thing that was happening to me. So, I made my next statement carefully. "Well, I met a woman yesterday named Mara. Said she knew my mom."

"And you don't believe her?" It didn't sound like an accusation. More like she was curious.

I shook my head. "It's just all so weird to me. My mom never mentioned anyone named Mara. But then my mom gave me this letter telling me to trust this woman. And that my mom needed me to do something that I'm not even sure

I can do. But she never told me why she hid it all in the first place." I huffed. "Really, I don't know why it pisses me off so much. She did this all the time."

"Do you believe that maybe your mother was protecting you from something?"

I rolled my eyes. "I don't need protection. I *need* answers." As Farrah wrote in her notebook, I went on. "And Mara keeps talking to me about things as if she knows everything about me and who I am."

Farrah peered up at me enough to still see her notebook. "Well, if she *did* spend time with your mother, that would make sense."

My jaw clenched. "Okay fine, but it just makes me uncomfortable. Because it's nothing I've ever known about myself." My temples throbbed from the adrenaline coursing through my veins.

Farrah stared at her notes, at me, her notes again, then back at me, and for the first time, she frowned. She didn't have an answer. "What is it you want to hear, Rylee?"

My fist clenched. "I want to understand why, for seventeen years of my life, my mom thought she needed to hide me from knowing who I really was. Who she was."

Farrah placed her notebook in her lap, folded her hands in them, and leaned forward. Her features softened again. "Maybe your mom saw how her work life had affected her relationships negatively. And she didn't want that for you. That she wanted you to have a life of your own. Not to be told what your future was. And as for Mara, maybe your mom thought if you knew of her, you would know that Mara was part of whatever your mother was doing."

Her answers made sense. My mom did have a reason for everything she did. Whether it was right or wrong. But how could not telling me be the right thing? I wanted to believe so much of what Farrah said. My mom wasn't an evil person, but she wasn't an angel either.

"Rylee, let me ask you something. How close were you and your mom?"

We weren't that close since I *literally* drove her to her death. That's what I wanted to say, but that's not what came out.

"We didn't see eye to eye much." I let my gaze settle on her odd owl figurines because, though they gave me the creeps, they wouldn't make me deal with the pain wrestling on the surface now. I wouldn't have to see the lifeless look in her eyes. Smell the rush of water as it attacked my lungs.

"Rylee. Rylee."

I turned to the voice in a sudden daze. "Huh?" I was still in Farrah's office. "Sorry." I blushed. "It's . . . It's still hard . . ."

"Deaths always are. But it's even harder when the one you loved died, and things were left unresolved. Is that what happened with your mom?"

I questioned her but then remembered she'd talked to my dad the day I'd come here.

"I killed my mother," I whispered.

"I don't quite understand what you mean. Can you explain?" Again, she asked this question like she wanted to understand. She wasn't accusing me. Wasn't upset.

It was instantaneous. The skin around my knuckles whitened. Heat rose in my cheeks. "I can sit here all day long and tell you that my mom neglected her family and that was why I was angry at her. That I always felt the people she helped were more important than me. But the truth is, I'm the real bad guy. I've said horrible things to my mom. I've gotten mad at her for stupid things. And right before we crashed, she told me that she wasn't going to be home for my birthday." As if someone turned on a faucet, I couldn't stop the tears from falling. "I . . . I told her if she . . ." My words faltered. "If she left to never come back." My face crumpled into my hands. "The last thing I ever said to her was that I never wanted to see her again. How could I say something so horrible?" But then I wondered, how could she have been so cruel to kill her family?

Farrah handed me a tissue. I wanted to tell her that the biggest part of my guilt had come from not understanding the visions that could have saved them. But it was easier just to tell her this, so she didn't think I was completely psychotic. This hurt the most, and this I'd never forgive.

"Your father told me a bit about that day, from what he could remember. But tell me exactly how you felt when you learned your family was dead."

I didn't want to do this, but I had to. I had to talk to someone or else I would go crazy.

"I shouldn't have gotten to live. But my dad got me out."

"And you wished he hadn't?"

"No!" I rasped. "Damian would have been able to grow up and have a life of his own. And my dad wouldn't have to spend the rest of his life in agony. Having people pity him because of his handicap. My mom might have still been alive, and we could have fixed this. Done this all together." I banged my fist into the arm of the couch. "I should have been punished for the things I said to her. For the things I didn't see."

The couch dipped at the end. "We've all done things we aren't proud of. When I was your age, I got pregnant but aborted the baby. Now the doctor told me I can't have any more children. I feel like that's my punishment. But we are human, and it's normal to feel this way. You might have said those things, but you didn't make those choices for your mom."

"I'm trying to move on, but I can't. My dad has asked me

twice now about that day. And every time, I freeze. I know he's not doing it on purpose, but I feel like he's trying to make me say it so I'll get over it."

Farrah made her way back to her chair. "I don't think that's it at all. When we ask for information from someone, we ask it because we want to know. But if we ask for it more than once, we *need* to know."

I couldn't help but wonder then. My dad was talking to me now. And only really about that day. Could he have been trying to get our relationship back on track so he could find out more about that day? Did he need to know so he could try?

"Is there something about that day your dad wants to know about and thinks you know it?" Farrah asked, bringing me out of my thoughts. "It's clear why you don't want to talk about it, but remember, your dad is dealing with this too. He might also have pain of his own in this."

I'd never thought about how my dad felt about all this, but she was right. He'd gone through that day, too, and if I told him what he wanted to know, maybe he would understand. Or maybe he would disown me. I handed the tissues back to Farrah but said nothing.

"Guilt is an unfair thing," she said. "To have your mom die before you were able to reconcile your relationship with her is heartbreaking. But as sad as that is, understand you have another chance to make things right with your dad. As I told you in the beginning, *you* have to want this. No one else."

But I would never be ready to lose my dad forever.

"Thank you, Farrah." I walked with her out of her office. "Can I see you in a few weeks?"

"I already have you down."

My dad's beat-up minivan waited for me in the parking lot. Twice I considered running back inside, but Farrah was right. This was his pain too. The heat cuddled me like a blanket when I jumped into the van. We turned on the main road when I'd decided to tell my dad about my session with Farrah, but he spoke first.

"I know I haven't been the best, well . . ." He rubbed the steering wheel, making the plastic squeak. "I'm sorry. I want to be better for you."

He took one of his hands from the steering wheel and reached for mine. I wanted to be happy about this, but after talking to Farrah, in the back of my mind, I couldn't help but wonder if he had an ulterior motive for the way he'd been acting.

I continued to stare at his hand on mine, too ashamed to look at him. "Does why you're wanting to be here for me now have anything to do with wanting to know what happened that day?"

The sigh that left him shattered every bone in my body. It hurt him to know his daughter saw him this way. But his words understood it. "I can't be mad at you for feeling that way. I've done nothing to show anything otherwise." We stopped at a red light. The broken five-minute red light. My dad took my face in his hands. "But I promise you, I would never do anything that heartless to you. I've done enough to your sweet heart already."

Silence spread between us as his hands fell. "I used to think you wanted me to talk about that day so I would get over it. But then Farrah told me that you might just *need* to know about that day."

"I never wanted you to feel like that." His shoulders fell as the light finally turned green. "But there is a part of me that does believe that if you *do* talk about it, you could find some peace as I have." A heartbeat passed between us. Something like confusion rested in his eyes.

"And maybe I will." I hoped saying that would ease his mind.

But that confusion had branded itself in his gaze. "You know that I want to know what happened that day, but now you need to know why." His eyes hardened. "After he hit me, I died. But then it was like five seconds later I was alive, and you and that guy were on the ground." He paused. "I just want to know why all of this happened. We were driving and then it's just blank. What happened to me? How did I survive? And why did I feel like I was in this black space and losing my soul even though I was dead? And you . . ."

I stared out the window. All he wanted was closure. I didn't know how he'd survived. I would tell him everything I could, but not about my mom. I wasn't ready to lose him forever. So, with a deep breath, I began the story I would never forget.

My dad's facial expressions changed about every minute or so as I told him about Nikolas running him over. About Nikolas's still unexplainable white veins and eyes. He cringed when I told him about what Nikolas had done to him.

"I still feel like an idiot for just sitting there." Even though he'd paralyzed me. The tips of my fingers burned as my fist pressed into my thighs.

"Sweetheart, you don't have to go on." But his kind voice couldn't stop the tears. It actually made them worse because of how thoughtful they were. I let the sobs consume me. All this pain spilled out. As if all this time my body had been cased in numbness and my tears the solvent.

"I don't want to tell you anymore, but I have to," I shuttered with a hiccupping breath. "I don't know if I was seeing things or what, but I could have sworn I saw what looked like a skull tattoo." My dad's eyes went wide. "What?"

"I remember seeing that in one of the moments I woke up. When he was lying on the ground. What else do you remember?"

I thought back through the haze of that day. "I saw this white smoke coming out of you and into his tattoo." It was so terrifying; I was sure to never forget it. "And you were disintegrating right in front of me."

My dad pulled into our driveway, turned off the car, and faced me. Desperation in his eyes scared me. "Rylee, how did you stop it?"

That was the part that was hard to explain. I was paralyzed, then I wasn't. I felt it, though. It hummed in every vein. It tickled every nerve. But I *felt* something holding it back.

It was magic. My magic.

"I screamed for him to stop. And then deep in my stomach, I felt this weird feeling. And then my finger started to tingle. I saw lightning and then I threw it at him." Chills ran down my spine thinking of his haunting eyes glaring at me. "Doing that pissed him off and he paralyzed me, but I was able to get out of it. And then I saw a water puddle, so I put my hand in it and shocked us all and everything went black."

"Hun, I'm so sorry all of this happened to you. But you saved my life. If you hadn't done that—been able to—I would have died. I'm so grateful to you."

He wouldn't have said that if he knew I'd killed his wife and son.

My dad's gratitude was sincere and his words true, but there was no resolve in his eyes.

"You want to know about before." It didn't come out as a question because I knew the answer. He'd literally been asking it. And I couldn't hold out anymore.

He cringed, staring at Drake's flickering pumpkin on the

front porch. "She just flew off the bridge like our lives didn't matter to her." He tore his gaze from the pumpkin and then to me, running his fingers through his hair. "What happened? What made her do that?"

My heart plummeted. Why did he have to know the one thing that would tear us apart? But if I told him, we could finally move on. My thoughts went back and forth. Should I or shouldn't I? Telling him the truth would either break us or make us stronger. I had a bad feeling it would break us.

"What makes you think I know?"

He turned back to the pumpkin. "I've seen how painful this has been for you. I may not have been there when I should, but I've seen how every time anyone says her name, you cry. Or how you can't even go to the garage because her paintings are in there. You blame yourself for what happened that day in some way. I can see it in your eyes. It's not your fault, but it also means you know what happened."

Though it terrified me, he deserved to know the truth. This was his life too. So, I told him everything about that day, from the visions to the last thing I'd said to her.

"I never thought my words would hurt her so much she would try to kill us," I cried. "I never thought what not understanding those visions would really mean. I'm so sorry for killing our family." My dad slumped, his arms limp and his eyes distant. Minutes passed, and he still said nothing. Like a stone statue staring into nothingness. I had done it. I had broken him. "Dad, I need you to say something," I pleaded.

His voice came, but at a whisper. "What happened wasn't your fault, Rylee. It was mine."

8

The next morning when I awoke at dawn, as usual, my dad had already left for work. He texted me to let me know he'd gotten to work fine. The silence between us was different this time. His comment still rang in my head. He blamed himself for what happened that day. Why? Knowing I wouldn't get that answer yet, I spent most of my morning cleaning the house, doing laundry, and finishing next week's homework. Which was a normal thing for kids in a private school to do. Plus, I was just two months away from being able to graduate early. My heart broke every time I thought of it because I never got to tell my mom. I'd told my dad I wanted to tell her.

Suddenly my phone pinged.

> MARA: Hey, I know we were just talking and all, and you might have a lot going on, but we kind of need to start practicing your magic.

I slapped my palm against my forehead. A timeline I wasn't ready for. I let my fingers hover over the keyboard, thinking. I wanted to do this, but then there was something my dad had said to me yesterday. That I needed to be honest with myself about *why* I was going to save the Fable world. I thought of my sessions with Farrah. Was I doing this because I was trying to make amends for my mom's death?

Another ping.

> CLAIRE: RY! Girl, I need a BIG fav! I signed up for this thing like forever ago and now I can't do it. It's to help that food bank downtown. I think you said your mom worked there. So, what ya say? Help a girl out?

Claire Banks and I had been friends since kindergarten. But of course, she'd never been to my house. I'd been to hers many times to tutor her. I knew Claire enough to know when she said she couldn't make it, she had a party to go to.

It felt like the universe sent me a sign. This was how I could start to heal from my mom's death. Maybe. I hadn't gone anywhere since my mom and Damian's death, and I had to change that. Starting now.

> ME: Sure, got you covered.

> CLAIRE: OMG! Be there @ noon!

I swiped back to Mara's text, reading it over and over again. What if I was doing this to make amends for what I did to my mom? Would that be so bad? I didn't know these people. But at the same time, they were just as human as the rest of us. They deserved to live. And if I could stop something from happening, then I would.

> ME: Sorry, it's been a little weird here. But I'll see you tommorrow.

Before I headed to the food bank, I wanted to practice some of my magic. Maybe if I got a head start, Mara would be happy about it. I would make it a bit easier for her. I sat on the cold wood floor of my bedroom staring at my hands. I thought it best to start with lightning because using flames didn't make any sense at all. I remembered back to when I'd asked Mara about what I could do if I wanted to practice magic on my own. That I had to tell it what I wanted it to do.

All I wanted was some lightning. Was that so hard? Suddenly, in my veins, just as it had on the bridge that day, electricity shot through my body. I wanted lightning. And in a second, there it was, but then it wasn't.

I tried again. On the bridge it'd lasted longer. This time I thought harder, focused harder on what I wanted. The lightning danced around my fingers. I stood, gazing around the room for the safest place to throw it. The only thing I could think of was my empty clothes basket. Readying myself, I aimed. The bolt of lightning ricocheted off the mirror, burst through a small hole it made in the window, and nearly missed a powerline.

I stared at my hands again, readying them once more. I needed more magic, more control. But as I focused, it was as if something held itself back inside me. Opening my eyes, the lightning was gone. I tried to bring it back, but it wouldn't come. My phone alarm chimed then, meaning I had to leave. Guess I would have to try more later.

It was thirty minutes until noon, and the bustling of downtown was in full swing. The sky was like a cloudless ocean. I wormed my way through the crowd. It was strange walking down this strip. I never wanted to explore this place. To be a part of it. But now, I kind of did. I let my eyes wander. All shops and buildings rubbed together like two papers in a book. I tried to focus on that, but the memories came without my permission. They weren't just buildings. My mom had tricked me into eating at the sushi bar, and it made me sick. I laughed.

More clothes and food shops. And then Sam's Pizza Joint. I laughed out loud this time. I could never forget telling my mom I thought that the basil on their pizza had to be weed. People started to stare at me, so I moved on.

I hurried through the strip, walking past an entire bricked market, the park, and a public art exhibit taking place at the museum. I soon found myself weaving through yet another crowd of people. I was beginning to remember why I never did this. But then, there was a small girl licking an ice cream cone. Her hair as bright and fiery red as mine. Her big green eyes stared up at her mom as we all waited by the crosswalk. I remembered instantly my dad getting me vanilla ice cream every Friday after school when I was younger.

Once I'd made it past the small Mexican market where my mom would get me a Spanish soda after helping her, I recognized the food bank across the street. I focused on the line of people. It had always been sad to see these poor people line themselves down the sideway waiting for food. Some having to be told there was none left.

Every set of eyes that met mine was like a small needle pricking my heart. For a small moment, I wished I could take away their pain. It was a hopeless thought as I struggled my way inside.

Thud.

A man with wild, hazel eyes and a wrinkled face met my gaze, his gray beard matted to his chin. Much like his clothes to his skin. His eyes pleaded for safety. For food. For a chance. My problems seemed stupid compared to his mountain of uncertainty. I didn't want him to feel this way. I wanted him to find peace. And then, unexpectedly, he smiled.

"Thank you, young lady."

And he walked on.

The soup kitchen was packed as it was on most Sundays. But that didn't stop me from seeing my mom everywhere. Her behind the kitchen line spooning out food. Boxing plates to take across town. Sweeping floors and wiping off tables. I'd only come here with her on Thanksgiving and Christmas. I stared at the walls as if they would move or something. The yellow was so calming. Not the lifeless peeling white. Because my mom never wanted that. Even the hardwood floor, my mom had put in herself. My throat tightened. But I had one thing to see before I got to work.

Back in the front entrance was the mural of my mom and Damian. Damian's picture had been his yearbook photo because it was the only picture he'd been able to take. Car stickers lined the red construction paper frame of his picture. I turned away. His last words blared in my head. *Sissy save me.* I missed Damian so much.

But my mom made me sob like a baby. Everything about her was beautiful. Her luscious red hair that shaped her round face. Her deep green eyes, bow lips, and adorable freckles across the bridge of her crooked nose. And what was funny, I looked just like her, other than my nose. So, when I looked at myself, it was like looking at a reminder of who made me.

I turned back to the photo. Gold glitter glue traced with green construction paper around her picture because it was her favorite color. And each corner had a paper lily around it. I knew of only one person who could do that.

"I understand why you didn't come." Cassie moved from behind the double auditorium doors. "No one blames you for that."

I knew she wasn't talking about my self-guilt, but I still stayed fixated on the pictures. "A friend of mine signed up to help you guys. But she can't."

"And you thought by coming here it could help you too?"

I turned to her now. "Kind of . . ."

I paused trying to think of what today taught me. The shops, the little girl, the food bank. It'd shown me what I missed the most, but I couldn't tell her that. I didn't deserve her pity because she didn't know the truth. I forced a smile.

"I think it has."

I'd spent the first few hours spooning out food, sweeping, then boxing up food. After a few more hours, Cassie asked if I could start packing the boxes into the truck. Heading out with a small box pressed to my side, I prepared to shield my face from the sun. But I didn't need to. The sun tried to claw its way through the dingy clouds. So much for a sunny day.

But then came a soft childish giggle. Stepping down and off the final step, I turned to the sound. A young girl giggled beside a puddle. Her tousled brown hair bounced as she splashed in the water, creating a rainbow that disappeared with the mist. Part of me wished I was that small again. To be so innocent to the world. Not to know heartbreak, pain, and loss. Then her mother came toward her with a bag of food, nearly dislocating the young girl's shoulder while scolding her. Maybe she did know pain.

Another hour passed, and I was holding the last box. I didn't want to let it go because if I did, it would mean I would have to go back home and face my problems, and I just wasn't ready for that. I sat the box down and stared at my hands. Thinking of earlier, maybe I should have started with just forming the magic and then messing around with it.

Since lightning didn't go the way I planned, I thought of my fire.

Closing my eyes, I told myself that I wanted fire in my hands. Nothing. I tried again and still nothing. What was I doing wrong? Was I not wanting it badly enough?

Finally, by the fifth try, fire laced around my fingers. Bright orange and red. I even felt a bit of heat from it. Now it was time to play. But just as before, it fizzled. I shook my head. Maybe it was for the best. Who knew what I could have done?

So, with no more fun, I picked up my box again.

"Our paths cross again, I see."

I yelped, my heart leaping into my throat. The box I'd been holding dropped hard on my foot. Pain shot through, and I screamed.

Instinctively I reached for my foot. Drake jumped into action, kneeling beside me. Though tears blurred most of my vision, I met his gaze. And just like the other times I'd seen him, his eyes showed nothing.

His tone remained expressionless as he asked his question. "Where does it hurt?"

Wincing, I pointed to my big toe. The way he delicately untied my shoe and took off my sock made me feel like he had done this before. He examined it, cautiously touching it like he knew what he was doing. His cold finger tingled against my flaming skin.

"Would you mind moving it for me, please?"

The small amount of movement sent a shooting pain up my foot. By the time I gathered the breath to tell him it wasn't necessary, Drake carried me to the edge of the truck. Being in his arms again reminded me of the first time he'd picked me up at the barn. Strong and never wavering. But still, in the last few days, he barely spoke to me and here he was doctoring me.

"It seems as though you have possibly just bruised it. But you should receive accurate advice from a doctor rather than listen to a novice such as myself."

I tried to stand but quickly fell back against the truck. "No hospital."

Helping me back into the truck, he said, "Okay, no doctor. I just need to go inside then for some ice."

It was difficult to think of nothing but the pain as Drake went away. But his voice quickly carried from the back room. Why was he here?

Minutes later, he returned with a small bag of ice. For the first time since he'd shown up, I was able to get a good look at him. He had his black hair slicked back as he'd had done when I first met him. He wore a dark-gray cashmere turtleneck under a maroon trench coat and black slacks with loafers.

"I wanted to thank you for the pumpkin." I took the already melting ice bag from him. "It nearly broke my neck." I chuckled. "But thank you."

"Why do you not prefer hospitals?"

Not a conversationalist. Got it.

Well, if he didn't have to talk about something, then neither did I. Plus, it wasn't something I *wanted* to talk about.

"There's a lot of bad memories."

"Like Liliana and Damian?"

Chills shot up my spine hearing their names now. As if it were a curse to say them. Or because the way he said their names sounded so detached. Like they weren't people at all. "It's . . . it's more than that."

"Do I frighten you?"

My brows knitted together. "What would make you think that?"

"You seem rather hesitant with me. As if I make you nervous."

I chewed on the inside of my cheek. "It's hard to explain."

"Please try."

At least we weren't talking about my fear of hospitals.

"You intimidate me." I waited to see if that phrase might offend him, but as always, nothing. So, I went on. "When I look at you, I don't know what . . ." This boy made me nervous in a way that had nothing to do with attraction and everything to do with not understanding him. It's like when he was around me, I became a completely different person. "I get nervous around you because I don't know what you're thinking or feeling. And what you say doesn't help with that."

His eyes remained trained on me. "I do not wish for you to perceive me this way. Understand that I am different than most people you may have become accustomed to."

"Or maybe you haven't found the right friend. A friend who could help you open up a bit."

Still, he gave away nothing, not even in his response. "And you believe that to be you?"

I would have been lying to myself if I didn't think it would be nice. But of course, I wasn't going to tell him that. "Who you choose to confide in is up to you."

"How have you become so accustomed to trusting people? Say my sister and myself as an example. You hardly know us."

"Honestly, I'm not." I thought about when I first talked to Farrah. "But I was always taught to give the benefit of the doubt to those who deserved it. When I look into someone's eyes, that tells me if I can trust them. There's this sincerity inside them. I saw it in Mara's eyes."

"What do you see in mine?"

His question nearly knocked the wind out of me. What should have been crashing waves of blue in his eyes, were calming seas that could carry on forever. I didn't want to lie to him; he already seemed so lost.

"It doesn't work on everyone." I was hoping that would be enough.

I kept thinking about his question. I may have not seen anything in his eyes, but that didn't mean I couldn't trust him. He'd pulled me from that fire. If he hadn't, I would have died. He was here doctoring my foot. And there was the pumpkin. These small things were enough for me to believe I could trust him enough to talk to him.

"Does your fear of hospitals have something to do with your past?"

He wasn't going to let this go.

"It's hard to talk about." I had to swallow the lump in my throat before I could continue. "My grandma meant a lot to me." I stared up at him then. "Why are you so interested in knowing?"

"I am trying to get to know you."

Why now? He hadn't wanted to in the small amount of time I'd known him. And why was it oddly comforting? "She died at the hospital," I said, not looking at him.

"It seems as if more is preoccupying your mind on the subject."

I huffed. "Don't miss much, do you?"

"I am rather attuned to my surroundings and others. I believe it to be a necessity."

That made sense now how he'd figured me out so easily when I first met him.

My words faltered. "I . . . I should have been able to save her. I should have understood what those visions were telling me." I focused on the orange leaves falling from a nearby tree. "Since that night I've tried everything I could to keep the rest of my family alive. And we see how well that worked." It bothered me that he didn't look shocked or sad.

"Why do you find yourself not able to accept what is not in your control?"

His question blindsided me, but I answered it the best I could. "Everything is in my control. Maybe not the last month or so. But if I can save this Fable world as my mom wanted, then that's a start. She spent her whole life saving others. Now it's my turn."

"So, you are doing this to redeem yourself for your guilt of your mother?"

He would understand. He was dealing with the same things with his mother. And maybe hearing what I had to say could help him in some way.

"In a way you're right, but in a way you're wrong. See, my mom wasn't around a lot when I was a kid, because she would go to different places to help people. And it hurt. Now I just wish I had more time with her. But all in all, I admired her for what she did." I chuckled, thinking of something cheesy. "So, I guess you could say now I'm walking in her footsteps."

"Rylee, from knowing you for this short time, I do not believe that you are doing this for amends. I believe that you do care for them in some way. And this does explain why you are here today."

I chuckled. "I guess if you want to look at it that black-and-white, sure. But a friend of mine asked if I could come and help her out."

My curiosity wanted to know why he was here. Based on how he'd been acting toward me, though, there was a sure-fire chance I wasn't going to get much out of him.

"You want to know why I am here as well?"

My mouth fell open. "How did you know that?"

"As I have told you before, I am rather attuned to people. And you have had a rather eager expression. So, I can only assume that is the question you would like to ask."

I was speechless. "Okay, so, um . . . I guess I just assumed you were told to come here. I mean you kind of give me this vibe like you don't like to be around people."

There, in his eyes, for one millisecond, was something like pain, or was it anger? But in another blink, it was gone. "If you must know, my sister sent me here. I nearly beat a man to death at a pub. She believed I could acquire compassion coming here."

"A bar? How old are you?"

"Eighteen. In the United Kingdom, the legal drinking age is eighteen."

"Why did you beat him up? Were you drunk or something?"

Without answering my question, Drake gave me his hand to help me down from the truck. In doing so, his jacket sleeve rose. Revealing a thick silver cuff bracelet around his right wrist.

"Where did you get that?" I asked.

He stared for a moment at where I had pointed as if he didn't know what I was talking about. "It was given to me when I was young."

"By who?"

But Drake only helped me foreword. "Best take you home before your father begins to worry." He threw my arm over his shoulder as we walked to the car.

His quick change of subject gave me a headache. "Drake, do you really believe not trusting anyone and being alone will make you happy?"

He didn't answer until he helped me into the car. "I do. But this belief comes from more than not trusting someone, Rylee." Before I could ask him what he meant, he closed the door, going to the other side of the car.

Drake had closed himself off, and I found myself needing to know why. Maybe it was curiosity. Or maybe I wanted to help him. Either way, Drake Sullivan was hiding something from me.

He turned the key in the ignition. "Why do you possess this need for me to find someone trustworthy?"

My fingers knotted together. I chose not to look at him. "Honestly, when I look at you, I see myself. I've always wanted someone to be here for me. And they never were. And it doesn't seem like anyone's here for you."

"Please do not look at me as a charity case for you. Or something for you to play with, if you will."

Play with? What was he talking about?

"Look, what's so wrong with being friends with someone who knows your pain?"

Drake let the conversation end at that as he drove down our street. Then a few minutes later, we sat awkwardly in my driveway. It was too quiet. My eyes wandered to my rearview mirror, hoping to find anything to talk about. Then Mara's yellow Mustang came into view.

"Do you really think Mara can teach me magic?"

"I do. She has traveled around the world to learn her craft."

"That's reassuring." Putting my hand on the door handle, I noticed the lights in the kitchen were off. "Well, I guess I should get inside. Good night, Drake."

"Rylee, I would like for you to understand that I do enjoy your kind company. Apologies for my behavior. I look forward to seeing you tomorrow. I will pick you up around seven. Is that alright?" I nodded. "Until then."

For the smallest moment, I could have sworn something lingered in his eyes. And it made me smile.

9

I didn't know what to expect when I walked inside my house, but I wasn't expecting the blaring sound of the smoke detector. Or a thin cloud of smoke traveling from the hallway. Where the hell was this coming from? Coughing, I tried to see if I could figure out where the smoke originated from. It had to be the kitchen.

Coughing through the thick smoke, I managed to find the culprit. The stove. So I wouldn't burn my hand, I reached for a mitten we always kept on the counter. Opening the oven, the smoke flew out and plumed a dark smog into the already gray air. I waved the smoke away, and a nearly black cake pan sat in my hand. I swore and threw it in the trash. This wasn't like my dad. He'd always get upset with me when I left the stove or oven on.

Even after defusing the problem with a fire extinguisher and opening the window, my body remained tense. The thick smoke didn't help. Where was my dad? I made my way to his room, wondering if he'd fallen asleep.

"Dad, why—" But nothing had been touched, and his room was empty. Closing the door, my brain went into overdrive. My next thought was to look outside. I ran to the front door to look at the side window. My dad's van remained in the driveway. Did he go see Chuck? I pulled out my phone to call him.

"Rylee?"

"Yeah, have you seen my dad?"

"No, why? Is that an alarm? Is everything okay?"

I panicked and hung up. I could only think of one other place. The living room. Even though the threshold between the kitchen and living room lights were off, maybe he'd fallen asleep there. My heart hammered against my chest in the darkness as I made it to the side table near the couch.

Once I found the lamp and turned it on, I screamed. Blood pooled on the floor next to his body. I searched the best I could through the smoke for the cause, but nothing had been touched.

"Dad!" Kneeling, I pressed two fingers to his neck. Where was his pulse? Placing my index and middle fingers on his wrist, at the base of his thumb, I tried to focus. He couldn't leave me. I needed him. The faintest pulse throbbed beneath my fingers. Letting out the largest breath I could, I reached for my phone and prayed I wasn't too late.

The consecutive beeps of the heart monitor were the only reassurance he was still alive. I'd done this to him, so I deserved to be here. Sleep hadn't found me as if to punish me. I hated the smell of this hospital. Now I hated it even more as the smell of my dad's blood from my shirt mixed with it. Curled up in the chair, EMTs rushed in a man wearing a breathing mask with a little girl crying by his side. A mirror image of my pain only eight hours ago. It was now six fifteen in the morning.

I was angry. Angry he didn't call me. Every minute his eyes remained closed, my chest grew tighter and tighter. If he died, I would lose my chance to make things right.

Suddenly a knock came on my dad's door. Gazing up, Drake stood in the doorway. I'd forgotten he told me last night that he was going to give me a ride to school today.

"Hey, I'm sorry. I meant to call you," I whispered as he came into the room.

"It is quite all right. My sister informed me of what happened. How is he now?"

His question came out as actual concern, which was odd, but at the same time comforting. "The doctor stitched up his head, but he still hasn't woken up." My heart broke as I thought of all the ways this could have happened.

Drake's voice brought me out of my thoughts. "My original intentions were to ask if you still required a ride to school."

I didn't want to go through the motions of school for eight hours. "He'll need me when he wakes up."

"The brain can only process so much at a time."

I watched the rise and fall of my dad's body as I spoke in a low voice. One, to keep my dad from waking. And two, because it hurt so much to say them. "Have you ever felt on your best day, everything in the world makes sense and nothing can go wrong? And then when you think of your worst day, everything around you seems to blur? The things you once thought were the truth, are lies. And what once seemed okay is hopeless. That's how I feel now. But I have to be strong for my dad because his life has changed more than mine. And now he's in the hospital because of me."

"Life is a complex mechanism we can never understand. But over time we learned to adapt and understand why things happen. You must believe your father's accident was not your fault."

"I wish it were that easy to do, Drake. I really do." I turned back to him because, for the first time since meeting him, his forehead creased with worry. After giving my dad one last look over, I took the seat next to Drake.

"My sister retrieved this from your home. I hope you do not mind."

Drake handed me my school uniform. I took it, thanked him, and ran to the bathroom to change. I threw away the soiled shirt. It was nice to have some company here, but I couldn't figure out why he was here. Coming back into the room, Drake stared at my dad, that worry still resting in his eyes.

"Drake, why are you here?"

His eyes softened. "I assumed you to be rather upset, so I thought you might enjoy some company. Though I might not be the best choice." His smile seemed so unnatural. Like he was trying too hard to do it. Did I make him feel uncomfortable too? "But I do wish to be mates."

It felt as if he'd put a small bandage over a piece of my broken heart. "I'm glad, but why?"

"I am not much of a person unless I meditate. Along with my emotions, it also provides my mind with clarity. I found my thoughts returning to the food bank. Seeing how kind and friendly you are. To people who are strangers. Like myself. That is what qualifies as a true mate. But please do not be mistaken. This, unfortunately, does not mean I will open myself up to you."

I could only take a deep breath in an attempt to hide my disappointment. I plastered on a fake smile. "We don't need to know everything about each other."

A low groan came from my dad's bedside. I almost tripped over a chair running to him.

"Daddy!" I laid my body on top of his as Drake went to call the nurse.

My dad swallowed hard and spoke in a slow and hoarse voice. "Hun, what . . . are you . . . doing here?"

"I need to be here."

"Punishing yourself with pain . . . isn't what I want."

A tall skinny brunette came into the room asking my dad all sorts of questions. So many I'd begun to drown her out. Between checking his vitals and asking how his pain was, I was going mad. I just wanted them to leave the room so I could figure out why all of this happened. Thirty minutes later, as the last nurse left the room, I was finally going to get my chance. I sat next to my dad, but he turned his focus to Drake rather than me.

"Would you mind taking Rylee to school?"

Drake stood. "Of course not, sir."

I stared at both of them. Drake didn't know me that well, but I found it hard to believe my dad thought I was leaving here without figuring out what had happened.

"Do you think I still blame myself for what happened to you?" I asked. "Is that why you're shooing me away? Because I don't anymore." Though of course I was lying about that last part. I just needed him to talk to me.

"No Rylee, that's not it."

He only ever called me by my first name when he was either mad at me or he was being serious about something. But regardless of his reasoning, I wanted to know the truth.

"Why won't you just tell me, Dad?"

The room stayed quiet. His face contorted as he thought. So, I remained quiet. But then after a few moments, he spoke. "What's today?"

"What does this question have to do with what happened to you?"

"Hun, just answer the question, please."

"October fourteenth. But I still don't know . . ." Then it hit me. "It's two and a half weeks before my birthday."

Drake joined in on the conversation. "May I ask what that means?"

My dad nudged me to tell Drake. My heart hurt at the thought. I wouldn't be able to hear her singing happy birthday to me and telling me to make two wishes. One, for the wish *I* wanted to come true. And the second, for someone else who needed a wish.

"I was born on Halloween. Which is kind of ironic now since I'm a witch and all. Anyway, every year my mom would make me a pink cake two and a half weeks before my actual birthday. The doctor told her I was supposed to be born on the fourteenth, but it didn't work out that way."

It was nice to see Drake smile. His teeth were white, but his bottom teeth were a bit crooked. Seeing it made me wonder how it was there. He'd never shown anything toward me, so why now? "What were festivities like on your true birthday?" he asked.

"I'd rather not talk about it if it's okay." Drake nodded, and I turned back to my dad. "Are you saying you were trying to make Mom's cake?"

"Yes. I went to the china cabinet to grab the plate you'd made when you were six. Do you remember? You said you wanted to feel like a princess on your birthday. And a princess only ate on a pink plate with rainbow glitter."

I laughed. "And Mom even got me a crown one year." I couldn't stop staring at my dad's bandaged head. "What happened after you got the plate?"

"Well, it was wedged between two other plates. As I was trying to move them, I guess my wheelchair hit the cabinet and your mother's great-great grandmother's vase hit me. You know the one I'm talking about. It could survive a nuclear war and be okay." Chills ran down my spine thinking of it, and I couldn't force a smile. "I had to grab something else to stop myself from falling too hard. I grabbed the door of the cabinet. And suddenly, everything, the cabinet and all, fell on me."

But when I'd found him, I found no trace of broken glass or wood anywhere around him. "You're lying. Why?"

My dad shifted his gaze to the bandage on his hand, then to the door. "He said . . . he said . . . he would leave you alone. That I was all he wanted."

Adrenaline coursed through every nerve in my body as my gaze went from Drake to my dad. "Who? Who attacked you?"

"Please just leave this alone. I . . . I can handle it."

I scoffed and pointed to his bandaged head. "Oh yeah, we see how well that worked the first time." I pinched the bridge of my nose, taking a deep breath. I didn't have a right to be angry at him. "I'm sorry. I just need to know what's going on. Please. I need to know everything."

There again was his pain-filled sigh, killing me.

"I wasn't lying when I told you that I was making your birthday cake. I was putting it into the oven when I heard noise coming from the living room. So I went to go check it out and there he was. He told me that he'd come back to finish me off."

I bit my lip trying to hold back the bile rising in my throat. "Dammit, who?"

"Nikolas." He all but choked out his name.

I couldn't speak. I couldn't think. Why had Nikolas come back?

"Did he tell you what he wanted?"

My dad stayed silent and his paled face didn't make it any better. "He wants...my...my heart..."

All blood rushed to my head. His heart. What the hell could Nikolas have wanted with that? What was he planning with it? Nikolas had to be stopped. I wasn't going to let anyone else die.

Drake asked the question that I couldn't. "Mr. Jenkins, why did you not choose to tell the police of this incident?"

"He'd go after Rylee," he whispered.

Maybe it was because I was in shock, but I asked him something that had nothing to do with Nikolas. "What did you mean when you said it was your fault that Mom died that day?"

The room fell silent as my dad shifted in his bed. "Because of what *I'd* said."

I moved closer to him. "What do you mean?"

"I know this might sound naïve, but I always thought your anger toward your mother was because you were a teenager. But I remembered that day. When she came to pick me up, she told me she wouldn't be able to make it home for your birthday, I'd gotten angry. I told her . . ." His words faltered. "I told her that if she broke your heart again, it was over between us." My dad took my hand in his. "Hun, I know we have a long way to go before we find our way back to each other, but I love you."

I rested my head on his shoulder. "I can't live in this world without you."

My dad sat up more in his bed now. "Rylee, always remember, it may seem dark now, but it won't stay that way forever." He kissed my forehead. "Now Drake, please take my daughter to school."

Drake stood as I kissed my dad goodbye.

"I'll love you forever, Dad."

"Forever and Always, Rylee."

IO

After school, I made my way to Mara's house to finally start my training. I'd asked Drake if he wanted to tag along, but he said he had some homework to do. So alone I went. When I'd first gone to Mara's house with my dad, there had been an eeriness to it. An unknown. But as I stood here now, waiting for her to answer the door after my second knock, I didn't have that feeling anymore. I still didn't know what my magic could do or how strong it was, but I understood myself more. I didn't feel like that part of my life was a mystery.

I pulled out my phone to text Mara.

> ME: Hey, I'm at your house.

> MARA: Sorry, grading papers and got stuck in traffic. Be there soon.

Well, I guess while I was waiting, I could look around.

Their grass was as green as you would see in magazines. Cut perfectly. Every bush had a place. I wasn't saying that I didn't like Mara's house, but sometimes, old things were better. I found myself staring at my house longer than I meant to, and I knew why. Because of what happened there. Of *who* was there. Nikolas had escaped from prison and was after my dad. And that was part of the reason I was still standing out here waiting for Mara. I would get her to teach me magic so I could stop him. I couldn't understand why Nikolas wanted my dad's heart. What did my dad ever do to him? Electricity ran through every nerve in my veins. I turned away. There was nothing I could do about it right now.

Stepping back onto Mara's porch, I let my fingers glide with ease along the thick white oak railing. My fingers trailed up to the beige-trimmed screen, which would be used to keep the rain from coming onto the porch. These people thought of everything. After a few minutes or so of looking at plants and sculptures, I sat in one of the two lounge chairs with a chess set between them. Picking up the remote by the chess set, I had no idea what it went to, but I pressed the on button anyway.

And then came the sound of water. A small bamboo waterfall hid nestled in the corner of the porch. But the sound grew louder by the second. The louder it grew, the clearer a forgotten memory became. The rapid water taking both my dad and me back and forth. Him trying with all his might to push through. But the water held on to us as if it had hands. Until finally it threw me loose of my dad's grip and my head smashed into a rock.

Everything went black.

"Rylee, are you okay?" Looking toward the voice, Mara stood on the top step. Her brows knitted together.

I turned, still dazed. "Wha . . ."

"Are you okay?" she asked again.

I shook my head to clear it, and it doubled as my response.

She reached into her satchel for her keys, dug them out, and unlocked the door. "Look, we'll figure this out, but until we do, we need to focus on getting your magic stronger so we can stop this war."

"Yeah, because stopping a war is better than stopping one guy, even if it's for my dad's sake."

The heat from the handcrafted fireplace welcomed us in. Mara motioned for me to sit on either the white leather couch that matched the chairs on the front porch or one of the red satin armchairs, both separated by an ornate glass-bottom table. I chose the satin chair, letting my finger slide across the velvety texture.

In the corner of the room on an easel, under a spotlight, had to be a photograph. The brushstrokes showed such patience and dedication. Such gentleness. How lively the tigress and her cubs played in water was anything but breathtaking.

"Who painted that?" I asked, not able to look away.

"Drake." She rolled her eyes. "If he cared for anything, he'd be good at it. He's been painting since he was seven."

Wow, she really didn't like him.

"He has talent." I pointed to the painting. "Why wouldn't he try to do something with it?"

"I don't bloody know," she huffed.

I hoped she wouldn't shut me down as Drake did. "Can I ask you something?"

She smirked. "You want to know why I'm such an arse to my brother?" I let my silence be my answer. "Look, it's no secret Drake and I don't have the perfect sibling bond, but he didn't ask to be the way he is. I know he can be more, and it pisses me off that he won't try to be better. I mean, he's smarter than me. Just don't tell him I told you that."

I chuckled. "I won't." Then my tone became serious. "So, you know why Drake's the way he is?" My heart pounded against my rib cage. In my ears. This was it. I would know him more. What he was hiding.

"My brother has trust issues, but I think you can see that. That's one reason why he keeps himself so closed off."

"You don't have to tell me."

"Rylee, I wouldn't even think of telling you if I couldn't see the good in you. You care for others. My brother needs people like you in his life."

"*You* seem to care for him too." I bit down on my lip.

Her brow furrowed. "I don't want him dead if that's what you mean." She deadpanned. Though I barely knew both Mara and Drake, it broke my heart to see a sibling bond this broken.

"So why is Drake the way he is?"

"He suffers from what's known as emotional detachment disorder. He can meditate to help it, but it only lasts a few days. I think he saw some therapist when he lived in London." I immediately thought of my therapy session with Farrah. This also explained Drake's attitude yesterday. "But I think the straw that broke the camel's back was what his best mate, Marcus, did to him last year. Stupid wanker."

"What happened?"

"I told him that boy couldn't be trusted."

Mara chewed on the tip of her thumbnail, staring at the fireplace. After a moment, she stood, then went to the cart behind the leather couch, which was short enough to see over. She removed the cap of the square container full of scotch and poured herself a glass.

"You want some?"

I had scotch before with my grandfather but didn't think now was the time.

"I'm good, thanks."

Mara took her glass and sat back down in her chair. "So where was I? Oh, yes, Marcus. Drake and Marcus had been best mates since year one." Mara took a sip of her scotch. "Well, last summer, Drake decided to tell Marcus the truth about himself, and it didn't go well. A few days before school started, some police officer came by telling me that Marcus had said Drake beat him up and then Drake harmed himself."

For a second, I found myself wondering if that was the same guy Drake had told me about yesterday.

"Did this happen at a pub?"

Mara shook her head. "That was something else entirely."

"Okay, what happened next?"

"Well Marcus had lied about what Drake had done to him. But then one of the officers showed me a video of Drake *showing* Marcus the truth. Drake went overboard even by my standards."

"Drake can't feel or show emotions. So I don't understand. There aren't many ways to prove that. It should have been obvious."

Mara swirled the liquid around in her scotch glass. "That wanker cut himself. The officer talked to kids and teachers at Drake's school. They told him Drake wasn't right in the head. So the officer said since we couldn't keep him under control, they were going to send him to a place where someone could."

My breath caught. "Where did they send him?"

She took a large gulp of her scotch, drinking the rest of it down. "To an asylum." She stared at the empty scotch glass for a moment.

"I didn't know they still existed."

"They don't. But with the right money and knowing the right people, you can do anything you want."

"So it was like an underground kind of place?"

"Yes and it's a place I wouldn't send my worst enemy."

She'd clenched her jaw so tightly, I thought she might break a tooth. "He was there for a month. My parents told me they didn't want him in there, but they didn't want him home either. So off to Canada we went. I was glad he was out. That place is like one of those places you would see in horror movies. They played with him like he was some toy."

Those two words. *Played with.* The same words Drake had said to me. Something had happened there. They'd done something to him. But Mara didn't know, and Drake wasn't going to tell me. I wanted to know so badly, then I looked at Mara. Maybe some dark corners didn't need light.

"I thought me having to see a therapist for an hour was scary. I can't even begin to imagine what that must have been like for him."

"But it worked out for the best. I'd also seen you in my visions but didn't know why."

Was that why they'd come here to protect me? Was I in danger?

"One thing I don't understand is, if Drake can't feel emotion, then how can he hold on to his past pain?" I asked.

"The Council, Selena, and Nathan are still trying to figure it out. But from what they've gathered over time, Drake has *only* been able to feel *some* negative emotions."

Hearing all of this broke my heart. To have to live with this every day was something I couldn't even start to imagine.

She stood from the couch. "Now enough sad crap. Are you ready to learn magic and save our world?"

"Yes!"

"Then let's get to the backyard and get started."

The sun had sunk below rooftops by the time we stepped into the lush grass. After a few steps, the grass turned into a cobblestone walkway. Tiny rustic lanterns guided the pathway to an octagonal white gazebo in the center of a lush brush of camellia, hyssop, and cyclamen. And growing were snowberries. I almost forgot why we were here.

"I don't mean to pry or anything, but how can your parents afford this stuff if they work with a group of Fables humans can't know about?"

"Nathan and Selena," she corrected. "When the Council was formed, they knew they would run into the problem of money. So, every four years when there's a new president, the Council helps him out in *magical* ways, and they get paid. Looks like they can bend the rules for themselves but not for anyone else," she muttered and then snapped her fingers, and the breathtaking landscape disappeared. "Now, let's get started. First, you need to understand magic and how it works. Let's start with your Magic Form."

"What's that?"

Mara rolled her eyes. "You're very impatient."

I blushed. My mom would always call me out on that. "Sorry. Go on."

"It's called simple magic. It's pretty simple, no pun intended. It's easy beginner's magic. Over time you harness it and make it stronger. Even the most experienced Fables still use it. Once you accept your Magic Form, which is the way a Fable's magic is released, your powers *slowly* become stronger."

"Like yours was in your hands and mine was on my fingers?"

She nodded. "There are three different forms. First, there's yours. Touch Magic. You feel the magic with your fingers. The second is mine, which is called Sphere Magic. That one's pretty self-explanatory. And last is Mind Magic. This one's tricky and rare. It's more doing with the mind than telling your magic what you want it to do. Like the other two forms." Mara held open her hand, and a flaming orb rested in the center of it.

"But every time I try to use my magic, it's like it fizzles out." I fixed on her bright flame. "I tried telling my magic what to do like you said, but it just doesn't work."

"You need to think of magic like riding a bike. Your arms and legs determine if you're going to ride the bike or fall off it. If your muscles tense or your eyes focus on something else, you will lose momentum and fall. It's the same way with magic." Mara extinguished the flame orb. "Hold out your hand and close your eyes." I did as I was told. "Now, I want you to think of what you want in your hand. Like what you want your arms and legs to do when you ride. Nod when you're ready to continue."

I wanted flames.

As if someone had used shock paddles on my chest, a warm sensation flooded through me. But it was pumping too fast. My breath couldn't keep up.

"You have to work with it, not against it. Give in. Guide it where it needs to go," Mara instructed.

The heat remained as I let it charge my magic. It filtered through my veins like water through a hose. And as the heat reached my fingers, I nodded to Mara.

"Good, now think of what you want to do with it. Like what you would want to do with your arms and legs. It's an extension of yourself, only it is less tangible. Until you let it out."

I wanted to throw it. The safest bet was throwing it to Mara so she could block it. Coming to this conclusion, I let the heat consume me again, but it wouldn't reach my fingers. I closed my eyes tighter, hoping it would help, but nothing happened.

"Mara," I huffed. "Your advice isn't working."

She frowned. "What do you do the most when riding a bike? Other than pedaling and steering."

"I don't know."

"It's breathing. It isn't enough to know it's there, but you have to release it. Like you would a breath. Now close your eyes again, and this time focus on your breathing."

Breathe in. Breathe out. I wanted flames, and I wanted to throw them.

And this time, with a long exhale of breath, the heat reached the tips of my fingers. Prying my eyes open, flames crawled around my hands like . . . Just like the fire at the barn. Images of the barn fire assaulted me. I didn't want these flames anymore. And just like that, the flames blinked away.

"I . . . I can't do this."

Mara frowned. "I'll be damned if I let you give up. You just started. The flow of magic is constant and effortless. Like breathing and like your emotions. You had your flames bright and strong until you realized they were there. You got scared and they vanished. What were you thinking about?"

I blushed, thinking about how childish this might sound to her. "The last time I touched my flames they burned me. So, I thought they would again."

For a second I thought I saw pity in her eyes, but the annoyed expression she had reserved for me returned. "Your flames can't hurt you if you harness them. But, other than telekinesis, when you release your magic, the link between the witch or warlock is broken. Therefore, the magic no longer knows where it belongs." Her eyes softened. "You have to relax."

"Relax," I repeated.

"Right. Now let's try one more time. Focus on your breathing. Let magic rush through you. Let your arms and legs control your bike."

Breathe in. Breathe out. The heat tickled every nerve in my body. Like a warm fire filling my veins. And as I opened my eyes, flames danced around my fingers.

"I did it!"

"Now, take that and throw it into this firepit." Mara waved her hands, and a firepit appeared. I concentrated. My fingers focused on the pit. The first attempt hit off toward her house, which Mara had to put out. The second nearly hit Mara. But by the third time, I'd finally gotten it into the pit.

"It's about time." She snorted. "But keep at it." Mara and I walked back to the patio. "I'm going out of town for a few days. I talked to Lucas earlier, and he told me about Nikolas. If I'm right in what I'm thinking, based on what your dad told me, that means the Council is up to something."

"How are you going to make them tell you anything?"

Mara smirked. "You'd be surprised to know what I can do." She turned back to me, her eyes softening. "Do you think you'll make it without me?"

"I'm sure I can." Though part of me didn't completely believe that.

II

It'd been five days since I'd learned some of my new magic, and the Fable world wasn't wrong when calling it *simple*. But there was something different about *my* magic. Even sitting here in my living room trying to do it, it felt like something kept my magic from reaching its full potential. And if I was right, my mom and Mara didn't know anything about it. Or else they wouldn't have asked me to save a world.

At least Mara would be coming home today. I would tell her what I learned about myself, and she would tell me what she learned about Nikolas. So, all I could do right now was try to do as much magic as I could.

Breathe in. Breathe out. I wanted to turn on my lights.

Darkness swallowed the living room. Lightning had become one of my most-used powers so I would master that one first. Even though my magic held back, electric-like ants ran through every tense muscle in my body. I let silence and my breathing melt away the tension that had built in my shoulders over the last few weeks. Opening my eyes, I marveled at the illuminating sparks flickering around my fingers.

Rylee. Rylee.

Adrenaline spiked in my blood as my head whipped to the voice in my head.

"Who's there?"

He laughed but didn't appear.

Taking a deep breath, I tried to keep my heart from exploding out of my chest and my lightning from leaving my fingers. I had to keep breathing, I reminded myself as I eased up from the couch.

"You might as well come out." I turned the corner to where the china cabinet met the doorframe to the hallway.

Oh, how I've missed you. Are you ready for your turn, my dearest Rylee?

I stopped breathing. That voice belonged to *him*. How a voice I'd only heard once became so identifiable, I didn't know. That raw, deep, hypnotizing voice from the man of my nightmares. Nikolas.

"I'm ready to play if you are." Not ready at all, I removed myself from behind the living room wall and stood exposed in the hallway. Nikolas stood in front of me.

"And so we meet again." He bowed, his overdramatic beige trench coat billowing behind him.

"Too soon if you ask me," I snarled. In that same second, I breathed the lightning into my hands. "What do you want?"

"I think you know." He smirked, taking off his trench coat to reveal white veins illuminating his light complexion. I would've been lying to myself if I said they weren't the least bit intimidating. Even more so as he stalked toward me. And as he did, I noticed he wore the same bracelet as Drake. The only difference was, his had what looked to be a slither of white crystal around it. Why was he wearing it too? What did it mean? Why was his different from Drake's? Was there one made for humans like Drake and one for Fables like Nikolas? But Nikolas's voice brought me from my thoughts.

"Now, why don't you just be a good girl and give me what I want and all of this will be over."

"What the hell makes you think I'll give you my dad's heart?"

He inched closer. His white eyes narrowed into slits. "Why does it matter so much to you?"

My chest and throat couldn't find air, but the lightning still trailed around my fingers as he drew closer. All I had to do was throw it at him. I wanted to throw lightning.

But in one blink, Nikolas vanished.

"Where are——" Before I could finish my sentence, Nikolas balled a fist full of my hair into his hand and yanked me backward.

"The hard way then." Nikolas's breath reeked of licorice as he yanked harder. "It didn't have to be this way."

The force he used to throw me made my body slide halfway down the hallway. My side slammed into the half wall of the dining room.

"I love the hunt, my dearest Rylee." He had that perfect psychotic I-am-about-to-kill-you laugh that I would have expected from a movie. "I won't stop until I get what I want."

I couldn't understand it. Nikolas said he was after my dad. So why come after me now? Was this some lesson he was trying to teach my dad? Like because he didn't give Nikolas what he wanted, he would mess with me? I wanted to move, but the blow to my ribs made moving nearly impossible. So, I lay there praying maybe he'd gotten his fill and would just walk away.

"Are you really going to give up that easily? I'm even giving you a fighting chance here."

"I don't"—I slung my arm around my side—"have what you want."

He reached for me again, but this time he didn't go for my hair. His fist jammed into my chest with such force, the world around me spun. My breath had left me almost completely. I could have sworn I actually felt his bony fingers gripping at my heart. He wanted my heart too?

Even through the dull pain, I tried to feel the magic inside me. But nothing. Where was it? *Breathe . . . in . . . Breathe . . . out . . .* Something sparked at the tips of my fingers, but it wasn't enough to do anything. I had to keep him distracted until I had enough energy.

"I've heard of you, you know. So powerful." He threw my head back, and for a moment, I thought he was going to bite me, but he only squeezed harder, making my eyes water. "You're not. Not yet. You should be thanking me."

"I . . . don't . . . have . . ." I screamed, electricity swimming through my veins and heart. The more he squeezed, the quicker my heart sped, and the faster the magic spread.

The lightning flying around my fingers made me smile, and Nikolas must have noticed because he said, "Why are you so happy?"

Without a second thought, bruised ribs and all, I released the lightning from my fingers, sending a convulsing jolt to Nikolas's body. After he released me, I collapsed to the ground. It was done. Nikolas wouldn't be able to hurt us anymore.

"Poor girl, you know nothing of me." Rather than lifting me by the hair, Nikolas chose my throat, wrapping his bony fingers around it. "Par—"

I had no idea if this would even work, but it was better than dying. So I closed my eyes and let the heat of my flames trail through every muscle in my body. Starting from my toes. Then in seconds, to my throat.

Nikolas screamed, grabbing his hand. "What the hell?!" For an extra measure, I kicked him in the groin. It was the second best thing to magic.

With my head throbbing in my ears, I ran to my room.

I tried to remember where I left my phone. Magic still hummed through me searching. That psycho was going to find me before I could even find it. But then, on the edge of my desk, my phone lit up with a text message.

"Paraseum!" His finger trailed along my cheekbone.

No magic coursed through my veins now. No words would leave me. Not even a muscle movement. I couldn't even feel the tightening sensation of my throat as Nikolas gripped it and threw me on the bed.

He took his place at the edge of my bed, glaring at me. I prayed someone would either run in and save me, or he would kill me. But neither of those two things happened.

"Can't have you drawing any more attention. Now, that was fun. I've been counting down the days until I saw you again, Rylee. I would have been waiting forever if I hadn't gotten myself out." His white eyes felt like daggers to my soul. "You know, you ruined something special for me and your old man that day. I don't like people ruining my plans."

Every passing moment he sat nonchalantly on my bed was as if he'd taken a knife to my chest, twisting it slowly. Finding some sort of assurance in this terrifying game he played with me was difficult. Praying at six o'clock in the morning, knowing my dad wasn't home, that Drake would come and check on me seemed like a pathetic hope at this point. But it was the only one I had left.

"Your mother was a smart one. I just wish I knew why. Why *you*, out of all these other Fables in this world." He waved it off. "But in my line of work, I'm not allowed to ask those questions, so, oh well. It's going to be fun, though."

Had someone hired him to kill me and my dad? And if so, who?

Nikolas stood from my bed and stalked over to me. His mouth was so close to my ear, his lips grazed it when he spoke. The tightening of my throat slowly returned. As had the clamminess of my hands. But still not enough motion to do anything useful.

"Today is the day you die," he hissed.

Though I couldn't *feel* it, I could *see* his hand going into my chest again. This was it. I was going to die if I didn't get out of this. I had to tell my magic what to do. I wanted fire. I wanted lightning. I wanted anything.

I could feel the invisible clutches of his curse lifting. I didn't know how, but it was. Fire and ice ran through my nerves, building and building as if it were a volcano about to explode. I didn't want to die. It continued to build to the point of being unbearable. I wanted to let it all go.

The next thing I knew, a blast of fire and lightning threw Nikolas across the room. His body crashed into the wall. I let myself steal a glance at him, but he was gone.

Minutes after he left, my body remained still. Not because I was still paralyzed, but because I didn't know what to do. I watched the small flames burn out, blackening my wall. He was here. Just feet away from me. Anger festered inside me as I remembered how hopeless he made me. How I had control over myself one minute and the next, he took it away with just one word. It was six thirty when I found the courage to pick up my phone from the nightstand. I should have called the police, but they couldn't protect me from a monster like that. So I had to let that be *my* job. He could hurt so many other people if I didn't stop him, and I couldn't let that happen.

With every monotone ring of Drake's cell phone, panic clawed at my throat. Once he answered, his voice was as neutral as his ringtone. Of course, he would tell me to call the police, but as in my head, I explained my thoughts on the matter. I waited for him to attempt to console me. But even after asking him to tell his sister to come over, he said little. He did surprise me when he told me he was coming over with her.

After telling Mara and Drake everything that happened, Mara spent thirty minutes putting a protection spell around the house. Once done, Mara sat exactly where he had. I could still envision his bony fingers tracing my cheekbones. How his hot breath sent unnerving chills down my spine. When Drake came into the room and closed the door, panic overcame me.

"No! Keep it open." I never wanted my door closed again. It was the only peace of mind I had left. As Drake sat, my attention for a small moment went to his wrist, where I knew his bracelet was. I thought of telling him about Nikolas's, but a part of me didn't want anymore things to worry about.

With that in thought, I turned my glare on Mara. "Where the hell were you? I thought you were supposed to protect me."

She scoffed. "I was. It's not like Drake could talk to Aurora."

With panic still rattling my bones, I'd forgotten all about Mara going to talk to Aurora. "I'm sorry. I was just so scared. After he paralyzed me, I thought I was going to die."

"It's fine. I'm glad you're okay."

"Yeah, my magic helped me out. I've kind of been in this

situation with him before. And when I released it, he flew across the room. When I looked back, he was gone."

Drake had been the one to speak. I heard actual concern in his voice. "You said *before*. When was this?"

"The day of the accident. He'd paralyzed me then too. But I got out of it with my magic's help."

Mara had a curious expression when she said, "Seems like it works when it needs to." She moved a bit closer. Her brow furrowed again. "I know you've only been doing your magic for a few days, but have you felt like it's kind of, I don't know—"

"Not as strong as it should be. I was going to tell you about that. Is that what you found out from Aurora?"

She narrowed her eyes. "Do you remember when I told you that your mum took some precautions with you?" I nodded. "Well, Liliana thought someone would try to go after your heart one day because something about it makes it special. She had also wronged someone, and she was afraid they could hurt you. So, she made a second heart to cloak your real one. But to make it believable, it had to *feel* like a real heart."

I had two hearts inside of me? Why was it every time my mom's name was mentioned now, I learned more and more that she'd kept from me? When would I not hear something that wouldn't rock me to my core or change my life? Why couldn't it just be something I already knew?

"Okay, so what does this heart and the lack of my magic have to do with Nikolas and Aurora?"

Mara huffed. "It's no secret your mum didn't want you to know you were a witch. But she tried so hard to keep you from knowing about it that she tried to stop it altogether."

"What are you saying?"

"I'm saying that when your mum cloaked your heart, she blocked most of your magic from working."

I stared at my hands, flipping them back and forth as if they would tell me it wasn't true, but I knew better than that. I knew my mom better than that. Heat burned my cheeks, and it had nothing to do with my magic. Or in my mom's hopes, lack of magic. I thought back to her letter. How she'd said she never wanted to lie, and something in her past kept her from telling us the truth. But this wasn't the right way to go about it.

"Mara, Nikolas knew what my mom did."

"And that's what I learned going to see Aurora. The Council is trying to get him to take out that fake heart to unlock all your magic, but I don't know why."

This was all more than enough to think about. "So, I get why he's going after me if my *real* heart is special and all, but why go after my dad's?"

Mara shrugged. "All I know is they want both of your hearts."

Drake's expression remained impenetrable as a stone wall. "I agree that most of the Council's practices are rather questionable, but I cannot believe them to be this malevolent."

Mara forced a laugh. "You've only seen the Council like everyone else has. You've heard of them as everyone else has. I worked alongside them." Mara's lip curled when she spoke again. "Don't forget about their origin of a soulless. They made Fables like Nikolas for their gain."

"What's a soulless?" I looked from Mara to Drake.

"I know of the Fable and its practices but do not know how to defeat it yet," Drake said.

"Practices? Are you talking about like when I saw him taking something from my dad?"

"Yes, a soulless carries no soul and is a miserable Fable created by the Council. If a parent partook in the craft of dark magic, the Council would curse the next-born child of the parent who committed the crime. Or the parent themselves if they do not have another child. For these . . . well it is rather difficult to call them Fables, but for them to feel something else, they must harvest. Taking the emotions and soul from their human and, or Fable victims, but only lasting for a short time."

"But wait, if the Council is this powerful group of Fables, then why do they need Nikolas?"

"I love Liliana," Mara said, folding her arms, "but I wish she would have told you something. A soulless is the only one who can take protected hearts."

So she *was* trying to protect me.

"Is there a way then to stop the most powerful Fable in existence?" I bit the inside of my cheek.

"No there is not," Drake still stared out the window. Like he didn't want me to see what he was thinking.

"Drake, don't lie to the poor girl."

His expression didn't change when he looked at Mara. "We do not know of any. Or know of who may possess it. So, I do not see the reasoning in giving her hope."

"Dear Lord, someone better tell me something."

"Crystal is a very dangerous weapon in the Fable world," Drake said. "It is the only thing that keeps them from coming back to life. There is one crystal that can kill *most* Fables. A rainbow crystal. But to kill a soulless, you must have a white crystal. As I said before, they are not easily acquired."

"You know I can find some." Mara grinned. It was a bit unsettling how happy she seemed.

"Well, I don't want to kill him. There has to be another way. I just want people, Fables included, to be safe from that monster."

"Well, if you don't kill him, someone else will have to," Mara said. "For now, I will teach you all the magic you need to know. It will help you fight Nikolas. And"—she pointed to the locket around my neck—"it will help unlock that locket. These people need you to be alive to save them."

"So, let me see if I got this. We have a couple weeks left to learn *some* magic, kill a soulless, and save the Fable world. Shouldn't be too hard."

12

I tried to let the autumn leaves or passersby of the busy downtown distract me as Drake drove us to the hospital, but it wasn't working. I couldn't stop thinking of all the things that could go wrong. Everything bad that happened. At least I told my dad that I loved him.

Drake's Lexus stopped at a red light across from the hospital. My eyes wandered to the thirteenth floor. I couldn't remember the exact room location, but I prayed, actually prayed, he was up there alive.

"He said he enjoys the hunt," I said more to myself as Drake made his way into the parking garage.

"Who?"

"Nikolas. He said he wouldn't stop until he got what he . . ." This wasn't over. Although this wasn't the best thing to think of as good news, Nikolas wanted both of our hearts. Which meant he wouldn't stop until he got what he wanted. It also meant that I would have more time to figure out a way to stop him. "My dad's still alive."

No matter how many times I came to this hospital, the nightmares held in this place would never change for me, and anxiety found me the moment the front doors opened. Every scent, every nurse, and even patients reminded me of the countless times I'd been here. But then, as if the universe twisted the metaphorical knife a little more, an old frail woman, skin hanging off her bones, smiled at me. Her straight gray hair hung down the same way as Grandma Ana's. As if she could have been her sister. Oh, how I hated this hospital.

Drake's voice brought me out of my dark thoughts. "I see that pain still lies here." Drake had also turned his focus to the woman in the hospital bed.

I continued to stare at the woman as I answered, "Do you remember when I told you I hated hospitals?"

"Yes."

"*That's* why." I pointed to the room where the woman was. "That's the room where my grandmother threw herself out the window and I watched her do it." I could almost hear my cries as she folded her arms across her chest and fell backward out of the window. "This wing at the time was from the seventies, and so they still had windows." I clenched my fist.

Drake ushered me forward as the nurse eyed me.

"I could have saved her." I released my fist.

"You seem to hold a lot of guilt with your visions."

"Are you saying that it's just my fault then?" I snorted while trying to squeeze past a sick patient's bed—out in the aisle waiting for an X-ray—and a group of talking doctors.

"No, I am saying that it is not your fault at all."

An EMT rushed past us, hugging an IV bag.

"I'm not following you."

"You have only had your visions for seven years. In the years of your adolescence. You have not matured them enough, I believe, to let them validate your family's deaths. To feel guilt."

Drake pressed the button for the elevator. Waiting for it, I thought of his comment. A small part of me wanted to believe it. To say that, yes, it wasn't my fault. I didn't understand them because I hadn't had them that long. But the other part of me knew better.

"When I'd first had my visions." We stepped inside the elevator and I pressed the button to the thirteenth floor, "I thought, and still do, that I was having them for a reason. That I was supposed to do something with them. Because most of them were about other people I knew. Though I haven't had those types of visions in a while."

"That is what many seers believe."

We dinged on the sixth floor. As the door opened, a lanky young mother and her son holding a *Get well soon* balloon shuffled inside. Pressing a button for the seventh floor, my thoughts went to Drake's comment. Was that what I was called? *Did* it make me more special? Not that I wanted any more pressure than I already had. I wanted so much to ask him what he meant, but the little boy had his eyes transfixed on me with a huge grin. After what felt like an eternity, we dinged again, and the young mother and her son walked out.

As soon as the door closed and we moved again, I turned to Drake. "So, a seer is what they called Fables who can see into the future?"

"Yes. It is still puzzling to me, but it seems as if in older times, it was instilled in the seer to serve the Council."

"What do you mean?" I asked when we stopped again. This time an older man in scrubs, who appeared to have a limp, waddled inside.

"Looks like we all have the same stop," the man said without turning around.

"Seems like we do," I said, Drake's expression as featureless as always. Was this feeling only because it was somehow part of my ability? The way Drake and Mara kept talking about the Council, they were a group of people I didn't want to cross.

A few moments later, we stopped again. I let the man out first, hoping he'd either go the other way, or if he went our way, we could walk behind him so he couldn't hear us. But as he walked out, he hobbled out in the other direction.

"Drake, are you trying to tell me that the Council gave us this ability so we could one day serve them?"

"Yes. The Council was not as thoughtful to their kind millennia ago."

A boy rushed past us after what I assumed was his sister. "Aurora and her people haven't been the Council long then?"

"No. She has been in command only a decade." He paused, letting a man walk between us. "The gift of a seer and even the creation of a soulless came from her great-great-grandparents."

"You seem to believe the Council is good, but Mara doesn't. Why?"

We were finally in the wing where my dad's room was.

"Aurora has proven herself to the Fable world in my personal opinion. She is fixing problems created from the past."

"Like what?"

"She is working on making a way to send criminal Fables to a prison world they will call the Omega."

"Do you trust them?" I asked in disbelief.

He shook his head. "I am a man of fact. They have given evidence of their change."

"Okay. But before this world was even thought of, where did the criminals go?"

"The Council back then would rip out their souls and throw them into the Tomb of Lost Souls."

"If you believe the Council is so redeemable, I want to

know your opinion on the Council wanting me and my dad's hearts."

"This is a rather perplexing matter. I do find it odd, but in the same regard, they have had reasons for everything they have done even if we do not agree."

My heart hurt to know that my gift could be used for someone else's gain. It was also unsettling that Drake didn't seem to care if I might die, but again, I had to remind myself what Mara had said. And how Drake *had* saved me from that fire. So maybe all hope wasn't lost.

"Drake, do you think Aurora will try to use me too?"

"I do not believe so. You seem to believe that you are not good enough to do things of your own accord. But this does explain why you try as hard as you do. Why it is one of the reasons you are so compassionate. You want to understand people. You want to help them. And help understand yourself."

Butterflies fluttered in my stomach. "You've known me for only a short time, but when you talk about me or my personality, it's like you've known me forever. How is that?"

"When I find something interesting, I tend to notice more." But he didn't smile. Didn't wink. Which only left me to think he saw me as he would see a science project. And I was strangely okay with that.

"I see you have spoken to my sister."

I raised an eyebrow. "What do you mean?"

"Normally, your face is rather bewildered by my lack of expression. Or in the wake of my previous statement, you would ask me to explain why I feel this way. Now it is as if you have accepted it."

I bit my lip. "I guess it just makes sense."

If he could show his emotions, he would be raising his eyebrow. "And I assume she spoke of Marcus as well?"

"You guys might have a weird relationship, but she does care about you."

"If only I believed this to be true."

"She did get you out of that asylum."

Drake stopped walking. I hadn't even realized what I'd said until seeing his face. His deep-blue eyes became those crashing waves I'd hoped I'd never see.

"I'm . . . I'm sorry . . . She didn't tell me anything and I'm not gonna—"

"And I will not tell you." He stormed off.

Five minutes later, I found Drake standing by one of the soda machines, staring at it blankly. I thought of walking away—giving him some time and going to see my dad myself—but I couldn't leave him like this. So, with a deep breath, I made my way over.

I put two quarters into the machine and pressed the button. "You can never go wrong with Coke." I still didn't know how to interpret his silence. But I hoped he wasn't angry.

Once the can was dispensed, I opened it and took a sip. I was never good at small talk, so right to the point, I went.

"I'm not asking you to tell me about what happened. I'm not even going to tell you to deal with it. All I'm doing is trying to be your friend. Why can't you see that?"

He turned back from the machine. "I do apologize if I was out of line. You are too kind for a . . . soul . . . like mine."

"You're too hard on yourself. I have baggage too. Look, let's pretend that, that didn't just happen, and go see my dad, okay?" Drake nodded. I couldn't know why this hurt him so much. I couldn't know what happened. I was okay with that, but I wanted so much to take away the pain he felt for it. To see him smile once. If only.

Once we made it to my dad's room, it was comforting to

see an officer standing outside. I guess he finally chose to tell them. My dad's door was open, TV blaring the sports channel, of course. So we made our way inside.

"Excuse me, ma'am, but I can't let you through unless you're family," said the bodybuilding officer.

I reached into my purse for my wallet to show the officer my ID when my dad's raw voice came from within the room.

"Roman, that's my daughter and her friend. Let them in."

Roman turned back to us. "My apologies. You can't be too careful nowadays." He moved aside.

"I am going to wait out here," Drake said. "To give you privacy with your father."

I made my way inside. A small part of me wondered if he didn't want some space from me after what just happened.

I hated the smell of the antiseptic burning my nose. I hated seeing my dad in this bed, but at least he was alive. His smile was lazy and tired as I hugged him. He winced. *Had* Nikolas gotten to him without the officer or doctors knowing? Because he could teleport. I knew that much from our fight earlier.

"Daddy! Are you okay? Does your stomach feel weird? Do your veins feel like they're on fire or something?" I had no idea what it would have even meant if he felt any of it, but I needed to know something.

He chuckled, which turned into a deep cough. "I'm fine. You just squeezed too tight, and one of the needles pinched me. I'm glad you're here, though." I tried to meet his eyes, but I couldn't. "Are you all right?"

"Of course, I got my hero to protect me." I chuckled, hoping my words were convincing enough for him.

His eyes remained dark. "Hun, what's wrong?"

"It's nothing." I tried to pull away, but he held his grip.

Not telling him this wasn't because I didn't trust him, but because *if* I told him, it would show him how weak I was and that I couldn't protect him as I promised.

"Please don't do this. Don't shut me out," my dad pleaded.

"That's . . ." My words caught in my throat. I gazed up at him. "That's not what I'm trying to do, Dad."

"Then what is it?" He pulled me closer into him.

"I . . . I feel weak," I whispered, thinking of my fight with Nikolas. "I'm afraid I'll fail you, and I can't do that again." I burrowed my face into his chest.

"Rylee Cornelia Jenkins," he started, pulling me close to him again. "You listen to me and listen good. You have never and will never fail me or anyone. You only fail if you don't try. I've always *tried* to teach you that your worth is not measured by what you have alone, but what you *do* with what you have is what matters."

We let the silence surround us and I breathed in the scent of him. I loved him so much.

"I have something to tell you." I slowly pulled away and looked up at him. If we were going to fix us, I couldn't lie. So, I told him about Nikolas breaking into the house. Of our fight and how I'd lost. How Nikolas had paralyzed me with just one word. How terrified I felt knowing he could kill me.

Disapproval and worry swam in his dark tone. "And you didn't think to call the police?"

I rolled my eyes. He noticed, his stern fatherly eyes questioning me. "What can the police do? This guy can keep them from moving."

My dad rose from bed higher. "I'm coming home tomorrow."

My heart sped up. I didn't want my dad anywhere Nikolas could find him. At least here he had some sort of protection. "I want that, I do, but do you think you can stay here? Just until we find Nikolas."

His eyes softened. "It doesn't work that way." He rested his hand on my back. "Everything's going to be okay."

"I won't screw this up again."

"What are you talking about?"

"I lost my chance to make things right with Mom. I don't want to do that with us."

"Look at me." He lifted my chin. "You and your mom might have had your problems, but she knows you loved her. And *I* know you loved her. You did nothing wrong with your mom or me. *I'm* supposed to be proving myself to you. Not the other way around."

"But why would you want to? I was a horrible daughter. Who only thought of herself. How can you even look at me?"

My dad cradled me into his chest. "You are not a horrible daughter."

I let my head rest there working up the courage to tell him what Mara and I found out about Nikolas and my magic.

"I need to tell you something else."

"Of course. I'm here."

I lifted my head from his chest and told him what my mom had done to protect my real heart and my magic. "The Council wants Nikolas to take out the fake heart, so I have full access to this real heart and the magic, but we don't know why. Mara's going after Nikolas."

My dad's body stiffened. "I don't want *you* going after him then. I know you want to help, but do not go after this man. Let Mara do that."

"You don't understand. *I* have to stop him. He'll continue to hurt people if I don't. I'm the only one who really can."

He raised his voice only slightly, but it was the most I'd

heard from him for as long as I could remember. "No! You will not leave me alone."

Those words broke my heart while at the same time healing it if even possible. All I wanted was to feel like my dad was here. Like he wanted me. And here it was. He feared being alone just as much as I did. I knew all too well how this feeling was, and I loved him too much for him to know how it felt. I wouldn't go after Nikolas, but at the same time, if I had to, I would fight him if it came to that. But that, my dad didn't need to know.

"I promise, Dad. I won't go after him."

13

On my way back home, Mara texted me saying she'd be waiting for me in her backyard. I had to learn more magic. I didn't know how she would take it when I told her I wasn't going to go after Nikolas, but by the you-better-take-this-seriously look on her face when I made my way to the backyard forty-five minutes later, I didn't think she'd take it too well.

"I'm ready to do this," I said, stopping in the center of the white gazebo. After studying her face closer, I'd read it all wrong. Her brow was furrowed in worry. "Does he scare you too?"

She huffed, turning to face me. "Of course not." She waved her hands then, making everything disappear. "But let's not dwell on that. Let's focus on what we can do now."

"Which is magic."

"Right. Now one of the more important spells every witch or warlock needs to know is how to create a shield."

"Okay, so how do I do that?"

She rolled her eyes. "You need to stop being so impatient. It could get you killed."

I pinched the top of my hand, avoiding her gaze. "Sorry. Show me then."

She placed both of her legs apart in an A-frame stance. Her arms the same, but hands inches apart cupped outward. And as she did so, I couldn't help but notice the weight she had lost in her face and stomach. Mara wasn't overweight by any means, but this version of her appeared as if she'd lost at least twenty pounds in the weeks since meeting her. Her eyes more sunk in. Her cheekbones more sharp. Her stomach flatter. But she still held the thickness in her arms and thighs. I couldn't help but feel sorry for her. Wondering what kind of toll this was taking on her.

"I want you to throw some fire to practice your magic. I'm going to make a shield around me. You need to watch how I make it because you'll have to do it next."

"But how can I if I have my eyes closed to use my magic?"

Mara released her stance. "You have to keep them open. In the real world, you have to be alert of everything around you." I said nothing. "Look, you can't be scared of what you don't try."

"Fine. But if I die, it's your fault," I joked.

Breathe in. Breathe out. Heat circulated through every nerve in my body like hot cocoa running down my throat on a cold December evening. Staring at the dying flames around my fingers, I knew their lifelessness had been my mom's fault. But what I did have would be enough to stop Nikolas.

"Stay focused," she yelled. "Be one with your magic. You have to control it. Breathe as you release."

Mara readied herself again.

Throwing my hands in front of me, the fire released from my fingers like small, erratic fireballs. I had to tell myself it would take time, but in the back of my mind, all I could think of was what Nikolas had said. *I heard you were powerful.* I shook my head. I had to focus on Mara, not myself.

As my sporadic fire flew toward her, an orb grew in her hand. The farther she drew her hands from herself, the larger the orb became. In a matter of seconds, the fire hit her orb in a small explosion.

"It'll take some practice, but it's something you need to learn if you're going to fight Nikolas." I cringed at the mention of his name. More because I felt guilty for lying to her. "You want to try it?"

"Uh . . . sure." I tried not to look as guilty as I felt. "So how do I stand again?"

Mara showed me the pose again, but all I thought about was Nikolas and my promise to my dad. She'd been so good to me. After this, no matter how pissed she would be, I was going to have to tell her.

"All right. I'm going to go easy on you. I'm just going to throw some water. Are you ready?"

I couldn't handle the guilt eating at me.

"Mara, there's something I need to tell you."

"What?"

My shoulders released a mountain of stress as I let the words go. "When I went to check on my dad in the hospital, I told him everything that happened and what Nikolas wanted from us. He made me promise I wouldn't go after him."

"And you told him that you couldn't do that, right?" My boot had started to make a dent in the grass. "Tell me you told him it's your job to stop him."

Something in the way she chose to say it hit the wrong nerve. "And why the hell is it? I didn't ask for this psychopath to attack me. I'm seventeen years old for crying out loud. What do I have any damn business in going after a man like that, huh?" Heat flushed my cheeks. I didn't need to say that, but it was true. Why couldn't Mara do it? She was stronger, and training me only wasted her time.

Mara glared at me. "That's a promise you shouldn't have made. He wants *you*, Rylee."

"Oh, I'm well aware of that. But I made a promise to my dad, and things between him and me . . ." I broke off. "You wouldn't understand."

Her laugh was almost cruel. "You think you and Drake are the only ones who know anything about broken families? Well think again." Her eyes darkened. "So, am I supposed to fight him too?"

"No, I told my dad I wasn't going to go after him or pick a fight with him. But if he comes after me—that, I can't help."

As the silence fell between us, I thought about Mara's comment. She'd never cared about Selena, but what if her bitterness was actually sadness?

"I'm sorry, Rylee. It's just . . ." Her eyes glistened, but she blinked, and it was gone. "I miss your mum, and this whole magic locket is enough in itself, and this bloody bastard comes and tries to ruin what your mum wanted. It just hurts, is all."

I made my way to her. "I'm glad she had a friend like you."

"More like my mother." Mara groaned. "Okay, enough. We need to get back to work. We're going to do some magic first and then get into doing the shield. You ready?"

"Ready as I'll ever be."

Once I made my way back to the other side of the yard, I faced Mara. Every muscle in my body stiffened. Nikolas stood in Mara's place. My heart sped like a jackrabbit.

"How did . . . You can't . . ."

"Relax, it's just me." It was Mara. "We don't have much time for you to learn a lot of magic, so I thought the most effective way to learn was by doing it with the person we're hunting. So here he is." She threw out her hands. "Now that you know, give it all you got."

"I don't get a minute to breathe?"

"No. You never do in real action. Now come on. Show this wanker how you feel about him. And remember, keep your eyes open."

Breathing in and out, electricity made its way through my heart, veins, and then fingers as I stared into the sightless white eyes of the man who swore to take everything from me. The man who'd tried more than once to take away the man I loved. Heat intertwined with the electricity coursing in my veins. I wouldn't let him get away with it. I would stop him.

Before I knew what was happening, my fingers released erratic spurts of fire and electricity. Nikolas grinned, waving his hand, and the objects torpedoed at me. I panicked but managed to tuck and roll out of the way.

"Get up!" Mara yelled, Nikolas's form still making my heart hammer. "Use your shield."

I dusted off the grass on my shirt and pants. I knew this wasn't him, but if it were, I would have to survive. Suddenly, air whizzed past me.

"What did I tell you! Keep your bloody eyes open."

Flames danced around my fingers again, but my muscles ached, my magic seeming drained and weak; I had to keep going.

"Come on, Rylee, breathe and go with what you know. I know you're tired, so I'm going to throw fire at you, and I want you to use your shield." She transformed back into herself. "Just take a deep breath. Listen to what's around you that can hurt you."

Mara cupped her hands. An orb of flame was so blindingly bright, I almost had to look away. I readied myself as Mara taught me. With each breath, the shield wall slowly formed in front of me, but the magic in me didn't let me have control of it all. My body wanted to let go. But *I* couldn't.

I placed my hands in front of me to keep the shield up just long enough for the flaming orb to crash into the wall. I fell to my knees.

"Rylee!" Mara ran from across the yard and kneeled next to me. "Are you okay?"

"I'm fine." I pressed my hands to my knees to ease myself up. I'd prove to her that I was okay. But in standing, I was far from it. "I forget sometimes I'm new to this." She eyed me. "I'm fine."

She huffed. "Fine. You can sleep it off on my couch if you want."

"I'll take you up on that." The bit of sun peeking in through the trees hit my locket, and I noticed something faint, a marred scratch on the surface. "What is this?"

She took the locket between her fingers, allowing me to see it closer. It was what looked like the start of a faded swirl of a *J*. For my last name.

"Ah."

"What?"

She handed the locket back to me. "The more you use the locket, the more the engraving will show. We're getting there. It's just going to take some time. Now go. Get some rest."

The scent of lilies engulfed my nose again, but with it, too, came the smell of licorice. Music I didn't quite recognize played in the distance. Then I saw him. Nikolas held what looked like a stuffed red-bodied phoenix while stroking the bird's head, fingers brushing through a bright blend of yellow and black feathers.

"So sad he won't show his true self."

And then came white light.

My eyes shot open, but I remained still. Who was the *he* Nikolas talked about? It didn't make sense. My chest tightened as I thought of the first vision bright lights and a popcorn stand. Then Nikolas showed up saying something. What did he say? It wasn't that long ago. It was an apology, I thought. But for what? And now this vision. What was it trying to tell me?

"You better be good." I heard someone's voice, but my eyes couldn't put a face to who it was. "I have to find Nikolas. Until then, try and not be a total arse." That was Mara for sure.

Though I couldn't see his face, I could make out the sincerity in Drake's voice. "I am good. Should be for a few days. I thought it best for me to better myself for a while. To be there for Rylee."

"Whatever." Mara's footsteps faded with the closing door not far behind.

"You can wake now," Drake said, reentering the room.

I turned myself over, sitting up on the couch. "I didn't hear much honestly." He smiled. It alarmed me because I wasn't used to seeing it, but I found myself missing it when it faded.

Drake made his place on the edge of his coffee table much like he'd done when I'd first met him. The only difference now was that curiosity settled in his eyes. "Does me being this way make you happy?"

"If it makes *you* happy, then yes."

His brow furrowed. "These feelings are false."

"Drake, doesn't it get lonely feeling nothing all the time when you can feel something with just some more work?"

Drake threw himself up from the couch, storming to the fireplace. He grabbed the poker and turned the logs. Even with his emotions, he was frustrating. Still closing himself off to me. We had to make headway somewhere.

"I should not be angry about your ignorance, and I say that politely. But I assure you there is no simplistic way for me to apprehend my emotions, not in the way you see them. I also will not allow you to use my moment of vulnerability to pry into my life."

Enough was enough. "All I've tried to do is be here for you. But *I'm* the only one trying. I'm the one sharing my thoughts and feelings. I understand you can't express yourself all the time, and I'm trying to get used to that. I understand you've been hurt in more ways than one, but so have I. And the saddest part is, I heard it all from your sister. *You* should have told me. I know you're going to call me pushy or whatever, but I don't care. I just want you to finally hear me."

Drake kept his back to me. As if pouring my heart out to him meant nothing. After all that, was he really going to say nothing? I let a few seconds pass before I spoke again.

"So, nothing? You don't care enough for our friendship to even acknowledge what I said?"

Silence.

A small piece of my heart broke as I stood. There was something different to this pain, but somewhat familiar, like when seeing my dad hurt, or even that man at the food bank. I hurt so much more for Drake and his pain. I just wanted to take it away. It was odd because I should have been angry that he still chose to shut me out. All I wanted was for him to be happy. Maybe he was right. I cared for people. People I didn't even know. That's why I was doing this. That's why it hurt so much. Because I cared about him too.

Drake still said nothing as I grabbed my jacket and headed to the door. When my hand rested hesitantly on the door handle, a small tear fell.

"I want to take you on a tour of my home. Will you let me?" Drake asked.

I wiped my eyes. "What?"

As I turned, a playful smile drew across his face as he stood in the large atrium of the hallway. "I would very much enjoy it if you would accompany me on a tour."

I had no idea where he was going with this, but the reassuring thought was that he didn't let me leave.

"I would like that."

He first took me to the living room. Though I'd seen it numerous times now, I never truly paid attention to its features. It was spacious with high vaulted ceilings. A cream-white couch under the front window caught a ray of light that revealed soft motes of dust in the room. Around the couch someone placed a few expensive pieces of artwork. Drake's piece was still my favorite. Two other couches sat in the middle of the room with a dark wooden table in between them. The room itself seemed like something I would see in a historical president's house.

Walking down the hall to the kitchen, I still didn't know why he was doing this. The white-tiled floor in the kitchen went well with the light-gray cabinets, the up-to-date silver appliances, and the gray marble tops. After finishing with the kitchen, we headed up the stairs, where Drake chose to finally speak. Nathan and he both enjoyed history, so Selena let them design the house. The only thing she wanted was a modern kitchen.

The second floor had three bedrooms and one bathroom. "Would you like to see my room?" Drake had already started making his way there. Without answering, I followed.

The scent of cinnamon was the first thing to welcome me into the room, reminding me of the first time I'd met him. How he'd stared at me like I was some alien. I laughed to myself. His walls were deep-blue, just like his eyes, and laced with an elegant white trim. His bed sat to my right. A black iron-rod bed with a blue comforter to match the walls. The bed was made in military form. Even the desk, night table, and chairs matched.

I stared at the alphabetized bookshelves and neatly placed art supplies. "It's not just you that's proper, is it?"

"I take it that you are different?"

I laughed, trailing my fingers through some of the books that were mostly about art history or anatomy. "Yeah, you might have to kick a few things around to find what you're looking for, but I got a system."

I could feel his eyes on me as I wandered around his room, but he didn't say anything. This meant he was thinking, and I needed to know what about.

"Why the tour?" I asked, holding a drawing of what appeared to be a pair of phoenix wings.

He took himself away from the door then. "It allowed me time to find the words to say to you. I have seen more darkness in the world than need be. And it is difficult for me to fathom believing there is good left. That is why I find myself so reluctant with others."

"But I'd hoped I'd shown you I'm not like them."

"You have. You are a wildflower in a field of weeds."

I picked at the corner of the picture I was holding, thinking. "A wildflower, huh? I still feel like a weed."

Drake took the drawing from my hand. "Well, weeds can still be remarkably unique."

I stared up at him now. "This belief for others—where does it come from?"

And there it was, resting in his blue eyes. Sincerity. "I do not need emotions to know this truth. But you need to believe in you as well."

I wanted to believe that so much. Even though my mom blocked my magic to help me—to hide it from anyone who wanted it—I still felt like she blocked it because of me. Because she didn't think I would be strong enough.

"You must understand something," Drake said, taking me from my thoughts. "Regardless of belief, I cannot portray every emotion you require. But I also would like it if you could spare me your patience. You are good for me and me for you. I know it."

His words were like glue filling the cracks in my heart. And my heart warmed. "I've known that since the day I met you."

14

It'd been a week since Mara left to find Nikolas. All I could do was practice my magic. The engraving of my initials hadn't changed, and my magic still wouldn't work with me. I was beginning to panic knowing that we only had a few weeks left to save these poor creatures. I couldn't and wouldn't fail. At least Drake was there to help in any way he could. Since we talked, I couldn't say Drake opened up to me entirely, but he wasn't trying to shut me out.

The day after Mara left, my dad came home like he said he would. Right away, he gave me this strange vibe. That night I told him I would make him dinner, then I heard him on the phone with someone. At first, he wouldn't tell me who he was talking to. But by the third night, I found out he was asking about Nikolas. When I asked why he was asking about him, he just said he wanted to make sure someone was looking for him.

But as the days went on, my dad got weirder. During class, he would text me asking if I was okay or if I'd heard from Mara about Nikolas. I hadn't. Then he would text back telling me to come straight home. When I did, he'd be on the phone asking more things about Nikolas. I couldn't understand it. He'd told me not to bait him, but that was exactly what he was doing. By Monday afternoon, I was looking forward to talking to Farrah.

Farrah closed the door and routinely grabbed her notebook before sitting in her chair. "So glad to see you, Rylee. How have you been? How's Mara?"

I couldn't tell her everything, but there were ways to dance around it. "Where do I start?" I chuckled. "As I'm sure you heard on the news like everyone else, the guy who put my dad in his wheelchair escaped prison."

Farrah didn't write anything down. "I did. How are you dealing with that?"

Between trying to deal with my dad, my magic, trying to save a Fable world, and Nikolas, I couldn't even begin to think let alone know how to feel about all of it. So, I let my silence be my answer. Farrah wrote something in her notebook. Probably something like *carries the feeling of hopelessness*. It was what I'd write.

"I can only imagine what you're going through, but I'm glad you're okay. Where's Mara in all this?"

"She's gone to find the guy." I fidgeted with the end of her couch, avoiding as much eye contact as possible. I was afraid she could see I wasn't telling her everything.

Her initial silence made me nervous. "But that's the police's job. Why would she be out looking for him?"

I had to meet her gaze now to throw her off. "But isn't what she's doing just another form of protection?" I plastered on a tense smile.

"It seems reckless." She leaned in closer. "How old did you say she was?"

I had to take a moment to think about her question. She said she was ten when she had her first vision. And

Drake was eighteen. "She's in her late twenties, I think. Why?"

"It just seems odd for a woman her age to do something so naïve as to run after someone she doesn't know who is dangerous."

I chuckled. "Mara's anything but predictable. But she's very smart." Farrah still eyed me. I had to get her talking about something else. "Well on another note, my dad's out of the hospital."

Farrah wrote something down in her notebook again. "So, things are going well?"

Maybe not the right topic change. "They are and they aren't."

She tilted her head. "I don't understand."

"We got to the point where we're finally being open and honest with each other, but it feels like it's too open. Like he wants to know my every move. It's getting a bit suffocating. I feel selfish for thinking this, let alone saying it because I wanted it for so long. I thought this was what I wanted. To have my dad around. To care enough to check on me. To set some ground rules. But it's not."

Farrah's scratching pen was the only sound for a moment. "Sometimes when we realize something that we have done wrong and learn the way to do it right, we tend to overdo it. Not that we mean to. Your dad loves you; there's no doubt in my mind of that. That's why he's acting this way. And as your feelings go, you aren't wrong to feel them. You didn't know what to expect with this shift in your relationship. But neither did he."

She was right, but there was more to it than his borderline overprotectiveness. Almost like he was trying to do something more, and it angered me. "He's been calling the police asking about this guy, and it pisses me off. Just the other day, he made me promise I wouldn't go after him. And now that's exactly what *he's* doing. He keeps asking me if I've heard anything from Mara. It's like he's hoping to find something." Hot tears streamed down my cheeks as I went on. "It's like when he gets the information he wants, he's going to go after this guy himself. And yes, I know he really can't, but you get what I mean. He's trying so hard to prove himself to me that he's going to get himself killed. Leaving me alone again, and this time I'll have no one because I let them die."

She let the room stay silent. "Rylee, we've talked some about your mother, but I want to know about you and your dad. What was it like with you and him?"

I wiped at my eyes. "He used to be my best friend."

"What do you mean *used to be*?"

"I remember once, when I was little and my dad had this really beat-up truck." I laughed at how silly I looked then. My big head peeking just over the steering wheel. "He had me sitting in his lap. The truck was parked, and he let me move the steering wheel back and forth. And he kissed me on the head saying . . ."

"What is it?"

I took a deep breath. "He said, it'll get harder when you're older."

This had been the first time I didn't see Farrah write something down in her notebook. "What do you think he meant?"

"I have no idea." In a daze, I stared at the green shag carpet. "We did everything together. But by the time I turned seven, it's like I wasn't enough for him anymore."

Farrah's pen filled the silence in the room again. "Your bond with your dad is stronger than I think you realize."

I turned away, not wanting her to see the hurt in my eyes. "So, it means I'm finally enough for him?"

"When someone we love dies, it sometimes puts a lot of

things in perspective, and maybe your dad knows he's done wrong with you and needs to make it right. And that you never know if you have tomorrow."

I stared out into Farrah's large back-office window to the skyline of downtown. "I went downtown a couple weeks ago for a thing for one of my friends. I thought it would help me heal. I hadn't gotten out since their death, but the whole day I realized I wasn't healing, but missing. Missing what I used to have. Now my mom is dead. And my dad's trying but trying too hard. I just don't know."

Farrah wrote something in her notebook and then set it in her lap.

"Do you feel to blame for what happened to your dad?" she asked.

"Why would you ask that?"

"You believe you're not enough so you didn't think you could have saved him. So, it would make sense if you feel to blame. And you feel to blame for your mother's death as well."

"I did try to save my dad, so I don't feel to blame for what happened to him. But my mom . . ." My words faltered. "I . . . I . . . could have stopped that accident."

"How?"

I had to be careful with what I told her. After thinking for a minute, I said, "Before that day, I would have dreams of rushing water. Or I would hear someone screaming but didn't know who the voice belonged to. Or I would see faces but hear nothing."

Farrah wrote in her notebook again. Probably writing this time, *this girl's crazy*.

"Do you believe, because you didn't know what these dreams meant, it stopped you from saving your family?"

"Yes. I mean how else could you explain it?"

Farrah stayed quiet as she thought. "Have you ever heard

of survivor's guilt?" I shook my head. "It's when someone feels guilty to have survived when others didn't. Like your mother and brother. It seems like you've used these dreams that have no true effect on reality as a way to justify your guilt."

Drake had said that I shouldn't focus so much on the impact of my visions, and here Farrah was saying the same thing. Maybe they were right. "But I just don't know how to find that peace with so many things left unsolved. Like the why."

Farrah wrote in her notebook again. "You seem to focus a lot on the why of things."

"I just don't think that things happen without a reason." Depression started to set in.

"We cannot control the actions of others no matter how hard we try. We have to find a way, though, to help you understand that you had nothing to do with what happened to your mom and brother."

I had to talk about something else. "I finally told my dad about that day."

Farrah wrote in her notebook, and this time I knew what she was writing. It was what Drake would do when he didn't want to talk about something. *Avoids sensitive topics.*

Farrah put her pen down, her eyes softening again. "If you don't talk about what's bothering you, you can never fully move on. You know that, don't you?" Suddenly, my phone buzzed.

DRAKE: Your father had to assist his mate Chuck with something and asked me to come and get you. I will be waiting outside when you are ready.

"I want you to know that both you and your dad have

your hearts in the right place but still have a way to go if that's still what you want."

"It is. It's just sometimes I feel like I'm going backwards."

Farrah set the notebook down in her lap. "Sometimes it does feel that way. Do you remember when you asked if something happened when I lived in Sweden?"

That had been so long ago. "Maybe."

"Well, you did. Anyway, something did happen." Farrah rose from her chair and walked to the picture of her with her parents on the wall. She came back, handing it to me before she continued. "Right after we took this picture, I told my parents I was moving to Miami to go to university there. My papa wasn't happy. He told me I needed to stay home and help with our family bakery. But I wanted more for my life."

I stared at the happy family, for a moment thinking of my own. "What happened next?" I asked, handing the picture back to her.

She took it from me, placing it on her desk. "The whole time I was in school, I never heard from my parents. But they did show up for my graduation. I told them I was sorry, and they said they were sorry too. After graduation, I still stayed in the States and interned at a local psychiatry office. My parents and I were talking again. But a few years ago, my mama died. My papa and I stopped talking again after the funeral. Part of me felt like he blamed me for her death because I wasn't there to help them, and her heart gave out from exhaustion. It wasn't until a few days ago, when I told him I was pregnant, that we started talking again."

My eyes widened. "Congratulations!" For a small moment, it was as if I saw my mom in her eyes seeing that same glow she'd had when she'd told Damian and me that Christmas morning. My gut knotted, and I swallowed the sorrow that reminded me it wasn't just Damian and my mom we lost. We lost the twins.

She rubbed her belly. "Thank you."

Suddenly I remembered something she'd said on the first day I'd met her. "You told me when I first saw this picture that everything isn't always what it seems. At first, I thought you were only talking about me and my dad. But you were really talking about you and your family. Weren't you?"

"Always remember that though you may stumble backward sometimes, it's the persistence you have that will keep you going. And I see you have plenty of that." Farrah glanced over when her phone lit up. "Well, that's all our time for today. See you again next week?"

"I wouldn't miss it."

15

As Drake drove me home, I thought of my session with Farrah. I did need to deal with everything that had happened since my mom's death—my guilt, my pain—but something more held me back. It had nothing to do with survivor's guilt. My eyes wandered to Drake. The one person who could understand this confusion with or without his emotions. My friend.

"Thanks for picking me up." I kept my eyes trained on the windshield wipers as they swept against the light rain. "Hope it wasn't too much trouble."

"It was not." He turned up the heat. "I do hope all went well with Farrah."

"It did. I told her about my visions. Well, worded around them."

Drake stopped at a red light, his tone still giving away nothing in his words. "And she told you that their deaths are not your fault."

I stared at him for a moment, thinking he'd make a perfect psychologist with his ability to overanalyze people, but I didn't say that. "She said that I can't control what others do." I half laughed. "I ask myself why I can't move on when I *know* why. Other than my part, my mom drove us off that bridge and I can't understand why. So she was pissed at me. Why throw your whole family off a bridge for it?"

Other than those visions I saw. Those words I said to her before she literally drove us to our deaths, I feel like there's something more keeping me from moving on."

For at least two minutes, there was silence until Drake pulled off the main highway. I didn't ask where we were going because I thought maybe it was just a quicker way home, but it wasn't. Then I realized where we were going, and my heart quickened.

"What are we doing at the bridge?" But Drake just turned the car to the side bank and turned it off. My chest constricted as my body broke out in a sweat, and I peered into the rapid waters. "Answer me!"

"You feel as if you do not deserve to move on." Darkness shadowed his face even as the sun peeked through the clouds. Like he knew this pain. "But this truth is for Damian. The innocence of a young child. To never be able to live, love, or have a life of his own."

Why was he saying these things to me? These true, awful things. But then, his hands gripped my shoulders, and his blue eyes stared beyond me.

"Even if you had known what those visions meant, that does not mean you could have saved them. Those words you spoke were of only pure coincidental anger. You must find a way to move past this. Let go of the grief you carry."

I'd never let myself cry in front of anyone because I didn't want them to see me as weak, but I didn't care what Drake thought of me now as the tears fell and I pushed away from him. "How do I do that, huh? My mistakes are always around me. I'm my own mistake. They should be here, not me. They had so much more to offer than me."

"Must you continue to feel as if you are not enough?"

I sniffed. "Name one thing I've ever done that's mattered."

"You have helped me, so that is what I shall do for you." He opened his car door and stepped out into the mist.

As if nothing had happened on this bridge months ago, we stood on it, gazing at the water. Two people hadn't died on this bridge. Someone hadn't gotten ran over and was now paralyzed. No, everything seemed normal. Only for me, it never would be again. Walking past the first guardrail, something yellow flapped in the wind. It was a piece of caution tape. One true sign near the bent metal that had yet to be fixed. No one had to die that day.

Out of the corner of my eye, Drake surveyed my face, but he showed nothing now. Weird. But was it?

"They were such good people. Why did they have to die?" I asked.

"It was their time." His attention traveled to the water.

I followed his gaze, remembering something else about the water that had nothing to do with that day. "There's something I haven't told anyone about the day of my mom and Damian's funeral. Not even my dad or Farrah." I took a deep breath and continued. "I tried to drown myself. My dad was leaving to go back to work, and I knew I was going to be alone again." I was thinking of what I was about to confess to him. "Drake, there's another reason I wanted to be friends with you. And I don't think I've realized it until now. It has to do with my parents."

I was glad for once when Drake didn't show any emotions. "What do you mean?"

"I've told you that my parents kind of abandoned me as a kid. So, I guess subconsciously I started looking for someone who could . . ." Heat rose on the back of my neck.

"You believe that part of the reason you became mates

with me is because you do not wish to be alone? That and because I know how you feel whether I can show it or not."

I blushed. It made things a lot easier when he knew what I was thinking. "Are you mad?"

"You sell yourself short, Rylee. You may not prefer to be alone, but that is not why you preferred to be mates." He tried at a small smile. "But, if it makes you feel better, I will never let you do any of this alone."

Those words fluttered in my chest like a hummingbird.

"I'm glad."

Something wrestled in the trees in front of us. I shielded Drake with my body; because he was only human after all. A figure stepped out from the shadows slowly. White veins and the never-ending whiteness in his eyes drew a familiar feeling of fear.

"Rylee, you must call my sister, and tell her of Nikolas." Why couldn't I move? He hadn't paralyzed me. Those eyes. Damn those white, depthless eyes. "Rylee!"

This was what he wanted, but how could he have known this? How did he know we were here? Finally, I made the call, wishing I knew what he waited for and hating that I was probably playing into his plans somehow.

"Hey Rylee, what's up?"

"Get to the . . . the bridge . . . now. Nikolas is . . . is here."

Putting the phone back in my pocket, I could make out the faint hum of a sports car coming down the road. I prayed it would stop and see us. See Nikolas and call the cops and this would be all over, but I knew better. *Breathe in. Breathe out.* And with it came the fire.

"Allow me." Nikolas reached into his jacket. My hands rose toward him. "Relax, sparky. Just going to give us some privacy." He opened a vial, and odorless lime green fumes floated through the air. "Now no one can see us, and we can't see them." Looking back, the car had vanished. "Illusion spell," he said in response to my unspoken question.

A flash of light burst in front of us. "Don't start without me."

"Mara!" I squealed, running to her. "Thank God!"

She smirked. "You didn't think I'd let you and Drake fight him all by yourself."

We all turned back to Nikolas, who was rocking on his heels.

"Tell me what the Council wants with my heart." I said it with all the vibrato I didn't have. Electricity tickled my veins. I didn't need my magic to hold back now.

Nikolas laughed. "You should want this from me." He snaked his way closer to me, bridging the gap between us and the road. "I can let you be what your mother was afraid to let you be."

"Don't listen to him. That leech is just messing with you."

Nikolas sneered at Mara but spoke to me. "If I am, then tell me, my dearest Rylee, how can you unlock that"—he pointed to my locket—"if you don't have full access to all your magic?"

I placed my locket into the palm of my hand and stared at it. It still only had the vague start of *J*. Was he right? Would I get nowhere without all my magic?

"No! You know not of Rylee and her strength."

Nikolas laughed. "Ah yes, the boy of darkness."

"What is he talking about?" When my eyes darted to Drake, he barely met my gaze.

"It is nothing. Do not worry."

"Well then, if you're not going to tell her," Nikolas went on, "back to the matter at hand. I've been waiting for you to come to this exact place. And my seer friend showed me today was the day. I want you to die exactly where your mother and brother died."

Lightning trailed around my fingers. No one would die today. Not even Nikolas. He would be locked away somewhere he couldn't escape.

"No one dies!" I let my fingers fly as lightning shot in erratic spurts toward Nikolas, but all he did was blink out of the way, reappearing in the same place.

"Come on! I can make you better."

"No!" I threw another storm of lightning, and again he evaded me.

Mara's hands moved around an empty space, forming a dark amber orb. I expected her to throw it, but it was as if it appeared before him, causing him to crash into one of the guardrails.

Nikolas glared in my direction as he picked himself up. "I told you what would happen if your friends got involved." Again came the buzzing noise.

Mara was gone.

"No!" I screamed, throwing my lightning anywhere I thought would matter. Suddenly I heard a snap. Staring upward, my misfired lightning caused a larger-than-life tree to break, but before I could think of what to do, Drake's hand gripped my shoulder and pulled me away from the outstretched branches reaching toward us. The resounding crash would surely draw attention, if Nikolas hadn't used a spell to silence the noise around us and make everything invisible.

"You must focus," Drake said. "Do not let him win."

He always made it sound like it was so easy. I took a deep breath and let my mind wander, thinking of my next move. Nikolas wanted me to lose focus. He would use any chance he could to take my heart. He wanted to get inside my head;

that's why he talked about the nonsense. But I wouldn't let him. I had to be strong for my dad. For myself.

Breathe in. Breathe out. The heat that consumed every nerve in my body was beautiful. Welcoming. And powerful. Lifting my hands, I wanted to laugh. To think I once feared these flames, but they were mine and they would protect me.

"It didn't have to be this way," Nikolas mocked, coming closer.

"But I'm afraid it does."

Nikolas grinned so wide, I thought his cheeks would split open. "Then you need a taste of what I do." Nikolas pressed his hand to my head. Memories of my family flooded inside my mind. All things I'd seen and let happen to them. All things I could have stopped. "You know deep down Liliana didn't want you to know about that magic because she didn't trust you with it. Because look how well you did with the visions."

He was right. I'd been thinking this exact thing for a while now. I just didn't want to completely admit it to myself. Now it made sense. She'd known about my visions. She knew I hadn't learned to control or understand them. And that day—I'd seen that day, and still my magic had done nothing to help me stop it. She must have known that. She knew what I had, and I had failed to master the little bit of magic I'd discovered.

"Rylee, you must not listen to him."

Nikolas laughed as his hand moved to my chest. "Let me take away your problems, my dearest Rylee. Paraseum!"

Again, I couldn't move. His nails raked at my skin as if trying to claw into my chest. I couldn't breathe. Couldn't feel the magic humming in my veins. "I feel bad for the poor boy," he hissed. "He doesn't know how useless you really are. You can learn all the magic in the world, and I will still beat you."

Nikolas continued to claw at my skin. Was he right? I could still see the helpless look on my dad's face when he told me how hopeless he felt. If I could have seen my face when Nikolas broke in, I would have looked the same way. With just one word, he was unstoppable. I couldn't beat him. No magic I had could win. Drake and Mara both said he was the most powerful Fable in existence. A soulless was truly unstoppable.

The excruciating pain of where Nikolas had dug his nails into my chest erupted from my throat as the feeling returned to me. But Nikolas wasn't beside me anymore. He was across the street, and Drake straightened his body and hovered over me.

"Please listen. You can stop him. Your shield blocks his abilities for a short time. If you can get that up first, the rest will be easier."

I wanted to ask how Drake knocked out a soulless, but I just turned to him. "You don't understand. He's right. I'm useless. This magic isn't going to stop him. I've only survived because *he's* wanted it. My mom didn't want me to have this magic. That's why she did what she did with it."

Drake did something so out of character, I didn't think I would ever forget it. Taking my face in his hands, he stared deep into my eyes. So many emotions rested in his gaze that I couldn't decipher them all, and it was as if I looked into the soul of another. "You are not useless. You are taking me, a man who cares for nothing and no one, and showing me there is hope even for a lost soul such as myself. You have never given up on me. Even though I make it difficult for you. A useless person does not choose to save a world she knows nothing of. You care. That is why you fight harder than anyone I have ever known. Now show him what I see."

Something fluttered to life inside me, like the confidence I wanted to have, but I'd never known where to find it. I used my hand and Drake to pull myself up from the ground. I didn't know how much magic I had left in me. I readied myself and formed the shield in front of me. Heat, electricity, and now this new feather-like weight all gathered inside me at once. My hair twirled in the unexpected wind. Opening my eyes, ominous clouds swirled around overhead. Limbs scratching my face. No rain, only moments of thunder.

"Keep calm!" Drake's voice came faintly through the winds that went from a hard gust to a roaring gale. "Do not use anger in your magic."

"I am calm! Calmer than I've ever been." And I would use anger if it stopped Nikolas. Lightning struck around us now. One. Two. Three. I let the magic build inside me, letting it overflow my every thought and feeling.

You might win a battle, my dearest Rylee, but you will not win the war.

"I want you gone!" The magic released. It was as if all my anger and sadness had fused itself into a tornado that hovered above me. The fire sparked out in all directions. With everything I could manage, I threw the chaotic form. And now, where Nikolas once stood was a crater-size hole. I fell to my knees, screaming and exhausted.

Drake kneeled next to me. "It is okay."

I gave him a half-smile. "I'm fine."

"Paraseum!" Nikolas appeared in front of me, my body stiff. His fingers wrapped around my throat, but I felt nothing. "You didn't think I would be gone that quickly, did you? I've enjoyed the chase, my dearest Rylee, but all good things must come to an end." Nikolas grinned at Drake. "What should I do to you?" A knife I'd never seen before flew out of Drake's back pocket and into Nikolas's hand. "Guess I'll just have to kill you."

Nikolas raised the knife over his head. Though it was used to kill a Fable, a knife was a knife. I couldn't let Drake die. A mixture of emotions, of ice and fire, all boiled in the pit of my stomach and surged to my chest. Pumping the magic into my veins felt as natural as the current of blood that carried it. Before the knife swung into Drake's chest, I threw my electric current toward Nikolas. His grip tightened, and his body convulsed. The electric current coming from his body came in waves until I let him fall, and his paralysis fell away.

I hugged Drake without a second thought that he would do it back.

"Ry—" Before Drake finished, Nikolas made him vanish just like Mara.

"You have to make things so hard." Nikolas reached his bony fingers around my hair before I could back away. He wouldn't stay down. I saw his mouth moving, but only heard the all-too-familiar buzzing noise.

In one blink, his eyes went from brown to that haunting translucent white I knew all too well. From the base of his scalp, white glowing veins crept like cracks on glass, then to his head, shoulders, arms, and to his wrist. As clear as if he'd had it tattooed, the skull marking I'd seen on the day of the accident appeared.

Then my body crumpled to the ground.

I'd always heard when someone died, they saw their life flash before their eyes, but that wasn't true. The first thing that left was pain, replaced by numbness. Then came sorrow. Not even a speck of moisture could form in my eyes. And worry was no more. But I did feel a sense of sadness. Sleep beckoned me, promising to take away the sorrow. The skin around my fingers was nearly invisible. I closed my eyes to welcome my eternal slumber as Nikolas jammed his hand into my chest. But this time, I could feel that he'd broken through. He would get what he was after.

Then everything stopped as a bright light broke through the darkness.

Once I found my breath, Drake jumped out of a wall of glowing light. Rage, something I hadn't even seen in myself, burned bright in his eyes as he held the knife to Nikolas's chest.

"Drake, I don't know . . . what he did to you, but . . . you . . . you can't kill him," I rasped.

Suddenly, there was another bright flash. "Don't do it. He can't die. Not yet." Mara stepped out of the light. "We need to figure out what else the Council is up to first."

Drake hesitated but gave her the knife. Mara stepped next to Nikolas, pressing the knife to his neck. "Now you can either give up your powers, or I can stab you with this knife and you can die over and over again. Which one is it?"

"Do what you want. It's part of . . ." But before he could finish, Mara took the knife Drake had given her. She let the blade slash across Nikolas's tattoo. White blood bubbled up from it. She spoke something in a language I couldn't understand. Dark smoke seeped out of his tattoo and into Mara's mouth. "I'll hold on to your powers until I think I want to give them back." Mara nodded to both of us. "I'm going to take him back to my house. You two best meet me there. We'll figure out what our next plan is when you get there."

And in a blink, Mara and Nikolas were gone.

I tried to figure out what just happened. That's when Drake walked away. Subconsciously I grabbed his hand. As he turned to me, I'd never seen such pain on anyone's face. It was almost unrecognizable.

"Were you planning on killing him with that knife?" I waited for his answer.

When Drake finally spoke, his tone was so dark, it worried me. "We vowed to protect you, and that is what I will do." But his eyes expressed something else. Something had shaken him. I could still envision the hatred in his eyes as he held the knife to Nikolas's chest.

"Where did he send you?" He hadn't changed until that moment. "Look at me!" I pulled his face in my direction and saw a lost boy. Afraid of what, I didn't know.

He took my hands from his face, and I let them fall to my side. "He sent me away. There, a seer who worked for him showed me a future without you. I cannot live in a world like that." I couldn't understand what he meant. Had I truly made him see me as more than a friend? "You are the only mate I require. I do not wish to continue this monotony of life attempting to find others."

"You don't have to."

"I know. It just needed to be said aloud." He was silent. Then he looked at me as if trying to read my thoughts. "I do not understand where the instantaneousness of my sudden emotions came from. But, do you hate me for what I tried to do?"

"No, why would I hate you? One, you've saved my life twice now. And two, you didn't kill him." Sirens and red and blue lights flashed from just over the hill. "We have to go."

We ran to the car and drove in the opposite direction, leaving the evidence of an unnatural storm.

16

Confusion and pain wrestled in the blue of Drake's eyes as we drove in silence. I'd never been able to see him this vulnerable before. To see him biting his lip to hold back the pain. My heart hurt almost as much as it did the day of the funeral. As if I yanked it out of my chest, then jammed it back in repeatedly.

I remembered the rage-fueled look in Drake's eyes when he came back through the portal. As we passed by the grain field, I had an idea. There was one place we could go. A place where he and I could try to find answers.

"Would you pull over? I want to show you something," I said.

Without a second thought, Drake pulled over to the right side of the road. As the car came to a stop, I got out and he followed. Maybe it was because *I* was always this way, but I expected him to ask where we were going. He just blindly followed me.

Ash blanketed the ground. The wood from the loft lay broken and charred and mostly burned up on what was once the ground floor. Small shreds of books I'd loved and cherished for years were scattered throughout the once large space. Even my mom's bean bag chair hadn't made it. But then, something just a few feet from us flapped in the wind from outside. Kneeling to pick it up, the tears I'd tried to keep from shedding broke free. It had been the picture Damian had drawn of our family. Only the words remained. *My family.* Putting the piece of paper into my pocket, I rose.

"Might I ask why you brought me here?"

Though the image of the area had changed, the meaning remained the same. "When I found this place, I thought it could be something for everyone. A place we could all come to. My family and I would have picnics and build snowmen here. But there are bad memories here too. This is where my first boyfriend, AJ, broke up with me. This was where I found out that my grandpa Walter died. But I always felt like this was my home away from home. A place that could always give me answers." I gestured to everything around us. "This is where it all happened for me. I realized on the day of the fire, though I didn't understand it completely, that there was something different about me. That I was capable of something I'd never known was possible. I thought the day my family died, I was changed forever, but seeing all of this now, I realized the day this place caught on fire was the day I was reborn.

"When you came out of that portal, I could *feel* the hatred you had for what he'd done to you. I'm not scared of you, so don't think that. I saw in you what I knew I would realize about myself coming back here. I rose from my ashes that day, and you rose from someone else's. Figuratively, of course. This barn has its mixed memories and emotions, but it's still my safest place to hide. What I'm trying to say is, I didn't come here just for me. But for you too. In hopes that this place could help you understand yourself and be your solace as well." I took in my own words for a moment.

"Granted, it needs some repairs, but you and I can do that together if you want."

Drake's eyes focused on something in the distance for a moment. "You brought me to a place you cherish dearly. In hopes of helping me find my understanding." I didn't know why he was repeating what I'd just said, but when he opened his mouth to continue, I was hopeful. "You still care for me even though I can offer you so little." I opened my mouth to tell him not to think of himself that way, but he held up his hand to stop me. "Nikolas's seer showed me a war. I believe it to be the one that Liliana might have wanted to stop. Between humans and Fables. You had died. Havoc and darkness spread. A man I had never met was the leader of this group, and Nikolas was his right hand because you were not able to kill him. After learning of your death, your father no longer wanted to live. My parents and sister died trying to protect you. And I was alone. I found my way out of the portal and into our world.

"There was this unexplainable pain in my chest, something I have never had the pleasure of feeling until seeing that vision. You were correct when seeing the knife in my pocket, but I did not intend on using it. I believed it to be possible to find another way to destroy him without killing him. But after seeing the future, I knew there was no choice. I did not want Fables to be at war. But most of all, I did not want a world to exist without you. You bring more to other's than you know, Rylee."

I was speechless. He'd rather kill someone than let me die. I turned his face toward me. I wanted to see what he was feeling, and I wanted him to see the same in my eyes. "What you tried to do for me, though I am a bit freaked out about it, means a lot." I let the silence sit with us as I thought of my next words. "Did you mean what you said back there?" Heat rose in my cheeks. "About what I'm doing for you?"

He turned his gaze away from the clouds, then back to me. "Of course. You have shown me there are still good people in this world." He stared at the clouds again as his brow furrowed. "But there is something else that I do not quite understand."

"What?"

"From talking to Mara, you know that over time I have only been able to feel negative emotions. But it seems as if something about *you* is giving me different feelings. Nothing romantic, but I cannot quite explain it."

I didn't know what to say. I'd given him something he'd always been looking for. But in the back of my mind, I couldn't help but wonder, like I had with my dad, if Drake was only friends with me because of what I could offer him.

"Is that why you've been hanging out with me?" I bit the inside of my cheek.

"I will not lie; when I first saved you from the fire, I felt something strong inside you, but I did not understand its meaning. And then when I came to the food bank, it grew stronger. But over time I have learned to see you in other ways that have nothing to do with what you help me feel. I promise you this."

In his eyes again was that sincerity. Though it hurt a bit, he'd been honest with me even from the beginning.

"I believe you. Please always be honest with me, and I'll do the same for you."

I smiled and he nodded.

"I want to thank you for saving my life," Drake said. "I know of no one who has done this for me before."

"Not even your parents?"

The small light that I'd seen in his eyes died in an instant. "We should get going."

He stood to leave, but I grabbed his wrist. "Why do you do that?"

"What?"

"Why won't you talk about your family? I mean I know about Nathan and Selena from what Mara told me, but I know nothing about your real dad." Drake stared at my hand on his arm, and I pulled away, blushing.

"It is no different than you not wanting to share the past festivities of your birthday. It pains you in some way to have to answer it."

"I'll tell you then," I said eagerly.

A moment of contemplation rested in his eyes, but it faded as he spoke. "It does not work that way. Some are not as open as you. I beg you to let this go. To trust me, as I see you do. I am not telling you for reasons only for me to know. Sometimes obtaining all the answers means nothing if you do not understand them."

With every fiber of my being, I wanted to push him until he told me. But something about him carried this vague familiarity of myself in the last few years. Studying him longer, a deeper pain wrestled on his face. What happened to his father had broken him in a way I'd never seen in anyone, not even myself.

"I may ask a lot of questions, but did you ever stop and think you don't ask enough?" He didn't answer, but again, he was contemplating the question. "I know your family's hurt you in some way, but you're right. It's still hard for me to talk about my mom. So will you forgive me?"

A half smile touched the corner of his mouth. "There is nothing to forgive. But if it allows you comfort, then I do forgive you."

Drake was a perplexing person, to say the least. All I wanted was for him to open up to me. Not to be worried I would hurt him. I had to give him time, but how much was too much?

"There is one question I have that I think you can

answer. It's about something Nikolas said. That you were hiding something from me, and when he was taking my soul, the next thing I knew, he was across the street." He stared at me. "What are you hiding, and how did that happen to him?"

"Nikolas does not know what you do and do not know. And as far as how he got to where he was"—he pointed to my locket—"your locket did that."

I took the locket in my palm and tears built in my eyes. It was showing half of my initials now. It was working. Suddenly, my phone rang.

"Mara," I answered still smiling at the locket. "I got some great news."

"Nikolas is gone."

17

We were all back at Mara's now. I was sitting on her porch steps because the fight with Nikolas drained my magic, so I needed to regenerate. Mara and Drake stood at the bottom on both sides of the railing. The panic hung in my throat. This couldn't be happening. I thought back to the moment I thought I had him, but with one touch, he'd taken all that hope. I had to stop him, but honestly, I didn't think I could. And people's lives could pay for that.

My eyes wandered to Drake. If it hadn't been for him, I'd still feel like there was no hope. He was there to pull me back. He was always there. Every time death was at my door, there Drake was. And though all of that was comforting, he couldn't save me forever. I had to stop Nikolas. No matter the cost. If what Drake saw was the future, I needed to be strong and stop it.

I stood, holding the railing, but wobbled. My head spun, so I sat back down. "Mara, tell me again how the hell he got out." I pressed my hand to my head in hopes of stopping the spinning.

"His seer ambushed me when we got home. She's a witch, and a good one at that." Mara went quiet. "There's something else you should know."

"What?" I snapped, not meaning to.

"He has his magic back."

"I do not understand," Drake said. "You took his magic, so how could he take it back?"

Mara pinched the bridge of her nose, but didn't say anything. For once she was wearing on *my* patience. "What happened?"

"As much as I don't want to admit it, that seer got the upper hand."

"And that means what exactly?" I asked.

"She used dark magic to steal Nikolas's magic from me. She even took some of mine." Mara snapped her fingers, and everything disappeared. "You need to get stronger, and quick. He won't stop."

"I know you were preoccupied for most of Rylee's fight, but she has endured a lot." It was sweet to see Drake standing up for me, but he was telling her I was too weak. Less sweet. Maybe he was doing it because I saved his life?

"Stand up," she demanded, waving her hands at me.

"But I—"

"Bloody hell. Stand up!"

I did as she asked, and it was as if I'd slept a full eight hours. "How?" I made my way down the stairs and us all to the middle of the yard.

"Even though you can't use all of your magic it still works. You never lose magic. You personally just don't have all access to yours, so it makes you more tired and feels like you're losing it but you're not."

"Well that's good to know. So what's are our next move?"

"You need to learn how to teleport. Right now, you're new so you can only go short distances. As you get stronger, you can go from city to city, but that's about it. Strength will help with distance, but not knowing made you vulnerable today."

"Okay, so what do I do?"

"Close your eyes, tell your magic where you want to go, and snap your fingers. It's that simple." Mara took a long look to Drake as if studying him. And after a few more seconds she handed him a vial full of glowing white liquid. "Now that you know that you need to know how to fight a soulless."

I stared at the vial in Drake's hand and then remembered the one Nikolas had used on the bridge. "Is that vial going to do some magic thing to help me?" She nodded. "Okay, but what does Drake have to do with it?"

"For the potion to work, it needs a vessel, which'll be Drake. First I'm going to teach you how to be smarter than a soulless."

I wanted to see something in Drake's body language. His shoulders tensed or relaxed. Even in his face or his eyes. Something to let me know that he was okay with what we were about to do. Him taking the vial was the answer to that, I guess. But regardless of his lack of expression, I didn't want to hurt him. He was my friend.

"Will you make sure I don't hurt him?" I asked.

"He'll be fine. Now let's get started." Mara teleported from the back of the yard to the deck. "You must always pay attention to everything a soulless does and even what they may show you. Teleportation is one of their well-known abilities. You can do it too. You must be careful."

"But won't they just copy me?"

Mara rolled her eyes. "If you pay attention to their subtleties, then you should be able to attack them before they can do the same to you. You have to clear your mind." Mara nodded to Drake. "Give her some practice."

Drake drank the vial's contents. And just like Nikolas, I watched him transform. Drake planted both of his feet firmly on the ground. White veins seemed to glow against his light skin. That potion. Did it give him the powers of a soulless? The only difference now was, I didn't fear death, but there was a pain to it. Drake was no monster. He wasn't even a Fable. Seeing him this way was unnatural, but if this would help stop Nikolas, it had to be done.

I would be glad when it was over.

I waited for him to move and then, in one blink, he vanished. In another, he stood just inches from me, knocking me hard to the ground.

"Oh come on. Drake could have killed you if he wanted to."

"I'm sorry." Drake reached out to help me.

"Let's do this again. And this time, pay attention."

Breathe in. Breathe out.

Drake's foot inched to the left as the wind swirled around his face. A tendril of hair fell in front of his face like a blade of grass catching the breeze. I had to stay focused. His body shifted and he was gone. Again, he appeared in front of me, knocking me hard this time.

"What are you doing?" Mara asked.

Again, Drake held out his hand for me. "Sorry, I'm trying." I grunted as I lurched to my feet.

"Not hard enough. Since you seem to think this is a game, we'll kick it up a notch." Mara nodded to Drake. His veins glowed almost as brightly as Nikolas's. "Now focus, and if you do it right, Drake won't rip out your soul. Don't overthink it. Go!"

Drake's fingers twitched as he moved his left foot back. With my next exhale, it's as if I only blinked and appeared where I wanted to be. With another exhale, I turned, putting a shield around myself. Drake stalked closer, and heat rose in my fingers. I released the weak stream of flames at him, realizing what I'd done a moment too late.

He stood just inches from me. The heat now on my skin had nothing to do with my fire. I wasn't sure what I'd do if I hurt him, but he'd avoided my attack so easily. What did Mara give him?

"Not bad." Mara slapped me on the back. "If you can master that, you can use your magic to weaken him."

"Wha . . ." I shook my head to clear the daze. "I mean, yeah, but how do I stop Nikolas from taking my soul?"

Drake answered my question as he sauntered up the deck stairs with us. "It is much like a soulless itself. You must release your emotions. Think of nothing. Then nothing will be taken away from you."

"Well, I think that's enough for one day." Mara dusted off her pant legs even though there was nothing on them. "You should go home and get some rest."

"Yes, and I have other matters to attend to," Drake said.

I ran after him. "Where are you going?"

We walked across the street to my house. "To speak to Aurora of the seer's vision. I believe it to be of help somehow."

"Oh okay. Well, thanks for helping me. But can I be honest with you?" We stopped at my mailbox.

"Of course." His eyes now glinted with curiosity. Were his emotions back?

"It was weird to see you use magic."

"I figured it would be. May I be honest with you now?"

"Your honesty is always a breath of fresh air," I joked, but I meant it.

"You are very strong physically and mentally. I wish you saw this in yourself as well."

Heat rose in my cheeks. "Thanks. I wish I could too."

Drake came with me inside the house, which I thought

was kind of odd being that he'd just said that he needed to be somewhere else. But I didn't mind. Opening the front door, the aroma of baked goods welcomed us. For once my dad hadn't sent a dozen text messages asking where I was today, but the blare of the TV and banging of pans told me where he was. Butterflies filled my stomach. I had to decide whether to tell him about Nikolas.

As we made our way into the kitchen and I saw my pink hand decorated birthday cake sitting on the table, I knew I couldn't tell him.

"Rylee, I'm so glad you're home." I heard a sense of relief in his tone. "Not that it's a problem, but Drake, why are you here?"

"Well sir, something—"

"He was just dropping me off." I glared at Drake and pulled him into the living room.

Once there, I tiptoed to look over Drake's shoulders to make sure my dad wasn't eavesdropping. "Look I'm not ready to tell him. There is so much other stuff going on. I just need time."

"So, you wish to leave your father in the shadows as you were the entirety of your life?"

"No, but what's telling him really going to do? So I say, 'Hey, Dad, I fought Nikolas and then he got away.' What does that do for anyone? It'll just make him mad at me, and I . . . I just want to tell him on my own terms."

"Not everything can be what is convenient to you." Drake abruptly turned to leave, but I grabbed his arm to pull him back.

"He's my father. This isn't your story to tell him." I needed him to understand that if he told him, this would break us again, and I couldn't have that.

"If you wish to keep lying to your father, then you cannot be angry with lies that your mother has kept from you."

It was as if he'd taken a knife and stabbed me with it. All I could do was watch him leave the room. But after a moment realized that I needed to follow after him.

"Is everything all right?" my dad asked as we came back into the room.

"It is not, Mr. Jenkins."

"Drake." I threw myself in front of him. "If you care for our friendship in any way, you won't do this to me."

Nothing betrayed his emotions as always.

"Mr. Jenkins, I believe it in your best interest to know your daughter took on a rare Fable called a soulless. I believe you understand him better as Nikolas."

My dad's labored breathing sounded a lot like mine. I couldn't turn around. To see the anger, the disappointment in his eyes. "I told you not to go after him—to let Mara handle him." His voice was calm, which meant he was trying not to lose his temper.

His words struck a nerve, and even though I'd hoped to avoid this confrontation, I couldn't withhold the words. So I turned to him with fury. "I didn't go after him. He found *me*."

"But you didn't have to fight him." His eyes met mine now, and in them was pain. I was too angry to care. "Mara could have done that."

"Why does this have to be all Mara, huh? Do you really not think I'm good enough to win?" His face fell, but I was glad he was sad for once. I was tired of always feeling like I was the wrong one.

"I never said you weren't good enough. I just don't want the only family I have left to die."

"Oh, so you care about me now that everyone's dead and you don't want to end up alone, great. Thanks Dad," I growled. I knew that wasn't true, but I wasn't sure what else to say. I couldn't have escaped if I tried? I'm alive now? He wouldn't listen anyway.

"That isn't—"

"You know, it's funny how you're going on about me and Nikolas, when you're doing the same damn thing. Asking the cops about him and then even asking me, but yet you don't want me to get involved. That's pretty involved if you ask me."

"I'm trying to protect you."

I was so tired of hearing that. From him, from Farrah, my mom, and even Drake and Mara. I didn't want protection. I wanted answers. I wanted honesty.

"You know what, you asked once if it was too late to make this right. It is." Heat rose on the back of my neck. "I don't want or need your protection. Guess you should have thought of your life choices before everyone was dead."

As the room fell silent and my body was flushed with anger, I should have regretted the words I chose to say to him, but I didn't. Why?

Drake turned to leave. "Where do you think you're going?" I growled. "You started this; you might as well tell him everything I've been doing."

"I think enough has been said." Suddenly Drake's phone rang in his pocket. Pulling it out, Mara's name flashed across the screen. He met my eyes, and I only felt angrier. "I do sincerely apologize, but it seems I am needed." Drake stepped toward my dad. "It was nice to see you, Mr. Jenkins."

But my dad didn't answer.

"I will see myself out then." Drake stood in the hallway. I needed him to leave. "Rylee, I know you did not mean what you said. But your father is unlike most fathers I know of. He does love you."

As Drake closed the front door, my dad's bedroom door

did the same. I let go of the uncontrollable sobs as my back slid down the wall. My head replayed me telling him that it was too late. The shattered pain in his eyes tore at my soul. It wasn't too late, so why did I say that unless, deep down, a part of me felt like it was.

18

Sleep eluded me as thoughts of my dad, Nikolas, and even how mad I was at Drake swirled in my head like a tornado. I didn't know what to do about any of it. I wanted so much just to wish it all away. To let it be someone else's life. But it was mine, and I had to deal with it. Mara had sent me a text last night asking if Drake and I would meet her at a farmers market, so now I sat in Drake's Lexus.

"So, you forgive me?" I asked Drake, messing with the door handle.

"Will it make you feel better if I say yes?"

"Only if you mean it."

"I forgive you." Drake stopped at a red light. "May I ask you something?"

"Yeah, I guess, but I'm kind of scared to know what you're going to ask."

"Why is that?"

"Because every time you ask me something, it's about something deep I really have to think about."

"I see."

"But still ask it."

"I was curious what you might have meant when you said you wanted Nikolas gone."

Had I really said that? Yesterday's chaos had become spotty. "I just wanted it all to stop. Fables like him are monsters!" I chewed hard on the inside of my cheek, tasting metal. "And honestly . . ." I turned back to the door handle. "I'm not sure we can beat him. And don't get me started on this locket."

The engraving remained the same, and we were just a week away.

"What if we can't get this locket to work?" My throat tightened. "What if there are no more Fables in the world, then what?"

He took a deep breath. "I do not believe you will let that happen and neither will my sister." He turned down the heat then. "Is there anything that I can tell you that could help ease your thoughts?"

"Can you tell me more about that knife that could kill Nikolas, not that I plan to use it."

"Yes, I can. The chemical in the crystal comes from the planet Mars. It is lethal to a soulless. It is the only thing that can make them bleed and keep them from coming back to life."

Drake continued to talk, but I'd drowned him out. He knew a lot about other things, but when it came to Fables, he only ever spoke of soullesses. When I'd asked about me being a witch, he'd left that to his sister. Mara had said Drake couldn't feel emotions. To feel them for a small time, he had to meditate. Nikolas had to harvest. Mara had also said Drake could feel pain as he'd gotten older. Nikolas was the same way. And then I thought of yesterday. It was like he knew how to activate the powers that the potion gave him.

I could have sworn my heart had literally stopped.

"You're . . . a . . . soulless," I whispered.

I didn't expect an expression or change in his tone, and I didn't get one. "I understand why you would come to that conclusion, but we are nothing alike."

"I saw what you did at Mara's."

"That was her magic's doing."

"Roll up your sleeves," I demanded as he pulled into the farmers market parking lot.

Once he'd parked the car and turned off the ignition, he did as I asked. I took my pointer finger and ran it along one wrist, then the other. I pressed down firmly, hoping for a secret way to make the tattoo appear.

"So you don't have the tattoo," I huffed. "That still doesn't explain all the lack of emotions and meditating thing."

"My sister told you of my condition."

"But it all seems too coincidental."

"There is one thing that sets humans with disorders apart from soullesses. When a soulless bleeds, their blood is white."

Drake reached into his pocket, pulling out the knife he was going to use on Nikolas. Suddenly the same loud buzzing sound filled my ears, but when I turned toward the noise, I saw nothing. I then turned back to Drake, who had yet to move. I had no idea what he was doing until he started to cut his hand. Red blood bubbled up from the wound.

"Stop!" I screamed, grabbing a napkin from the cupholder in front of us and pressing it into his hand to stop the bleeding. Seeing the blood seeping through the napkin reminded me of the story Mara had told me about Drake and Marcus. I wanted to slap myself now for letting him go this far.

"I believe you, okay," I whispered.

"Thank you. May I have my knife back?"

"Fine." And I handed it back to him.

Once we got out of the car, Drake told me I could find

him at a picnic table. He then told me Mara was waiting for me on top of the hill. Walking up the hill, I tried to keep my mind focused on my lesson with Mara, but I found myself thinking of Drake. In the last week, Drake and I had grown closer as friends. And that was fine, I just couldn't understand his sudden on and off emotions. Did it really have something to do with me? I remembered what Drake had said to me in the barn. How he didn't want to live in a world where I didn't exist.

When Drake shared his feelings now, it's as if he were stating more. Something deeper. It was as if he were opening up and feeling more. His emotions seemed intermittent, like crossing wire. But I couldn't think much about it anymore as I reached the top of the hill, where Mara waited for me, and for some reason, she didn't look too happy.

"Hey, are you okay?" I asked when I made it into the center of the lush grass mountain top.

"Why didn't you tell me what Drake was doing yesterday?" she snapped.

"Excuse me? I don't understand why you're mad at me. And what does it matter?"

"Because it's what he *did*," she huffed.

"I'm not following you."

She groaned. "Because he went and talked to Aurora, you now only have *days* to stop or kill Nikolas and open that locket."

"What? Why?" My leg suddenly felt like noodles. "You have to be joking, right?"

"No, I'm not. So, you can thank my bloody brother."

Feeling returned to my legs as I spoke. "Look, don't blame him for doing what was right. I know it's not what we planned, and yes it's scary, but we can do it. Why is it such a big deal anyway? We'd just have to save the Fable world sooner than we thought, which isn't a bad thing."

She took a deep breath. "I didn't want to tell you more until everything was good to go. But that locket holds the key to something that can stop all this. I know you want to ask why, but for once, just don't because you knowing now could mean your death."

I'd never seen Mara so frazzled before. She was anything but melodramatic. "Okay, then what do we do?"

Her eyes wandered to a rock. "All we can do is teach you more magic. So today we'll start with telekinesis. But while you're doing it, I want you to think of what makes you angry."

"Drake said it was bad to use anger with magic."

"My brother doesn't know as much as he thinks he does. There is a way, that if controlled, you can use your anger in your magic."

"But why do I need to learn to use anger?"

"If you can control it, emotions are strength. A fast and powerful source of it. And maybe that can unlock the locket. I will not let Nikolas and the Council get what they want. Your magic is some of the strongest I've ever felt, but we can't let them have it. So this is our next best bet."

"Not to get a big head, but do you think I'm as strong as you?"

She grinned. "If you tell anyone else this, I'll deny it, but I think you could be stronger. I want to show you how to harness it the right way so it doesn't get out of control."

"Okay, cool."

"Great! Now I want you to think of something that makes you angry and focus on it but don't release it. Let it connect with your magic. Then release it slowly." Mara's eyes wandered. "I want you to pick up that rock." She pointed to a stone across the field. "And set it next to me."

"Okay, but how do I use telekinesis?"

"It's the easiest one. Just find an object you want to move, and like your fire and lightning, you must focus. Tell the rock where you want it to go. This is the only spell done with the mind."

I kept my gazed fixated on the rock Mara had picked out for me. It wasn't hard to find what angered me. I was angry at the uncertainty of Nikolas. I was angry that I might not be able to save the Fable world. I was angry with my dad too. Angry that he'd been so reckless about Nikolas. I was angry at myself for what I'd said to him. The boulder rose just above our heads as my anger continued to burn. I was angry at how hopeless I felt. The rock swayed.

"Stay focused. Control your emotions. Use them as channels. Don't flood yourself with them."

It was as if my anger jelled into my bones. Into my magic. As if the weightlessness in my fingers came from my emotions alone. The feeling was so overwhelming, so rejuvenating, that tears built in my eyes as I let the rock softly land on the ground next to Mara.

"See, it wasn't that hard. Just keep control."

I couldn't help but look at my locket, but nothing had changed. I hated how much Nikolas's words were playing in my head right now. It wasn't Drake's fault, but we were running out of time to save the Fables from war. Maybe we didn't have a choice. I couldn't tell Mara this, though.

"We have to keep working at it."

I wiped my eyes. "I know. I don't think I've ever truly said this, but I want to thank you for helping me. For protecting me. And for, well, being like a sister to me."

Mara playfully shoved me and smirked. "Well, if you're going to learn this stuff, you *should* be learning it from someone great at what they do." Her playfulness faded. "Listen, I know I might seem a bit hard on you, but it's because I see what you can do. And I want to help you get there." She drew a small reminiscing smile. "My father was the same way with me."

"Well, I'm trying."

"Rylee, you beat yourself up for nothing. You may get on my nerves sometimes with your impatience and twenty-one questions, but I promise you I wouldn't be doing this if I thought you were hopeless. Regardless of some promise." Yellow smoke formed around Mara. "Well, we won't find Nikolas by standing here. Call me if you need me, okay?"

"I will."

In a blink, Mara was gone.

19

"Rylee." My body shook. "Rylee, wake up." As my eyes fluttered open, I made out the frame of Drake's black hair and beard that was now growing in. "I am sorry to have kept you waiting. Would you care to take a walk?"

The market chatter faded as Drake and I made our way up the opposite side of a steeper hill than the one I'd been on going to see Mara. We strolled for a while without speaking, but all I could see were the dirt-covered molehills and the lush grass spots here and there. I wanted to see the market, but I had a feeling we'd be back.

Drake walked beside me. "How did training go with my sister?"

I chewed on the inside of my cheek. "Well, actually, she's pretty pissed at you. That you went and talked to Aurora. She says now we only have a few days to unlock this locket."

"I was never able to speak to Aurora directly, so I left an anonymous tip about the vision his seer showed me."

Visions like I had. Like I'd been having. "I can't believe I didn't think of this, to begin with."

"Think of what?"

"I've been having visions of Nikolas. My mom had always told me to think of my visions like they were warnings."

"And what do you think these visions are trying to tell you?"

"I think they're telling me where to find Nikolas. Where I can finish this and keep everyone safe."

"Then let us discuss them. Tell me of your first one."

I thought back to the first vision I had about Nikolas, which was when I set my barn on fire. "When I opened my eyes, it was like I could see lights, but it was like they were far away or something."

"What else?"

"I was looking at a popcorn stand when I heard footsteps behind me. And then it's like before when he was trying to take my soul on the bridge."

"Did he say anything to you? Anything that would tell us what he wanted?"

Again, I thought. He had said something. But what was it? The apology. So many things he'd said, and I couldn't remember what it was he apologized about. Frustrated, I fought the urge to complain and wished all of this were over. That it could just end and I could have a normal life.

"All I remember is him saying he was sorry. I do remember, however, someone screaming my name, and it wasn't Nikolas."

Drake and I fell silent once more. But even saying it out loud didn't give me an answer. And what did the other vision have to do with why he apologized or where we'd find him?

"Wait, I think I got it," I said. "What's the one place that has popcorn?" Drake stayed silent. "The movie theater. And they also had those lights outside. Maybe I was just seeing them from far away because I wasn't there yet." The more I talked, the more it started to click. "Nikolas couldn't get my heart the day of the accident because I'd shocked him. He couldn't get me at home because again I'd managed to attack him. And on the bridge, you stopped him." I took in a breath to slow my fast-beating heart. "I know what this is. It's his last stand. His last chance to get what the Council wants. And it'll be my last chance to stop him."

"That does make sense. You spoke of visions, as in more than one."

"Yeah, the other one was kind of short. Nikolas was holding a stuffed bird. I think it was a phoenix, and he said something like, it's so sad he won't show his true self. But I have no idea what it means."

Drake thought for a minute. "So we have lights, a popcorn stand, Nikolas holding a phoenix. But I cannot decipher what he meant in his last comment. Have you received your final vision?"

I bowed my head. "No. Dammit! I need to figure these visions out." My fist clenched. "I have to stop him!"

"You do not have to do it on your own."

He was such a good friend. "Thanks. Now if I can just learn to use my magic with my anger quicker, I should—"

Drake stopped walking and at the shock of it, I didn't even notice the large rock that made me fall backward. He caught me, and just like in the movies, our eyes met. The only difference was, nothing rested in his eyes. No spark or longing. But *my* heart jumped like a jackrabbit. I wasn't sure why or if the moment had spooked me, but within seconds of him catching me, he pulled me upright and I let the thought wither.

"I do not understand why my sister would recommend you using anger with your magic," he said after I told him about our training. He walked behind me, most likely to make sure I didn't fall again. "She saw what that did to our father."

I bit my lip as I asked my question, knowing he wouldn't answer it. "Why won't you talk about him?" As I predicted, he said nothing. I wasn't about to turn around and have another awkward moment, made more awkward because *he* didn't know it was. "If I've learned anything in my short time in therapy, it's that talking about it helps."

Another long pause hung in the air as we made it to the top of the hill. Grassy moss covered most of the ground beneath our feet. Bushes and trees circled the perimeter. The sunset rested just above the horizon. Drake and I took a seat on one of the boulders.

"My mom loved these sunsets. She used to say, with the darkness . . ."

"Came anew," Drake finished. "It was from a poem I read once."

We sat for a long moment.

"I have a birthday gift for you." Drake reached into his pocket and handed me two pieces of paper. "I asked my sister for assistance in finding you a gift. She thought you would enjoy these." They were two tickets to the state fair.

A huge lump caught in my throat. I hadn't told him about this, about why I didn't want to go there. "These are really nice, but I . . . I . . . ." My heart hurt to have to remember. "When I was a kid, my parents and I would go. I loved the spinning teacups but hated the Ferris wheel. But we just stopped going, and I don't remember why. And now, we can't."

"If it is too painful, I do understand you not wanting to go."

"No, I need to go. If I'm ever going to move on with life, I have to start somewhere."

We sat for a long while, watching the sunset. Most people would find this moment of silence awkward, and I used to, but now it was comforting. Sometimes saying nothing at all said more than any word could. But all the while, I couldn't stop thinking about Nikolas and these visions.

And that's when I realized the answer to all of this. If I could unlock this locket sooner rather than later, it would stop Nikolas. Of course this was only part of the solution. But I could send him away and everything would be ok. I took a deep breath and turned to Drake. "There's something else I think we need to do."

"What is that?"

"Nikolas has to take out my heart so I can have all my magic. I know you and Mara won't let anything happen to me." Life flickered in his eyes. "You believe in me. But Nikolas is right, and I can't do what needs to be done without all my magic."

"And my sister cannot know of this because she could try to stop us?"

"Yes."

"I understand the source of your anger comes from not being able to prevent things. You become angry because something happens to someone or something has already happened, and you cannot stop it. There is enough strength in your magic. You do not need anger to make it stronger. You have to let go of your guilt for your mother's and brother's deaths. You have to let go of the guilt for your father."

"Why are you telling me this?"

A mixture of terror and hesitation swam fiercely in his eyes. "Nikolas would not have been the first one had I killed him."

I tried my best to keep my expressions to myself, not wanting him to think something more of them. I should have been scared to know he'd killed before, but the remorse in his words told me everything I needed to know. How pained he'd been at the hospital when learning I'd found out about his time in the asylum. It was far from okay what he did, but he regretted it.

"I have *attempted* to trust two other people in my life," Drake said. "But do you know the difference between them and you?"

I didn't know what this question had to do with what he'd just told me, but I answered honestly. "I wasn't mean to you."

"That, yes, but also compassion and understanding. You do not perceive me as broken, as something to fix. Though I did believe that to be your intention in the beginning. For that, I am sorry. I trust that when I tell my story, you will not shun me. And, I hope, you will not call the police."

I tried not to squeal, but what he said made it difficult. He'd chosen me. I wanted to ask him why, but hearing his story was more important.

"You know the story of Marcus, but what you do not know is what happened after. Being in that asylum was unpleasant. Though I cannot feel emotions toward them, I could feel the love my parents had toward me, and it kept me going. But then one day Mara came to me and told me that Marcus had shown the police the video of what I had done to myself to prove what I had said. And that he had lied about me attacking him. His hope being to get me locked away."

"She told me the rest." I bit the inside of my cheek to hold my anger inside. "Your parents sent you here because they didn't want to deal with you. But they loved you so much, why would they do that?"

He shook his head. "I do not know. But before we left, I

went to his home. His parents were not there. He asked why I was there. Going on about how I was a monster, and I should be locked away for good. When he went for his phone, I took his life. I could not be locked away again. Things I would rather not discuss were done there. And I preferred never to have to endure them again."

I should've called the cops right then. That hadn't been long ago. I should've been afraid to know that. My words were low and rushed. "What did you do to the body?"

His knuckles tightened into a fist. "I had him cremated and spread his ashes along a lake he played in as a child. I had another mate make it look like Marcus had run away."

Anyone else would have run, but I wouldn't. Though I couldn't say that it was right what he'd done, that had been another life. Judging by the look in his eyes and sound of his voice now, he didn't want to be that way anymore. I hurt for him. If only feeling something for what he'd done to his best friend. I wouldn't have done it, but the past was the past. He'd tried to at least honor his friend in the end.

"Drake, I promise you, I will never share your secret with anyone."

"Thank you. But I must ask, how you do perceive me now?"

"I can't judge you more than you could judge me. I'm not going to lie and say it's okay what you did, or that I understand it, but what's happened has happened. I can tell you're not that same boy anymore. So, to answer your question, I see you as the same boy I saw yesterday and the day before that. Nothing you do will change that." Then it made me wonder. Despite trying to understand how I felt about this revelation, I felt inclined to know his thoughts. "How do you see me?"

He tilted his head. "I have told you of this."

"No, I mean how you *really* see me. The girl who's broken. The girl who can't get over what she let happen to her family. The girl who still feels like it was somehow her fault."

"You are not broken, Rylee Jenkins. You must know deep down that nothing was your fault." He gazed deep into my eyes. "When did you receive those visions?"

I had to think back. "The first one I'd had about the accident was a few weeks before. I think the second one was a few days later. And the last one was when I was in the hospital after the accident."

"Then there was no way you could have understood these visions because you did not have all the pieces. They came too far apart to remember them all."

"How does that explain my mom flying off the bridge after what I said to her?"

He took a moment to think about my question. "We know that Nikolas was there that day and wanted your heart and your father's. Was your mother acting peculiar that day?"

"Other than her eyes being crimson and her mind numbingly driving off the bridge, no." I thought about the rest of Drake's comment. "Wait a minute. You don't think Nikolas has something to do with it, do you?"

"What were the exact words you spoke to your mother?"

Bile rose in my throat. "I told her if she left . . . never to come back," I whispered.

Realization dawned on him, and for the first time, it was like I could read his expression. What I said meant something. "A seer. You see the future because you are a seer. A soulless has certain powers. One is to hypnotize."

It hit me all at once. "Nikolas."

"Nikolas must have hypnotized Liliana to run off the bridge. Nikolas wanted your family dead. If his seer watched you closely, there must be significance in that moment. Perhaps Nikolas hoped to torment you, or perhaps it is something more."

"But why kill my whole family just for our hearts?"

Drake only shook his head. "I have no idea."

20

The moment Drake said it, I knew it had to be true. With everything Nikolas had done, he'd had to have his seer friend help him somehow. They'd watched me and my family for years, maybe. But how could they have known so much? Questions swirled around in my head as Drake drove me back home. I didn't want to go there, but Drake said I needed to face my dad. I wasn't sure sorry would be enough.

The moon cast an eerie glow through the trees as Drake pulled into my driveway after six in the evening. I nearly cried when I didn't see my dad's Odyssey.

"Would you like me to walk you in?" He was getting ready to turn off the car.

I reached over, pulling open my door. "No, I'm good. I'll see you tomorrow."

I waited for Drake's headlights to fade before closing the front door behind me. I stood in my small foyer staring at the living room to the left, kitchen to the right, and the dining room down the long hallway. But this place didn't feel like my home. It always felt like I was just visiting. My muddy boots echoed on the hardwood floor. I had good memories here, but it's as if I didn't remember them.

I deserved this loneliness I was feeling now. I shouldn't have said those things to him.

I'd subconsciously made my way into the kitchen, where all the memories I did have seemed to come to life. My dad's apron hung over the back of one of the chairs. For the smallest moment, I wondered if he left for good this time. If what I said had been too much for him. Worse, if he'd taken his own life because of me.

"I'm so sorry." I slammed my fist on the chair. "I'm so . . ." A small piece of paper flew off the table then. It was in my dad's handwriting.

> Rylee,
>
> I'm sorry but I can't take you to your therapy appointment. Chuck needs me to go to Atlanta. I'll be back in a few days. I'm also sorry for not being there when you really needed me. I'm sorry you feel like it's too late.
>
> I'll love you forever and always,
> Dad

My tears splotched the ink on the page. He *was* leaving me. I shook my head. He'd changed, though. But if he really had, then why was he leaving like he used to when things got tough? If I believed he was changing, then why did I still doubt him?

Farrah would have been just the person to ask, but I would have to cancel, so I pulled out my phone.

"Hello, Farrah Alastair's office. May I ask who's speaking?"

"Hi, I'm Rylee Jenkins, one of Farrah's patients. Could you tell her I can't make it in tonight?"

The woman typed something on her keyboard. "Is there any other time I can make for you?"

"No, no, it's fine. I'll call back when I have another day open up."

"All right then. You have a nice evening, Miss Jenkins."

"You too." I hung up.

It felt like an eternity as I stared at my dad's note. Rereading it over and over again. My phone buzzed. I thought it could have been my dad, but it was Farrah's office.

"Hello," I said, setting down my dad's letter.

"Hi, Rylee, it's Farrah."

"Oh." I put my dad's note in my pocket as if she could see it. "Yeah, sorry, I can't make it. My dad had to go out of town and won't be back for a few days."

"You don't drive?"

Her question stabbed at my heart. "I . . . I used to. Since the accident, I just can't see myself behind the wheel right now. It reminds me too much of my mom."

I could almost envision her nodding as she answered, "And it makes perfect sense." She shuffled something around on her desk. "Well, the reason I called you was to see if you wouldn't mind doing our session over the phone."

"That's an option?"

"It's an option for the patients who can't get out. And since you can't . . ." She paused. "Then it seems like it applies to you."

"Um . . . well, sure. I guess."

"Good." She fidgeted at her desk again. Most likely looking for her pen and notebook. "So, have you and your dad been able to talk about things?"

A golf ballsize lump hung in my throat. "Can you believe that someone is changing but still doubt them?"

"Why don't you tell me what happened so I can give you an accurate answer."

I took a deep breath and spoke. "I ran into that guy, and I told my dad I wouldn't go after him. Which I wasn't, obviously. But then he gets mad at me for not telling him, then we go back and forth." I tried to swallow the lump. "I told him it was too late to change. And now he's gone to Atlanta to do some work, and in the back of my mind . . ."

"You think he's abandoning you again."

Even through the phone, I could make out her pen scratching against her notebook.

"What I'm about to tell you, you may not want to hear, but I think it's time I tell you," Farrah said. "You will continue to be angry, hurt, and confused if you don't deal with this pain. You can't bottle up these feelings anymore. Because if you continue down this road, it will tear you both apart, and you may not be able to come back from it. You see what your dad is doing. He runs away from his pain. You keep quiet. You don't want to hurt those around you, but it's unfair for you to have to hurt. You need to talk to him."

"I was sent here to talk about losing my mom. Not to help fix me and my dad." Heat rose in my cheeks.

"You're the one who's chosen to speak about your dad. I can see by talking to you that you've carried a connection more with your dad than you have your mom."

I scoffed. "You call my dad staying late at work every night spending time with him? Or how he would leave me with my grandmother who I loved more than anyone but wasn't stable herself? And when I got older, we acted like nothing ever happened. And do you wanna know why I don't have such a great connection with my mother?" I spat.

"I overheard my parents once. My mom had gone behind my dad's back and adopted Damian."

"And you resent your mom for that?"

"I don't resent her for bringing home Damian. I loved him. It was *how* she'd done it. Going behind my dad's back. Like his opinions didn't matter. It wasn't like he would have said no." I clenched my fist. "I was angry with her because I didn't feel like I was enough for her. That she would get this new kid and be able to start over with him. But she treated him just like she'd done me. So what the hell was the point to all of it? But"—I took in a deep, sharp breath—"even though I'm hurt by my mother, my dad does hurt more. It's like me and my mom were too much for him. Or maybe it was the pressure he felt toward not being able to give my mom the kids she wanted. I remembered my dad talking to Chuck once. He thought part of why my mom did charity work was to be with other kids because my dad couldn't give her any more, which is what my mom wanted."

"And you might be right." She paused for a long moment. Without being there, I couldn't tell what she was thinking. "Rylee," she started, "we've talked a lot about you and your relationship with your dad, but I think we need to think about what he's going through."

"What do you mean?"

"Think about how it hurts to know that you couldn't give the person you loved what they wanted most in the world. Then that other person goes behind your back and gets it from somewhere else."

"I've never thought of that," I admitted. "I've only ever thought of how it made me feel."

"And that's normal."

"But I don't understand. I was right there. The daughter they both created. Why wasn't I good enough?" My eyes stung.

"I know I don't know you very well, but I can tell you're good enough for anyone. I can't tell you why your parents acted the way they did toward you. I know you love your dad, so you need to talk to him before it really is too late."

"But what if sorry isn't enough this time?"

"It may not be, but he has to know how you feel, and you have to know how he feels. It's the only true way to start to heal. Once you do that, I want you to call, and I want to meet both of you. Will you do that for me? Will you heal?"

I took a deep breath. Both Drake and Farrah had been right. I had to deal with this. It would hurt, but that's what the truth did. I wanted my dad and me to have a relationship. I wanted to bake maple bacon waffles and burn them. Because it wouldn't matter. We would be doing it together.

"Yes, I want to."

21

A purple haze hung at the edges of my vision again. The stench of licorice with the aroma of lilies. Again I heard music, only this time I realized it was carnival music. Blurred lights twinkled, circling me as the music continued to play. My boots sank into the mud.

Nikolas's voice hissed through the blur. "Only one of us can win."

As his voice faded, through the blur came an image of a Ferris wheel.

I jolted from the bed. I knew exactly where Nikolas wanted to fight me. It was six fifteen in the morning on a Sunday, my eighteenth birthday, and I knew no one was awake right now, but I couldn't go back to sleep. So, for the next three hours, I lay awake thinking about my visions and trying to piece them together. Some things he did still didn't make sense. But then I thought of what I told Drake. Nikolas had to take my heart. When he did that, we had to find a way to make sure he couldn't come back and take what the Council wanted or hurt anyone else. Without killing him.

By the time nine thirty rolled around, I texted Mara and Drake. They both made it over within the hour.

"What was so important you needed to wake me up so blasted early for?" Mara yawned.

"It's ten." I checked my phone just in case my clock died.

She snorted. "Some of us are out late looking for a killer." I pouted, and she rolled her eyes playfully. "Sorry." She groaned almost as if she wasn't and was just saying it to make me feel better. "What's up?"

I told her about my visions of Nikolas. "I thought at first it had something to do with the movie theater. But I heard carnival music. Then I saw the Ferris wheel."

"You do not prefer them," Drake added.

"Exactly."

Mara rolled her eyes. "Great, can you let us inside your little scatterbrained head then."

I blushed. "Sorry. Well, the popcorn stand, the lights and music, Ferris wheel, and tickets Drake got from you, Mara."

Mara eyed Drake. "I never gave you any tickets."

"Yes you did. You procured them for me to give to Rylee. You even left a note."

Mara raised an eyebrow. "Note? What note?"

Drake reached into his pocket, pulling out a small index card. "We should have some fun. Even you, my brother."

"Well, I would have never written something that bloody nice." Mara laughed. "Plus, I was too busy trying to find Nikolas, remember?"

I bit the inside of my cheek. More was making sense now. "It's Nikolas! He's setting up our fight. His seer friend must've been helping him while he was in prison. So, she watched us, and then when he got out, he did the rest. So, he gave Drake the tickets. He's setting this up. And by the way, it sounds like only one of us will come out of this alive."

"Well, great then. We'll all go and end this." Mara stood.

"No," I whispered.

Mara spun back around, anger fueling her eyes. "What do you mean *no*? You're bloody barmy if you think *I'm* going to let you go after that lunatic alone."

"I will not let you go defenseless either," Drake added.

"First, I'm not defenseless. And second, I don't want to risk you guys getting zapped away again, to Lord knows where. And that's another question. How *did* you two get back to me?"

"It was simple. After I found Drake, I made us a portal back."

"But I never saw you," Drake said.

Mara huffed. "Yeah well, I was thrown somewhere different than you, but I saw you and made the portal. Nikolas had a wolf waiting for *me*. So I was a little weak. That's why it took me a second to get back to you."

Drake then turned to me. "I do sincerely apologize." He bowed his head. "We do not see you as helpless, but we know what Nikolas is capable of. We do not wish to see a mate perish because they did not have assistance."

"I've told you that you're powerful, but we still need to practice more magic."

"Preferably not with anger."

Mara glared at Drake. "What is it with you and being Mr. Goody Two-Shoes? You used to not care about what needed to be done." She turned her attention back to me. "Never mind. Fine, you'll learn magic without anger. Probably too late to learn a new way anyway."

I tilted my head. "What do you mean too late? Too late for what?"

"I just mean with what you said about Nikolas. We don't have time to be learning new things right now is all."

"Oh." At the mention of his name, I remembered what Drake and I realized yesterday. "Mara, Drake and I think

Nikolas hypnotized my mom to drive off the bridge that day."

"Why?" So, I told her Drake's theory. "But why the whole family? What did it matter?"

I shook my head. "I don't know. Maybe the Council doesn't like my family or something."

Mara's brow furrowed in thought. "Maybe because of what she did, they didn't think she deserved to have her family."

"What could anyone do that would bring death even to their family? Not even the Council is so cruel," Drake said.

"Again with this." Mara groaned. "Come on, think about it. What if Liliana killed a Council member to take something that wasn't hers, and *that's* why the Council went after her?"

"But my mom would never do that."

"Or she could have betrayed someone, and they made her run off the bridge."

"But that doesn't explain Nikolas needing our hearts. Or the Council part at all."

Mara threw her arm over my shoulder. "Okay, that last one was kind of a stretch." She chuckled. "But enough sad talk. It's time to get your birthday started. What do you want to do?"

"Yes, happy birthday," Drake chimed in.

"Thanks guys. What I think I want to do is learn as much magic as I can before I have to fight for my life tonight."

Mara headed toward the door. "That I can do."

I turned to Drake. "Can I talk to you for a second?" Mara eyed us both but then made her way out, closing the door behind her.

I picked at the hole in my sheet, letting a few seconds pass to make sure that Mara was really gone. "You know we have to do this, right?" He nodded. "And if Mara knew what we were doing, she would stop me. She hates them so much. She doesn't want to see them win."

"I know this. But she also in her scarred heart cares for Fables as you do. *I* personally though, find this war unnecessary."

I sighed. "Tonight, when Nikolas takes out my cloaked heart, I don't want you to go after him. Stop Mara. Keep her from stopping Nikolas. Can you do that for me?"

"Yes, but will you look at me for a moment?" My heart raced. He'd never asked me to do anything like this before, but I listened. He studied me. "After tonight, Nikolas will no longer be a problem to anyone."

I tore my eyes away. "I don't want him dead."

"But you know it is the only way to truly stop a monster."

Mara and I spent most of the afternoon working on my magic in her backyard. Still, it came intermittently. Nothing about my locket had changed either. But if everything with Nikolas tonight went as planned, that *would* change. But with every shield I made, every lightning bolt I threw, I thought of the secret I was keeping for Mara. I didn't want to, but as much as I hated him, Nikolas had been right. The plus side to all this was that I wouldn't die, but I was lying to my best friend, and when she found out, I was afraid she may never forgive me.

It was just past six when I made it into my house. The TV blared in the living room, which was alarming because my dad wasn't supposed to be home for a few more days.

"Rylee?"

"Yeah, it's me." As if it would be anyone else.

"Can you come into the living room?"

My dad turned the TV off, and all of the lights were on.

I took my place on our scratchy red sofa between the coffee table and big screen TV, while my dad sat in his beige recliner. Once I was seated, my dad reached beside his chair and handed me a small, purple satin box. "Happy birthday, hun. I know it's not much, but I hope you like it."

I untied the bow and unboxed it. Inside was a worn and brown leather bound journal. Embossed in a circle on the cover, were four charms you would see on a bracelet: A paintbrush for my mom and a chef's hat for my dad. A thimble for Grandma Ana because she'd loved to sew. A little race car for Damian; it was what he wanted to be when he grew up. My fingers ran over each embedded charm.

"I saw you writing from time to time when you were younger. I thought now that your older, you might want to write again," my dad said as I stared at the notebook. "Each one of these charms represents everyone you hold dear to your heart."

I continue to stare at the book for a long moment. He'd remembered something from so long ago. Tears swelled in my eyes. "I wrote to create another life for myself," I whispered. "But now, I think I just want to live the one I have." I smiled to him and tears too glazed in his eyes. "But I'll find its use one day." I dove to my dad for a hug. "Thank you, daddy."

"You're welcome."

I turn my face to gaze up at him. "I shouldn't have said those things to you."

He held up his hand to stop me and motioned for me to sit back down. "There was never anything in Atlanta. I was taking some time to think about . . ." His Adam's apple bobbed as he swallowed hard. "About what you said. And it did hurt me."

I had to remember the truth would hurt.

"So, what made you turn around?" I fidgeted with my book.

"Drake."

My eyes shot to him then. "Drake? What did he say?"

"He said that you loved me, and you were scared of losing me and being alone. And that you felt like I didn't want you." He knotted his fingers. "But you're right to feel the way you do. I should've been acting like a father to you from the moment you were born." He turned away, but I still saw the tear that fell. "It just hurts," he whispered.

Drake had brought him back to me.

"I understand, but you don't have to keep proving yourself to me."

He lifted his head, his eyes already puffy and red. "Do you think that's the only reason I'm doing this?"

"Honestly yes." I sat on my hands to keep myself from fidgeting. "Why else?"

"Did you ever stop and think it was because I love you and want to make sure you're okay? I know you don't need me. You never did. That was part of the reason I didn't spend much time with you. But I realize now how wrong that was."

What did he mean *part of the reason*?

"But Dad, that's what I don't get. One day I'm six years old and we're baking maple bacon waffles, having such a good time, and then *bam*, you forgot about me. Farrah thinks we're avoiding our feelings and not wanting to hurt each other. So, it's creating this rift between us. And she may be right. But I could never live with myself if something happened to you and we didn't fix this. I just want to know what happened. What did I do that made you think I wasn't enough to remember anymore?"

My dad buried his hands in his face, and his shoulders shook with uncontrollable sobs. "You are so much . . ." I made my way to the other side of the couch, placing my hand on his back. "I never wanted you . . . never wanted . . ." He looked up, his cheeks wet and his eyes red. "I never wanted you to feel that way. You *are* enough. Don't you ever let anyone tell you you're not."

And in his eyes rested sincerity. It was all I ever wanted from him. To know, to *feel* that I was enough. And here it was.

"Thank you so much, Dad. You don't know how much it means to hear you say that to me. And I know, in time, we'll talk more about things. But at least this is a start."

He took my hands in his, grazing his big thumb across my knuckles and staring only at them. "When your mother died, I was scared I wouldn't know what to say or do for you because I hadn't been your father for so long. But when things started to happen to you with Nikolas, I came off a little too strong, and for that I'm sorry. I might be late to the game, but can I still play?"

"I don't see why not. But you staying alive is all I want from you. Promise me you'll do that for me."

"Yes, if *you* promise to do the same."

"I will." I pulled away then. "There's something else I need to tell you, and I don't think you're going to like it." I told him about the visions of Nikolas and about my plan. "I know you're going to say you don't want me to go after him, or to let Mara handle it, but Nikolas isn't after her. Nikolas isn't her fight. He's mine, and I will fight anyone I have to, to keep my family alive. And he will be stopped." His eyes widened. "I will find another way. There's always another way."

"And that is why we named you Rylee."

"What do you mean?"

He dabbed at his eyes with the back of his sleeve. "You may not know this, but your mother was Irish. And the meaning of your name is *courageous*. She said the moment she laid eyes on you, she knew you would grow up to be just that. But you're right, I don't want you to go. I want Mara to deal with it. But I also know *you*. And if anyone can stop him, it's my courageous, magic-wielding daughter."

22

Kids and teens in costumes ranging from superheroes to doctors ran throughout the fairgrounds. Buckets and bags overflowed with candy, but I couldn't focus on the fact that it was Halloween or that it was my birthday. I could only ask myself why. Why had Nikolas wanted to come here? The bridge had made sense, but him coming here didn't.

"Maybe there is no significance at all," Drake was saying as we all made our way inside. "Not everything in life has an answer."

"Oh, come on, a guy as smart as you doesn't believe a psychopath has a reason for why this place means something to him?" Mara asked. "Even I have to agree with Rylee."

"The why is not of importance."

Mara stared at her watch. "All right, I'm going to check the perimeter for Nikolas. You guys remember the plan? Just act like you have no idea that he's here. He has to be around here somewhere, and I'll find him. We'll meet back in fifteen." Her eyes wandered. "How about the Ferris wheel?"

Her eyes narrowed then. "And don't do anything stupid." She ran off, disappearing into the crowd.

The carnival music played, the lights twinkled, and kids screamed. No one knew what was happening here. No one knew what danger they were in just by being at the fair tonight.

"Do you think she knows?" I pushed past a group of teenagers.

"No, my sister is not one for hiding her thoughts or feelings. Now let us stick to the plan."

Drake led me toward a tossing booth. After a young boy and what I assumed was his brother finished, Drake handed a husky man with a blue beanie propeller hat a five-dollar bill. His name tag read "Bubba." Bubba reached underneath his counter, pulled out five darts, and laid them down in front of me.

Taking one of the darts, I flicked my wrist back and let the dart go. It lodged itself into a bear's stomach. The second one almost hit Bubba. I wasn't good at this game one bit.

"Here." I handed my other three darts to Drake. "I think you might have a better chance than me." And just as I thought, he lodged all three around the center.

"Do you wanna buy more darts, buddy?" Bubba asked.

"How much would it cost to buy one of the animals?" Drake was eyeing something in the back.

"Sorry, but they aren't—"

Drake leaned in closer to the man. A loud buzzing sound made me jump. I turned, but I couldn't find where it was coming from.

"No woman should leave without a prize."

Bubba's eyes widened as he spoke. "You're right."

"I will take that one." Drake pointed to the last fire-red

phoenix hanging in the back. Bubba pulled it down, and Drake took it, giving it to me.

It was just like in my vision. But Nikolas had been holding the bird. And now Drake was holding it in real life. Did this mean that Drake was the *he* Nikolas had been talking about? I shook my head. Drake had told me everything. I knew that for a fact. Didn't I?

As we strolled away, I studied the bird, thinking of the vision and of why Drake had chosen it. "Why the phoenix? I wouldn't have minded the monkey or the unicorn."

A small smile curled the corners of his mouth. "When you took me to the barn, you spoke of how you were reborn from the ashes. That is the way of the phoenix. You are my phoenix."

I was *his* phoenix? *His* phoenix? As if he saw me as his own. I shook my head to get rid of the thought. He didn't feel that way. I didn't feel that way. But then there was the drawing of the phoenix wings I'd seen when he had given me a tour of his house. It had to be a bad choice of words. But then the scent of black licorice brushed past me, tearing all my thoughts away. Flames trailed around the fingers of my free hand. A weight pressed on my shoulder, though, and the heat and flames died away.

"He is trying to trick us, but we now know what this means."

"What?"

"He is here."

Drake turned back to face the backside of the lot. "It is time to wait for Mara."

The closer we came to the Ferris wheel, the more my muscles tensed. The more my throat swelled like the balloons the creepy clowns were making for the children, and I didn't know why.

"Will you do something with me?" Drake asked as the larger-than-life Ferris wheel towered over us.

"I can't get on that thing. I don't know why, but I can't."

He gave me a small, genuine smile. "I will not force you to, then. You can wait for Mara here. But going up will allow me to get a better vantage point of the grounds."

I didn't want to be alone waiting for Mara to show up, but I didn't want to go up there either. I weighed the options in my head, and going with Drake, I had a better chance of not dying.

I sighed. "Okay, I'll go."

But as we stood in front of the towering Ferris Wheel now, I couldn't move. I watched the lights twinkle around the frame. In my head I heard laughter and screams. It was then I remembered why I hated Ferris Wheels.

"Are you all right?" Drake had his hand pressed against the small of my back. All I could do was shake my head. "This was not the best idea I see."

"Its been so many years," I whispered, more to myself. "I was six when it happened." I thought back to that night. "My best friend, Tilly, and I went on the Ferris Wheel. We didn't want to wait for her mom, so we got on by ourselves. We got stuck, and Tilly got scared and tried to climb down but fell off." I stared back at the Ferris wheel. "I must have repressed the memory."

"You do not have to get on if you do not wish to."

With a deep breath, I said, "No, it's time."

We moved in the line and then to our seats soundlessly. The top of the Ferris wheel jerked to a stop when we reached the highest point overlooking the fairgrounds. Drake's head darted across the landscape in search of any sign of Nikolas, but I doubted he could see anyone specific this high up. Everything seemed to move, but we weren't going anywhere. I gripped the bar in front of me, fighting the tremble that shook my entire frame. Not a second later, a leather, cinnamon smell plumed around me, encasing me in warmth.

"It is all right. It all will be." He patted the back of the jacket he draped over me.

"What did you mean when you called me *your* phoenix?" I blurted. Trying to take my mind away from my current terror.

"It is a nickname of sorts. I felt like, as my mate, you deserved one. As if you might think of me to be *your* fox."

I laughed. "More like an owl."

"Why an owl?"

"Because when I think of you, I think of that wise old owl from a kid show I used to watch. I even think he was British."

He chuckled. "Then I am *your* owl."

In the beginning with Drake, this was all I wanted. To have normal friendly banter. But knowing him now, it confused me. "Something's changed about you. Since you came out of that portal. I mean don't get me wrong, I like you this way. I just . . . I don't know . . ."

His gaze wandered into the starry night. "It is you, Rylee. It is what I saw without you in that portal. You are the first mate I have ever had who has wanted to understand me. Who has wanted to care. I have tried meditating once this week, and it has not worked because my emotions have been rather sporadic. The best way I can explain it at this moment is, I still find no happiness, peace, nothing to care for, but with you, it is as if the world is shifting on a different axis. Though it is strange. I only feel an emotional connection to you."

If I hadn't only known this boy for almost three weeks, those words would have made me fall in love with him right there, but it did make our friendship stronger. He was finally letting me in.

"How do you know this is what you're feeling?" I asked. "Remember that thing you told me at the barn?"

He smiled. "Still feel as if you are the weed, I see." Then his smile faded. "I observe people for a reason. I can see it in your eyes. Hear it in your voice. I can see the way you act when others require comfort. Like your father. That is how I know what I am feeling even if I do not know how to show it."

I didn't know what friends did in touching moments like this, but hugging him was all I could think to do. "All I've ever wanted was for you to be happy." As he did when saving me from the fire and at the food bank, Drake embraced me. The only difference now was he wasn't trying so hard anymore.

After a moment the Ferris wheel moved again, and Drake and I pulled away.

"I want to thank you for bringing my dad back to me," I said with a smile.

"You are welcome. Seeing your father leaving reminded me of my own. I did not wish to see someone else in pain as I was."

"What do you mean?"

He took in a deep breath of the crisp night air before continuing. "There is a reason I encouraged you not to use anger with your magic. Jeremiah, my father, conjured dark magic in his anger. It drew him into an endless abyss of madness. I never spoke of this to my mother, but for years he would use me for experiments."

I gasped. "I'm so sorry. Why would someone do that to a child?"

"I do not know."

"If it's not too insensitive to ask, what were the experiments for?"

"I do not know that either." His eyes darkened. "But on my eighth birthday, I received one last present. And with the needle in my arm, I knew it not to be a teddy bear. My father's suitcases were waiting for him at the bottom of the stairs a few hours later. He had told my mother that my lack of emotional expression was too much for him to handle and he was leaving. But I knew the truth." He balled his fist. "Such a stupid bloody child I was. I ran after him and Mara. And it was what he said when he left that made me this way."

"What was it?"

"That if I truly wanted to have a life, I was to trust no one to know who I truly was. Because if they knew, they would never accept me. What was worst of all, is my father made me the way I am."

"What? He had the same disorder, and he still abandoned you."

"Yes," he whispered.

"I'm sorry. But you think with your mom knowing that, she would be here for you. I mean I don't even understand why Mara isn't. She's always seemed like she's mad at you or something."

The darkness lifted from his eyes, but only slightly, as if the change in subject made him feel a bit better. "They do what they can, but after my stepfather, Nathan, married my mother, Selena, they both decided to stay in London to be closer to the Manor. As for my sister and me, we never got along as children. Have you not ever wondered why Mara never refers to our mother as such?" I remembered back to how much dislike Mara had shown for both Drake and Selena. "She feels as if my mother paid more attention to me because of my disorder. And forgot about her."

"I think Mara cares for you in her own way." I let the silence lay there for a moment as Drake toyed with the bracelet I'd seen at the food bank. "Did your dad give you that bracelet?"

He stopped spinning it and just stared to it as he answered. "I have attempted to take it off, but no amount of magic has worked. It is as if he wishes me to have a constant reminder of the pain he caused."

"I remember seeing that same bracelet on Nikolas's wrist," I said. "But his was different than yours. I don't know what it all means."

Drake stared ahead when the Ferris wheel moved again. "Neither do I, but I wish I did."

Suddenly, something bright and white caught my attention.

"It's Nikolas!" I screamed as the Ferris wheel made it to the bottom.

It was as if time stopped; everything and everyone around us stood stock still.

"It's something *my seer friend* gave me. Freezes time. Pretty neat, huh?" Nikolas laughed as Drake and I met him in the middle of the field of frozen people. "I'm glad you both could make it here tonight."

"Rylee!" Mara pushed through the frozen crowd. "Get away from her!" Her nostrils flared.

"Oh that can't happen." He turned to me. "This is the end of the line for you and your friends, my dearest Rylee. I won't go easy on any of you." His eyes and spider-like veins glowed as he stalked to us. "Are you ready to play one last time?"

Heat writhed in my veins, my skin, my fingers. I threw my hands in front of me, not caring if the flames burned him or even myself. Nikolas avoided my fire easily. I swore under my breath. I was ready to have all my magic.

"You know, I can fix that," Nikolas mocked.

"Shut up!" Mara barked, throwing a dark amber orb.

I took a deep breath. Across from the dart booth where Drake and I played, I noticed a popcorn stand. It wasn't ideal, but I just had to weaken him. *Breathe in. Breathe out.* I kept my gaze fixated on Nikolas and used my telekinesis to lift the popcorn stand from the ground. I smirked with satisfaction when it moved and shot straight at my target.

"Oh, how foolish you are!" Nikolas growled, blinking away. He dodged the popcorn stand and let it crash into the ground.

I studied Nikolas's movements. His right shoulder shifted backward. My cue to move. Nikolas appeared behind me. I could do this; I just had to think. Something metal slammed into the back of my head. White clouded my vision.

Two Mara's made their way to me as I fell helplessly to the ground.

"Come on," Mara pleaded. "You won't lose this fight to a tin bucket."

Mara helped me up with one arm as my head spun. I had to keep going. "Where's Drake and Nikolas?"

Mara pointed to a carnival tent. When I made it to my feet, we ran after them.

Inside the tent, I saw nothing, which was never a good sign in any horror movie ever. "Drake! Drake!" The tent lights turned on, blinding us, but once our eyes adjusted, Drake sat in the middle of the empty circus tent, but there wasn't a scratch on him.

"Rylee, it is—"

"Your friend is so cute thinking he can help you. Par—" Before Nikolas could finish, a dark orb zoomed past me.

"Leave her alone," Mara snarled, then turned back to me. "Run!"

I took Drake's hand as we made our way back outside. Trying to catch our breaths, we stared at the entrance to the tent and waited for something, anything to happen. Seconds passed and nothing. And then something flew from the entrance.

"Mara!" I screamed as her body plummeted in front of us. I kneeled beside her, but her chest didn't rise and fall like I wanted it to. She didn't move at all. Heat flared in my veins. "You will pay for that!" I yelled as Nikolas stepped into the light. I let go of what fire I could, hurling it at him all at once until a billowing flame swallowed him.

Within moments, the space cleared, and Nikolas wasn't there. I turned, expecting him to be there, but of course he wasn't. And neither was Drake.

"So sad he won't show his true self," Nikolas yelled from a few yards away, holding Drake by the back of the head.

This was my vision. He *had* been talking about Drake.

"He'd rather die than let anyone see what a monster he is."

"Let him go!" I yelled, moving closer. "He has no part in this."

"But we all have a part." He snorted, throwing Drake on the ground as if he were a piece of trash. "Now it's time for you to see, dearest Rylee, that you can't be the hero." He stalked toward me. "I want to hear you beg for me to stop."

My heart thundered as he stepped in front of me. He reached his nails toward my chest. "Tell me why, Nikolas. Why did you—" I screamed when his nails pierced my skin. "Did you send my mom off that bridge? What does the Council want"—I screamed again, his nails digging deeper, tearing past my flesh—"with their deaths?" Nikolas didn't answer, and I no longer had the breath to ask.

"You think I had something to do with that?"

I tried to speak, but a bloodcurdling scream ripped past my throat, the pain blinding as he pressed into my ribs. When he stopped, the pain felt thick and dull, like a heavy weight pulling at the threads of pain making my breath shallow and my mind cloudy.

Nikolas screamed.

I no longer felt the weight of his nails crawling into my skin, and when I opened my eyes, a bright light was dimming to reveal someone in its place.

"You should learn not to mess with my mates," Mara said.

No, she couldn't do this. Where was Drake? Mara went to throw more magic at him, but Nikolas just reflected it. But then, Mara managed to suspend him in midair. It couldn't be over that easy, could it? Drake hadn't moved, and I needed him to stop his sister. She'd kill Nikolas, and he still needed to take out my heart.

"Drake. Wake up. Please wake up."

His eyes shot open, and he breathed in a rush of air.

"Mara's going to kill him. I need you. Can you still help me?"

He rose as if he hadn't just been tossed like a rag doll. "Of course."

Drake and I ran as fast as we could back to where Nikolas and Mara were. Mara turned her attention to us in that moment. "Guys, you need to go."

And with that moment of distraction, Nikolas broke free and grabbed her and said, "You should learn not to be so cocky."

"And why is that?" she mused.

"Because you forget what I can make you do to yourself with just one word."

I turned to Drake. As much as I didn't want to admit it, Nikolas had to die. He wouldn't stop, and being locked away wouldn't do anything for him. Just one word would ruin someone. I didn't want that for Mara. I didn't want that for anyone.

"You have to stop this, Drake. I take it back."

He stared at me for a long moment. "Is this truly what you wish?"

"Yes, you have to kill Nikolas." I whispered the last two words.

Drake withdrew the knife from his pocket, and we ran to save Mara.

"You have done enough, Nikolas," Drake said, holding up the knife.

Nikolas laughed. "The martyr now, are we."

"You and I both know I am far from that. Stop this now."

Nikolas's gaze wandered to Mara. "You know, the funny thing about magic is, everyone can use it. Everyone is affected by it. Even if they have the same magical abilities. Though of course it won't last long for *some* of us." Nikolas smirked. "Paraseum!"

We all crumpled to the floor as if our bodies were bags of flour. No magic. No motion. Nikolas laughed as he strolled over to me like a lion stalking its prey.

"I'm sorry it had to end this way," he hissed. "Who are we kidding, I've been looking forward to this for a long time. Say goodbye, my dearest Rylee."

Again came an emptiness as every emotion left me. The death I never thought I would have. But maybe it was better to feel nothing. Never to feel hurt again when someone betrayed me. Never to feel pain when I lost someone I loved. But then I would never feel love for the ones who still cared for me. I thought of Drake. How it felt never to feel any of these things.

My vision waned in and out after a few moments. Maybe it was because death was upon me, but a light rose behind Nikolas.

"Rylee!" I knew that angelic voice. Drake. But where was he and how? We were all frozen.

Seconds passed and there came clarity. What I'd seen behind Nikolas hadn't been light at all, but a person. A person I knew like no one ever had. It was Drake. Covered in the same daunting veins and white translucent eyes. This had been what he'd been hiding. This was what Nikolas and my visions had been trying to tell me. Drake Sullivan was a soulless.

"Preying on the weak is beneath you!" Drake growled in his angelic voice. He punched Nikolas square in the jaw, knocking him to the ground. "Take a deep breath." I did as he instructed. He laid a hand on my forehead. And like melting ice, my paralysis jelled away.

"I'm surprised you would let Rylee see you this way." At the mention of my name, Drake brought his gaze to me, but I kept mine away because I couldn't look at the lie I'd been told for so many weeks on my best friend.

"Time for this to end," Drake hissed.

"Then let's finish this," Nikolas agreed.

Nikolas threw his own punch at Drake. It sounded like thunder as his fist collided with Drake's face. Though hurt by Drake's lie, I couldn't let him die for me. I ran to Mara to check on her.

"Rylee, I know this is your fight, but . . . we all have to . . . fight together . . . to win."

"All right."

Helping Mara to her feet, I couldn't tell her how much my muscles ached or how unsure I was of this magic inside me. I was glad that she wanted to help, but I couldn't let her stop me from getting my cloaked heart out. Drake and Nikolas landed thunderous blow after blow, but Drake wasn't as powerful as Nikolas. He was wearing out.

"Come on, Drake, you gonna have all the fun?" Mara joked, throwing multiple fire orbs in his direction.

Drake teleported back to us and Mara tagged herself in.

"Answer me one question, then I don't want to hear another word from you again," I snapped. "Why the hell did you just try to stop Nikolas? We talked about this!"

He pinched the bridge of his nose. "Because he was going to take your heart, then your soul. He was going to kill you."

"Oh," was all I could think to say.

I had to stay focused now. Taking out Nikolas and my heart was the only plan I had, and it had to work. I could still do this. I just needed to get him alone. I needed to make sure he was tired of playing this game.

"Are you ready to end this?" I asked, not daring to turn back.

"Yes."

"Then let's go."

Drake placed his hand on my shoulder, then we teleported to Nikolas and Mara. I still felt the magic humming in my veins, though not as strong as I wanted. Nikolas held Mara by the throat, and I squared my stance, ready or not.

"Let her go, now."

He turned. "And why, pray tell, would I do that?"

The electricity trailed into my veins and then to my fingers. "Because of . . . this!" I released enough lightning that he had to put up a defense, but by the time he let Mara go, it hit him.

Once the shock wore off, he laughed. "You think your parlor tricks are going to do anything to me? You can't beat someone who can win with just one word."

And he vanished.

"Where is he!"

No nails ripped through my skin this time as Nikolas's bony fingers gouged my chest, squeezing my cloaked heart. His soulless eyes bore into mine. Drake stood behind him, while Mara remained behind me.

Nikolas glared. "Now is it time for this game to be over?" I prayed neither Mara nor Drake would move. Though I would rather die than feel this pain, this was the only way to access my magic. "One of you other heroes move, and I rip her heart out."

Suddenly there came a faint sizzling sound as if something was burning into something. It wasn't coming from me or Mara. I stared at Drake then, who pressed the white crystallized knife to Nikolas's chest.

"Then I guess I will have to kill you," Drake snarled.

Nikolas laughed. "You seem eager to."

Nikolas squeezed my heart again, making me scream in pain. I had to act fast. Drake wouldn't hesitate to kill Nikolas. I couldn't let him do that before I got what I wanted. I stared at the knife, then at Drake, then back again at the blade. And with quick hands, I stole it away from Drake. I pressed it gently against Nikolas's chest.

"I guess you're more like your father than I thought."

I gritted my teeth. "You know nothing about my dad." I twisted the tip of the knife into his flesh, making him wince. "He didn't deserve what you did to him."

"It's such a pity not to know the truth. How your best friend has kept this secret from you all this time."

"What are you talking about?"

"Nikolas, don't do this. Please," Mara pleaded, moving from behind me.

He held up a finger to stop her. "Don't be rash, Mara. I have served my purpose. Now since I'm going to die, why not?"

I pressed the knife deeper into his skin, feeling it break and trying not to cringe. "Tell me what the hell is going on."

Nikolas yanked at my heart and it moved, but not enough to rip it out. "Lucas isn't your father, but once this is over, you'll know who is."

Nikolas was psychotic, but he wasn't a liar. "Then who —" And with a gasp of breath, my heart left my chest. Nikolas smiled wildly, and somehow, the pain was almost nonexistent.

My cloaked heart lay bloody on the ground. Drake didn't hesitate to kill Nikolas. Within seconds, a bright white flame engulfed my vision. But with those white flames came a luminance from my locket. It had worked. The J was full and visible. The magic rushed like a bullet train through every vein in my body.

But something wasn't right. My body felt both like blazing fire and arctic cold. My heart beat too quickly, and I couldn't find my breath. White spots clouded my vision.

Maybe this hadn't been the best idea, I thought as darkness welcomed me.

23

"Come on, Rylee! Its been three bloody days. Wake up!" Mara's muffled voice echoed through the fog of my brain.

It'd been three days since when? I tried to remember what'd happened. Three days ago had been . . . my . . . my birthday. And Drake had taken me to the fair. It was all coming back to me. My fight with Nikolas. Him taking out my cloaked heart. And him telling me that my dad wasn't my real dad.

Anger slammed into my chest, making me gasp and clutch my shirt. "Hey, relax. That new magic took a lot out of you," she huffed. "I should be bloody pissed at you for what you did. He could have killed you."

As my eyes adjusted to the light in the room, I eased myself up. "I know what you would have done," I snorted.

Her jaw clenched. "But you couldn't have known that it would work, then all of this would have been for nothing." Suddenly a tear trickled down her cheek, but she wiped it away.

I removed the locket from my neck and handed it to her, and she studied it. "But it did work."

Her voice dropped even lower as she handed the locket back to me. "I should have told you about him. I'm your best mate, but you have to understand that Michael was never my secret to tell."

Michael. Was that his name? "It may not have been, but you know what family means to me." I clasped the locket back around my neck.

"You know it doesn't work that way. Liliana made me promise I would never tell you."

"So, when was I supposed to know? When I finally did this locket thing for you?" I glared down at my last name initialed on the locket. "And if my mom didn't want you to tell me, then how did Nikolas know?"

"All I can figure was the Council told him. Please, if you let me explain, I'll tell you everything."

I didn't know if I wanted to know. To think that for eighteen years of my life, my dad, though he wasn't the best, hadn't been the man who gave me life. But if what Nikolas and Mara were saying was true, it made sense to me now. How my dad had always seemed so distant. Why he'd always been angry with my mom. And why that Christmas morning . . . my heart sank. My dad hadn't wanted to be part of the Christmas photo because he knew that the twins weren't his. Damian wasn't his. And neither was I.

"Mara, where did you tell my dad I've been the last three days?"

"I told him we all took an extended weekend up to our cabin."

Suddenly, I realized Drake wasn't here. Though what he had done still hurt me, it didn't mean I didn't want him here.

"Where's Drake?"

"He went back home to . . ." Her words faltered. "Are you sure you're ready for this?"

I knotted my fingers. "Not one bit. But I need to know. To make sense of everything."

"Well, his name is Michael Bowden. Your mum met him on one of her charity trips. She'd gone to Ireland. Said it was love at first sight."

"Did my mom meet him when she was with my dad?" Mara shook her head. "Well, then how could she have cheated on my dad then?"

"I think she still loved him even after marrying Lucas. She'd come back a few years later telling him that she loved him and wanted to be with him. She said that Lucas couldn't give her what she wanted."

"But I don't understand. Why not leave my dad and be with Michael?"

"I don't know. She would never tell me. But then one day Michael was accused of things that shouldn't have even been called crimes, so the Council locked him away. When I'd come to see Liliana, to give her the locket, that's when she told me about Michael. But I'd already known about him. That's why I took the locket. I knew it could save him."

"Did my mom even know what the locket could do?"

"Yes. But after the Council found out *I* took the locket, I had to go into hiding. Which was coming to Canada and finding Liliana. Drake's ordeal was just a bonus."

"But wait a minute. If your parents work with the Council, and they told you to come *here*, wouldn't the Council technically know where you are?"

Mara bit her lip. "Okay, so I lied a wee bit."

"Please tell me your parents know where you and Drake are."

"Not exactly. See, they think Drake's still in the asylum.

And that I'm on the run. Which I was at the time. But I couldn't leave Drake in there."

"So, for the last year, they thought their son was in an asylum? Haven't they even bothered to check on him?" I scowled at her. "He thinks his parents abandoned him. And that you see him as a burden because you guys were told to come here."

"Look, I never said I was perfect. He did find *you* after all."

Hearing her say that hurt because I couldn't help but wonder again if he hadn't planned it that way to get something out of it. "Forget it. There's nothing we can do about it now. Just finish the rest of your story."

"Okay. So, after I gave Liliana the locket, I learned she was going to die."

"And you didn't try to stop it?"

"Your mother wouldn't let me."

"What do you mean she *wouldn't let you*?" I huffed.

"I told her Nikolas was coming for her because of whatever the Council thought she'd done. I also told her that I knew they were after you. She looked like she knew what that meant and told me that she'd rather me protect you than her. That I had to stick with the plan we'd made, and if I got caught helping, all of this would have been for nothing. So she told me once she was dead, I was to come find you. When I did, Drake confirmed to me you were wearing the locket."

I remembered how quick Drake had been to leave when he'd learned of the locket.

"So, let me see if I get this straight. That locket you stole was to help get Michael out. So why didn't you just tell me that?"

Mara pointed to my locket again. "If you knew about it too soon, it could have gotten you killed."

I shuddered at the thought. "Okay, but how can this locket help get Michael out?"

"The locket itself is a portal. And it can transform into things you need from time to time. So when you get there, the locket will turn into a temporary key to unlock the cage that the Council put him in."

"You said that since Drake told Aurora about Nikolas's vision, something was happening. What?"

"Well even before Drake screwed up"—she rolled her eyes—"Michael was going to be sent to that prison world that the Council has been working on. If that happened, there would be a war. His people will fight for him because they believe they are the right of the world while the Council is the wrong of it. And they aren't wrong. That's why I needed you. But because of what Drake did, Aurora has chosen to make Michael's trial tomorrow and then send him away after it. Look, I respect Michael. I owe most of my life to him, and as much as I hate the Council, I just want to keep this war from happening."

"But there's something I need to understand. Why are *you* trying to get Michael out? Other than trying to save the world from chaos."

"Can't that just be enough?"

I shook my head. "It's obvious how you felt about my mom, but why go through all this trouble for a man *I* don't even know?"

Mara gritted her teeth. "You of all people should know what it feels like not to be wanted."

"But your dad wanted you. Drake said you and your dad left together."

She laughed. "He wanted what I could give him. For years my father treated me like I was his lab rat. And you know the strangest part; I have no idea what the bloody hell he was even doing. I just blindly followed him like a lost little puppy. After a few months, when he realized that I couldn't give him what he wanted, he abandoned me too. I'd kill myself before I went groveling back to Selena, so for the next three years, I tried to survive."

"And you were only thirteen?"

"Yeah. I'd found an old warehouse to sleep in. On one of my nights heading home, I saw someone in a shop making something out of what looked like leather. I didn't know who it was until a young lad no older than three and his mother, I assumed, walked in. When they did, the man turned around. It was my father."

My eyes widened, and my heart sank. "He made a new life and left his old one behind."

Mara turned away, her arm sweeping up at her eyes. "I could smell the magic on all of them."

"Did you go and see him?"

"I did. And I burned them all alive." She shuddered. "I can still hear them scream in my sleep sometimes." She gritted her teeth again. "Am I proud of what I did, no. But I will not say I'm sorry."

"Does Drake know the truth?"

"No," she whispered.

I didn't know what to think of Mara's story. It scared me to know she could kill someone like that. But most oddly, I understood. Somehow. That realization scared me too. "I can't imagine what you were feeling. But where does Michael come into all this?"

She sighed. "It was a few days later, and I was lying low in the warehouse. Well, the police started snooping around. One thing led to another, and they figured out it was me. I'd stolen my father's credit card and they used that to find me. You don't have to tell me how barmy that was. So I used that to make a run for it. I don't know why, but I found myself in

Ireland. I went to the first place I could think of to find out where the inn was."

"And that's where you met Michael?"

"Not right away. I did a few things here and there that, let's just say, a girl like you shouldn't do. Anyway, during one of my—let's call them extracurricular activities—I ran into one of the officers who had worked on my father's case. He went after me because, apparently, my father had a brother he never told us about. The next thing I knew, the man was hit over the head and being dragged away."

"Michael's men?"

She nodded. "Michael told me he'd been watching me for a while. That he'd seen so much potential in me, and he asked if I wanted a family that would be here for me. At sixteen, I couldn't say no." Mara paused, staring off. "You might hear a lot of things about Michael, but he's a good man. He saved me and showed me what evil truly was. He gave me a family that cared."

I chewed on my bottom lip. "Did he ever say anything about me?"

"Only that he wished Liliana would have wanted you to know him. So now that you know our story, you know I'll do whatever it takes to protect him. No matter the cost to me. But I needed to know from you, will you help me now that you know everything?"

Mara didn't have to tell me her story, and Michael didn't have to protect her the way he did. But both things happened. I had to do my part now. For my mom. For a man I'd never met—my father.

"Let's do this."

24

Sweat soaked my sheets when I awoke from a nightmare of Nikolas killing Drake. My heart pounded in my ears. Had I been crying? I laid in bed for a long while, thinking about Michael and wondering why my mom never wanted him to be a part of my life. From the way Mara had talked about him yesterday, he didn't seem all that bad. But at the same time, I knew my mom well enough to know she had a reason for everything she did. Drawing myself from bed, I had to put myself in the mindset of today. Today I was going to save a man I'd never met but who'd given me life. I also had to tell my dad what I knew. I didn't know if I was ready for that.

In the kitchen, it broke my heart to see my dad having a hard time pulling the biscuits out of the oven. His wheelchair couldn't get close enough for him to reach inside, and when he leaned awkwardly, I fought the urge to tell him to be careful.

"You're making a lot of noise this morning." I reached into the oven to get the biscuits for him.

"Sorry, hope I didn't wake you." Once the tray was on

the stove, he took his biscuits off the pan and put them on the cooling rack.

I went to make my coffee then. "No, I was . . . already up."

He rolled over to the table, putting fresh biscuits onto a plate. "So, what are your plans for today?"

I came to sit at the table. "Dad, there's something I have to ask you, and I need you to be honest with me."

He stopped and let his hands fall in his lap. "Of course, hun, what's on your mind?"

I wondered what I was even going to tell him. Maybe the truth. I was going into an unknown world, and I was afraid I wouldn't come back again. I needed to make sure we were okay. I wanted to make sure that everything I thought I knew wasn't a lie.

I bit my lip, holding back my tears. "Over the years things have changed between us. I know we're both to blame for that, but I think it's time you hear my part of the story. I can't leave here without you knowing everything."

He reached across the table. "I want to hear it."

I didn't know what any of this was going to mean, but I needed to say it. "All my life I've felt like you guys didn't want me. Mom did her charity work, and I felt like those people were more important than me. Then with Mom gone, you were always working at the restaurant. That just left me and Grandma Ana. But by spending time with her, she taught me things that, honestly, you and Mom should have. I'm not going to lie and tell you that I understand why you guys acted the way you did, because I don't. I'm telling you this because I need you to understand why I also come off the way I do. It killed me when I was younger to watch you leave me. It kills me even now to know that I could lose you. I just want you to want me."

My dad's eyes watered, and his chin trembled. "You

know how I feel about you. I'm trying now. I love you with every beat of my heart."

I took his hand, squeezing it. "I know that now, but there's more to it than that."

"Okay."

I took a deep breath before speaking again. "The day of Mom and Damian's funeral, I tried to drown myself. Mom and Damian were dead. You were leaving me again. I felt so abandoned. But you were the reason I came back up. I'm fighting for you because I don't want to be alone. Because I love you and because this world needs people like you in it. I just couldn't leave here knowing things were uncertain between us. I love you, Dad."

His tears came in streams. So many emotions swam in his eyes. I wanted to ask what he was thinking, but I couldn't bring myself to do it. He sat there for a long while, staring at me, crying, and it took all I had not to cry with him.

"You're more than I could ever dream of. I never knew you felt this way. I was only ever thinking of providing for you. I never stopped and thought you needed me in that way. Ever since you were little, you were always so self-assured. And as you got older, I didn't think you needed me anymore. But I was wrong to think that way. Hun, you don't see what I see. You don't need us like you think you do. You became who you are on your own. Yes, being around your grandmother when you were young helped establish compassion, but the rest was you. I know we've had our hard times. I'm also sorry for the things I said in anger. I was angrier with myself for not being there for you. I shouldn't have left you alone. I'm the one who should be apologizing. I know everything's going to be okay. We will be okay."

"But how do you know?"

"Because you're Rylee Jenkins." He said it as if it carried some magical meaning. And he had that loving twinkle in his eyes. The eyes that never could have been mine. I had to tell him about Michael, but if I had to tell him, I had to tell him what I would do today. With a deep breath, I told him everything, and I didn't leave out much.

"His name is Michael Bowden." All color drained from my dad's face. "And it makes sense now. How you always seemed so distant. The small comments you would make when I was a kid."

My dad kept his gaze fixed on the front yard. "She met him when she lived in Ireland. She'd told me that it was over, but then kept going back to him. I knew she loved him. And when you were born . . ." His eyes darkened. "He was gone. I told your mother I would be the best father I could, but I . . . I . . ."

I kneeled next to him. "It's okay. I understand."

"No, it isn't. I've always wanted to tell you, but I was afraid if I did, your mother would leave me. I loved you both too much for that. But you have to understand how much it hurt to see you every day. To look into those sweet green eyes that were his. I tried for the first few years. But as you got older, I saw more and more of him in you. I told myself I wouldn't be like him. I would be a good father for you, but every time I saw you, it reminded me of what I couldn't give her. And that was unfair to do to you. You were a child."

I didn't want to do this. To tell him the truth, to hurt him. But Farrah's last session kept coming back to me. I couldn't keep sparing my dad's feelings.

"It *was* unfair. Because of that, I thought you didn't want me. I thought I wasn't enough for you. And now I don't feel like I'm strong enough to save a whole world of creatures I don't even know. I don't feel like I'm enough for my friends. Like Drake. I'm sorry, but you did that to me. You and Mom damaged me." I didn't want to see the heart-stricken pain in his eyes, but he needed to hear me. "But do you want to know something you did that Michael didn't?" He stared up at me with his swollen eyes, ready for the next blow. "You stayed."

He sobbed. "I just left you."

I reached for his hand. "I didn't see you bring home a suitcase."

Darkness broke our heartfelt moment. It was as if someone had thrown blackout curtains over the sky, and with it came a screeching noise. I ran to the window, covering my ears, but I couldn't make out anything. Only silhouettes of our houses.

"What's going on out there?" I asked.

"Rylee?" my dad cried as I ran to the hallway, grabbed my coat, and ran outside.

Dark figures hovered in the sky, and the screeching noise echoed around me, looming over the neighborhood. From the corner of my eyes, my dad wheeled himself out of the house.

"Get back inside! You'll be safer in there," I screamed, remembering the protection spell Mara had put on my house after Nikolas broke in.

I started to go back inside with him when the dark figures all came after me. One of them grabbed my ankle, and within seconds, it turned black. Pain writhed in my leg.

I needed it to stop. God, why wouldn't it stop? But then came my relief. Drake stood over me with a hand mirror flashing in their faces.

"It causes them pain to see themselves." Drake helped me up from the ground. "Come on, we must get you inside." We ran to Mara's house, and I prayed we wouldn't die before we got there.

25

As we made it inside, one of the creature's hands wedged between the door, giving Drake no choice but to let me go as more creatures made their attack. The door pulled us back as we pushed it forward. I tried not to focus on the searing pain crawling up my leg and repositioned myself to press my hands on the door. As the door continued pushing us back and forth, something shined from my chest. Caused by light coming from overhead in the hallway. My locket. I noticed the J then. Remembering I had all of my magic now. And that's when an idea sparked. I had no idea how well this would work, but it was better to try it than die.

"Drake, move!"

Without questioning me, Drake did as I asked. I stared at the front door, readying myself to use my telekinesis. The magic chasing through my veins now felt like crystal-clear water rushing down a waterfall. Like the smell of the first days of spring. It was odd how right, how natural this feeling was to me. But it was finally all mine. And with no effort at all, the front door slammed, and the lock turned. I collapsed, and it wasn't from overexertion this time.

"Mara!" Drake yelled from the foyer. "Your assistance is required." He took me in his strong arms again, taking me into the living room and setting me down on the couch.

Mara made her way up from the basement. Her eyes widened but then turned icy, and she glared at Drake. "How could you let this happen?"

"I did not know this would happen."

"Mara!" I screamed as if someone were trying to eat my insides. "What . . . are those . . . things?"

She examined my leg as she spoke. "Those are the Hex."

"Make it . . . stop!" I screamed again. I didn't want this anymore. Why wouldn't I just die already? As my head tossed back and forth, I noticed Mara held a small book. *Dark Magic.*

"I wish you would not use that."

"Do you want her to die?" she snapped at him.

"No." He bowed his head but not before his eyes met mine. The worried look in them broke my heart. But was his concern just for me or for his sister?

Mara flipped through the book, finding what she needed. Once she did, she turned to Drake. "Go to the basement and get some wolves' blood."

As Drake went away, something didn't feel right. Like someone had shot me up with Novocaine. My body went into a convulsing fit, electricity surging through me.

"Take deep breaths for me," Mara instructed.

Breathe in. Breathe out. I did this for a few more seconds, and the convulsions stopped. But the pain continued as Mara held me down.

"Drake, come on!" Drake appeared in front of Mara with the blood.

Mara pulled a vial of green liquid out of her pocket and

mixed the two things. "Now, drink all of this and close your eyes." She handed me the vial. "Then I'll count down from five and jam my hand into your chest."

"But the . . . It hurts my . . . leg."

"The Hex's curse has nearly reached your heart." Panic must have been noticeable on my face. "You have to relax. The more you panic, the quicker your blood flows to your heart. Now drink the vial."

I did as she asked. She started counting down from five. Then, her fist jammed into my chest. When Nikolas had first done this to me, the pain was excruciating. But now it was as if my heart were on fire while freezing over, then beaten with a mallet.

Something didn't feel right. I felt like I were falling.

"Remain calm," Drake cooed.

How could I be calm when Mara had to be ripping every organ from my body and clawing at my skin? I tried to breathe, but it felt like my own blood choked me. Darkness consumed me, then the world disappeared.

The sun hit just over the powerlines now, which meant it couldn't have been past three when I'd finally woken up.

"You both need to go now. I can hold them off," Mara said. As my eyes adjusted, I examined my leg. I felt fine, and my leg looked fine. It was as if it never happened.

I tried to sit up, but it was a worthless effort as I fell back down. "Mara, I can't go without you."

Mara walked to the couch to sit next to me. "I'm the one they want. I'm also the only one who can deal with them." Her eyes softened. "You are good enough."

My eyes watered. "How do I open a portal?"

"Open the locket and tell it where you want to go."

I stared at the locket. "But you never told me where Michael was."

"It's called Prim Cave. But something you need to remember is, you can only open one portal at a time. The portal stays open for a little bit." She stared deep into my eyes. "You can do this." And then she stood.

Footsteps carried from the hallway. Light and graceful. *His* footsteps.

"Drake, I don't want you to come." I pinched my locket to avoid meeting his gaze.

"Is this because I lied to you?"

I never thought I could hear an angelic voice sound so sorrowful. I could tell him that I was mad at him. That I didn't trust him to go with me. I was hurt that he lied to me, but it wasn't why I didn't want him to go.

"You can live a life now. Don't you want that? If you go with me, you could lose all that, and for what? You said I gave you something, so what kind of person would I be if I just took it away?"

"*You* are my mate, Rylee. If I have learned anything from you, it is that we help our mates when they need us most. No matter the cost. You cannot sway me."

I thought of my dad, and I didn't want this again. I didn't want him to help me because he felt obligated. "I'll let you come with me if you answer me one question, honestly, which you usually do." I paused, wondering if I truly wanted to ask him this. "Are you doing this to prove yourself to me? Because if you—"

"No, only to be what you have been for me. A mate."

"Well, then I guess it's time." And with that, I took a deep breath and stood, feeling the energy return to my body. I opened my locket and told it where to go. I turned back one last time to see Mara, hoping it wouldn't be the last time I saw her.

The stench of rotting fish welcomed us as we made it through the portal in one piece. Lights didn't illuminate the cave when we jumped out. Drake and I pulled out our phones. The light bounced off the walls. Rainbow-like crystals glistened off the cave walls.

"These walls are laced with rainbow crystal," he said.

"But they can't hurt me if I don't touch them, right?"

Drake shook his head. "If you are close to the crystal, as you are now, it weakens your power. We best keep moving."

We walked in silence for what felt like miles. It was as if the walls were beginning to cave in around us. And the rotten fish smell was giving me a headache.

"Rylee, we have not talked about the fair, and since this is a rather long walk, I thought it best to take this time to do so."

Honestly, I wanted to forgive him. To pretend that he hadn't completely betrayed my trust, but I couldn't. I'd trusted him. I'd bonded with him in a way I'd never been able to with anyone. I'd let him into my little world, and he shattered it.

"If you wish for me to leave you be, please say so."

I stood closer to the wall. "Did you know about my birth father and this whole cage thing?"

"I did not."

We continued to walk through the narrow cave as I gathered my thoughts. I hadn't thought of having this conversation now. Especially not in a place where you could die or lose all of your magic.

"Do you know why I was able to forgive Mara?" He shook his head. "Because even though she didn't tell me about Michael, it wasn't her secret to tell. Just like it wasn't her secret to tell me about you. Yes, it's a lame excuse, but it was better than yours. *You* lied to me for a selfish reason. You didn't trust me. You weren't protecting me from anything. But what hurts the most was that I'd grown closer to you than Mara. You'd finally opened up to me. And you *pretended* to be a soulless. All that effort for a lie. If you cared for me, why would you lie to me?"

Saying these words out loud broke my heart to know how true I'd been with someone I'd barely known. How raw and exposed I'd let myself be. Yet another time I got close to someone and they hurt me. I tried not to think of the last time I'd been this vulnerable as my gaze wandered to Drake's darkened expression. Although I was hurt by what he'd done, I'd wanted Drake here because, through all of this, I couldn't see having anyone else by my side. And maybe that's what hurt the most.

Drake spoke softly and carefully as if not to frighten me. "Will you allow me to explain how I became this way then?"

"I do want to know," I admitted.

He took a deep breath. "I told you my father made me this way. You see, a soulless is created when a parent studies dark magic. The Council punishes the next-born child, or if there is not, the person. Thus, I was created."

"But you said your dad was like you."

"I had to, how do you say, throw you off." He took a moment to think of his words before he went on. "But at the age of ten, after my father left, things took a turn for the worst for myself. I spoke to my mother and Nathan about odd things that were happening to me. The lack of emotions. This was when my parents took me to see Mr. Tinley. He studied Fable medicine. I had expressed my concerns to him. He explained a way that, for a short time, I could feel something. After every session, he ended it by making me say words. Much like what you heard Nikolas speak. He said using these words around humans or Fables would allow me momentary bliss." I cringed, thinking of the words that Nikolas had been using. Even if I didn't know what all of them were, knowing what it had been doing for him was kind of disturbing. "I do not have to proceed."

I waved him off. "No, go on."

"I harvested my first soul, meaning I took it, using the words he taught me. But what Mr. Tinley did not mention was what would happen if I took too much of the soul. I did not know until someone died. I have learned to harvest only half. After telling my mother, she made me an appointment to see him again. Mr. Tinley made a list of ingredients I needed to make a serum. That is why I go to the farmers market. The serum I take helps me control myself enough not to kill when I harvest."

"What's in it?" I asked. "How does it help you?"

"Inside is a pinch of white crystal, which weakens me, and I cannot take more than I need." He paused. "I hope by hearing my story you understand me a bit better."

I turned away. "I care for you, but I can't be friends with someone who doesn't trust me enough to share themselves completely. Who lies to me. Yes, I would have been just as scared to know what you are. But Drake, did you ever stop and think if you had told me who you were, we could have had a true friendship that wasn't built on a lie?"

"To see the terror in your eyes when Nikolas had broken into your home, I began to question that."

"What do you mean?"

"I could only imagine what he attempted to do to you. But the way you saw him, spoke of him after, I was afraid to have been seen the same way."

A hard lump caught in my throat. "I know you didn't ask to be that way. But if you truly trusted me, then you should have told me. I think what hurts the most is how stupid you made me feel. You cut your hand to prove me wrong. You went out of your way to make the lie seem true." I needed to know something that could either make or break us. Depending on if he lied to me or not. "Have you ever used one of your abilities on me?"

He didn't meet my gaze. "Twice. Once for my hand. And the other for my tattoo. I hypnotized you to make you believe that was what you were seeing. That was the buzzing sound you would hear. Only my . . . victims . . . can hear it that way." He cleared his throat. "But those are the only times I have used them. I swear to you."

I gritted my teeth, strutting farther ahead, but he kept my pace with ease. I remembered the fair and the man at the booth. "Did you hypnotize that guy at the fair too?"

"Yes. Please understand my hesitance. I needed to see if you could keep my secret about Marcus. And if it was a success, I would have told you about myself."

"Waiting for the other shoe to drop isn't trust, Drake. Someday you have to trust someone completely. And it doesn't look like that's me."

"But you know everything now." Even without meeting his gaze, I could make out the pain in his voice.

"Yeah, only because I found out on my own." A lump rose in my throat again. "But regardless of whatever is going on with our friendship, I need you here now. I want you fighting by my side."

"And I thank you."

We walked a few more miles before we spoke again. Every muscle, even the ones I wasn't using, felt like I was just moments away from a charley horse or about to just fall flat on my face. I hoped the charley horse would come first. Less humiliating.

"Why does it smell so bad down here?"

He laughed. "I read once that mermaids inhabited this place, but pirate witches exterminated them all. Now the

Council uses this area as a holding cell for Fables awaiting trial."

I canted my head. "What are pirate witches?"

"They hunt for nearly extinct Fables and sell them to the highest bidder. Most of the time this is the Hunters Grimm."

"Who's the Hunters Grimm?"

"All that has been said is, they are a large community of humans who hunt and kill Fables for sport. They believe those Fables to be a harm. The leader is a warlock who cares not to be one. Only using his magic to torture other Fables to do his bidding."

"Wow, that guy sounds like a real piece of work."

Cackling laughter echoed in the distance.

"What the hell was that?" I asked.

Drake and I eased through the tunnel. "I do not know, but it is best to be on alert."

26

The farther we ran through the tunnel, the louder the singsong voice grew. My throat burned like the fire that I played with, but I had to keep running. Her words were almost audible, which meant we were getting closer. Once we made it to the voice, our backs hugged the wall. A red-haired woman stood in the middle of the room, laughing over what looked to be a dead fairy. The sparkle of its wings had long since died out.

Afraid to walk closer, I examined her the best I could from behind. She had greasy dreadlocks pulled to one side of her head. Her white shirt and blue jeans hugged her skin. Mud caked her boots, which were full of holes.

"Is that a pirate witch?" I whispered, turning back to Drake.

"Yes."

Something shiny reflected in the crystal. The witch had taken a knife and held it to the fairy's wings. I couldn't let her do this. But I also couldn't let her know I was here. My eyes wandered upward to the jagged roof. If I could just break some of it off I would be good to go. *Breathe in. Breathe out.*

Again, my new well of power made the task easy, and a chunk of the rock broke like I wanted. But then the rock froze in midair. The witch's head had been the only thing to turn. Her eyes glowed a devilish red as she glowered at Drake and me.

Without one word, she released a screech so piercingly loud. With our hands pressed to our ears, the witch engulfed herself in a thin cloud of odorless dark amber smoke.

I shrieked at the sight of a seven-foot-tall creature glaring in my direction. The beast's face looked like someone had forced it through a meat grinder and spewed out an irregular ball of a head. Her left eye moved near her nose, whereas her right eye was more to the right of her ear. Her arms and body looked like stitches and a staple gun pulled them together. She smelled like she'd just rolled in cow dung and doused herself in sewage. She exhaled, and her breath came in a plume of stench.

Drake stood in front of the beast first. He turned soulless while speaking his language. The beast just stared at him as if he had two heads. He tried to harvest her soul, but she was too big for him.

I had all my magic now, so I needed to use it. I closed my eyes to concentrate when my body lifted into the air. The beast's arm gripped me in a vice. I tried to use my hands as leverage, but she laughed and threw me against the wall. My body snapped as it slumped to the ground. Something hard fell on my left side, and I groaned but didn't move.

Drake ran to me. "Are you okay?"

In a matter of seconds, it was as if the heat in my body had gone up a whole twenty degrees. "Something . . . something isn't . . . isn't right . . ." I breathed.

Drake examined my side, and his eyes widened.

"What . . . is it?"

"A piece of the crystal."

"Am I . . . going to . . . die?"

"You will if we do not get it out now."

I stared back at the beast, which had been perfect timing because she ran toward us. Without a second thought, I formed a shield around Drake and me right before she hit us.

"Try to . . . take it . . . out!" I almost screamed.

Drake took two fingers, slowly digging into my side for a few moments. "I cannot get it." He took them out slowly.

I could feel the shield close to breaking. I had no choice. I had to finish this fight and just pray I didn't die.

"Help me . . . up," I rasped.

He didn't question me. Then holding my hand to my side, he said, "Remember to keep your eyes open to your surroundings. And we must hurry."

I had to think of what to do now. Throwing the fire would just piss it off, so I had to be creative. I let the fire release from my fingers and made a circle around the beast. The creature recoiled from the flames. I turned back to Drake, and a large gust of wind came forth, causing us to be thrown back against the wall. I didn't know what else I could do. Was this truly going to be my end? To die a horrific death by a seven-foot-tall monster? The heat continued to rise on my skin. But if I was dying from this crystal, why didn't I feel weak like Drake said I would?

Going to stand, my hand landed in a small puddle of water.

I turned to Drake, a thought coming to mind. "You said mermaids lived here. Is there any chance some of the water is still around here?"

"It is possible."

"I need you to distract her. I need to have all the focus I can for this." I took a deep breath in and out.

I had no idea if what I was about to do would work, but I had to try for both of our sakes. Closing my eyes, I breathed in not for concentration, but to find the water around me. Finding them under the crevices of rocks. In nearly dried-up streams and in dark, hidden places. When I opened my eyes, hundreds of water droplets hovered in front of me. I manipulated them, forming them into a sphere. And once finished, I held it in my hand with a smile. So this was what it felt like to have magic. Now it was time to end this.

"Drake, look out!" I hurled the large orb at the beast, but it only momentarily stunned her. She reached for Drake as she'd done to me, catapulting him across the cave floor into the wall.

I ran in his direction, almost falling on the wet rocks.

"Are you okay?"

He tried a half smile. "I am fine. You must focus on her. You must harness all the water here. Then fuse that with your lightning."

Panic crawled in my throat and down my spine. "I don't think I can do that."

Drake took my face in his hands. "I believe you can do anything your heart desires." His hands felt so warm. Even with the rising heat of my skin. "I will help you."

Drake and I stood together. The beast stared at us. Most likely wondering who to go after first. Drake ran toward the beast. She stomped at him as if he were a bug, but he teleported out of the way. I closed my eyes; I didn't want to see what could happen, and I needed to focus. I repeated the actions earlier to retrieve the water. Only this time, I made the sphere three-fourths the size of the beast for good measure. Once formed, I let it hover just above me. Then with both my hands free, I formed lightning. Sparks flew in different directions as I threw them into the water sphere. I yelled for Drake to get out of the way.

As the sphere crashed into the beast and it plummeted

over the edge, I felt, for once, something was finally going my way.

My chest burned and writhed with pain as Drake and I ran down the never-ending cavern. I didn't know if it was from the disorientation of being thrown hard against a wall, having a magical crystal killing me slowly from the inside, or me just feeling like I was in a bad dream, but I could have sworn the crystallized walls were closing in on us. But this was no bad dream, and that was exactly what was happening.

We ran so fast, so hard, it was as if I'd swallowed hot coals. My body temperature rose, and I could barely breathe. The walls were only inches from crushing us. We'd made it to the end, though, and with a leap forward, we made it out. I stared back at the closed-off passageway. At least we still had the locket.

Drake sat me against the wall. "We must get this out now. I need you to take a deep breath and try to sit up."

I winced as I attempted. My arm rushed to the left side where the piece had nicked me. Drake lifted my dirt-covered shirt just above my rib cage. His eyes went wide.

I screamed. "Take it out! Take it out!" But before he could, darkness swallowed me.

I stood in a field of sunflowers. The sun shone brightly, warming my cold body. Not a cloud in the sky. Off in the distance, a melancholy voice hummed a song I'd known even before I was born. Only one person knew that song. Only one person sang it as if she were a songbird herself.

"Mom!" I cried, running toward the woman whose head barely peeked over the heads of sunflowers.

The woman turned, smiling. "Sunflower, how did you find me?"

"What's happening? Last I remember I was with Drake. But I must have passed out from the pain."

She frowned. "Rylee, you're dying. But I'll make sure you go back."

I turned away. Was this her version of heaven? Off to the left of the sunflower field stood my grandparents' house with a wraparound porch and a screened-in patio. To the left was the barn I played in when I was a child. Horses galloped in the acres behind the house. Everything seemed too perfect. This couldn't be real.

"If I'm dying, then are you the real you?" I took a step back.

"Yes. I died that day on the bridge. And I know you have a lot of questions for me." Her chin trembled. "But we don't have much time together."

I took one step closer. "Why didn't you tell me about Michael?"

She shook her head, letting a tear escape. "I won't spend my last moments with you talking about a man I didn't love and who didn't love you."

I didn't understand. My dad and Mara both said that my mom loved Michael, but she was saying she didn't. But she was right. If these were my last moments with her, I wouldn't waste them.

I ran to her, giving her the biggest hug I'd ever given her. Embedding to memory the smell of coconut lotion on her skin. The way her hair felt like silk. And as my tears fell, I hated this because it would be our final goodbye.

"Oh, Rylee, I'm sorry for everything. For the way I acted toward you. But you have to know it was for the best that you hated me. So many times, I wanted to hug you and tell you everything was going to be all right. But I was afraid if you got close to me, you would get hurt."

"But your letter helped me understand. Well, kind of anyway."

My mom's eyes questioned me. "What letter?"

"The one you wrote me and told Dad to give to me."

She thought about what I said. "I honestly don't remember it, sweetheart." She took her hands in mine. Why hadn't she remembered something that had changed all of our lives? "But we can't worry about that now. I should have told you about Michael, about you being a witch, but you have to understand, you carry something very special inside you."

"I know, Mara told me."

She stayed quiet, but so was I. With only moments left with each other, we sure had a lot to say. "I've been the worst mother to you, and here you are still wanting to say goodbye. You haven't wished this all away." She waved her hand around us.

"Why would I want to? If anything, you should want *me* to go away for how I treated you. And for not being able to save you and Damian. I'm so sorry I couldn't understand my visions."

My mom kneeled to me, wiping a tear I didn't know had fallen. "I've been watching you. I see that you blame yourself for that day, but I want you to stop. I swear to you, that day had nothing to do with you and everything to do with me. I don't blame you for telling me never to come back." I turned away from her words, but she took my face in her hands, drawing me back to her. "No, look at me. Those were words of love, not hate. One day you'll understand my actions all these years, but I need you to promise me that you'll stop blaming yourself and your visions."

"I can't do that. If my visions can help people and I can't figure them out, I can't help but blame myself."

My mom sat me down on Grandma Ana's front porch

steps. "By now you know I've done a lot of things that I'm not proud of. Things I kept from the people I love to protect them. And for that I'm sorry. That's my guilt. Something that I could have controlled and made right. But the visions you had were something you couldn't control. Us dying wasn't in your control. The only thing in life, Fable things or not, that you can control, is yourself."

I thought back to Drake and Farrah. How they'd both said the same thing.

"Sweetheart, you will lose people along the way, but it is what you do with the time you have with them that matters. So, the question is, have you spent more time feeling guilty for what you can't control? Or have you been enjoying the time with your father like I had intended? Have you and your father gotten closer since you both found out about this magic or have you both let it stand in the way?"

I thought of her question but didn't have to think too hard.

"The magic at first was challenging, but I do think it brought us closer in some way. Like we had to learn some new things together. But I've spent too long in the past. Feeling like I'm not enough. Dealing with my abandonment issues. I've just now been able to talk to Dad about how I've been feeling. It's just hard. So, it's not just about guilt. And I . . ." My words faltered as my eyes met my mom's. "I miss you so much."

She placed my hand in hers. "I miss you, too, sunflower, but my death wasn't your fault. You said what you felt, and never feel sorry for that. You are not responsible for Damian either. You did all you could. And Grandma Ana chose to jump out of that window. Rylee, let it go. Let it all go. Stop giving yourself the guilt so you can hold back the pain."

I stared into my mom's eyes, and they didn't carry anger. Didn't carry annoyance, but they were full of love. She was right. Everyone was. It wasn't until I saw my mother's smile that I saw it. The smile I'd wished for all my life. The smile that said I was good enough for her. The smile that said she was always with me. It was the smile that said I love you. The same smile I also saw on my dad's face when he thought I wasn't looking. And it was then, that I understood what my mom had always said to me. They did what they did because they did truly love me. Sacrificing our relationship in exchange for my safety.

"All this time, all I could seem to do was focus on what went wrong and why," I said. "How I could have fixed it and if *I* was the problem. I became so focused on the pain from the past, that I forgot to enjoy the now." My lip quivered. "But I . . . I can't stop fate. I've spent too long wishing I could. I won't let that be my life anymore. I promise."

I stood to hug her, but when I did, I couldn't smell her sweet scent of coconut. Everything around me had started to fade without me noticing it.

"Rylee, there's something you need to know about Mara." My mom was almost invisible.

"What about her?"

"She's the one who—"

But she'd faded away, and her words were lost in the wind.

"Mom! Mom!"

27

Drake's angelic voice called for me to wake, but I needed to go back. I needed to know what my mom had wanted to tell me.

Drake helped me to my feet. "I thought you sure to be dead."

I couldn't feel the pain in my side. Pulling up my shirt, it had healed. "Where's the crystal? Can you heal too?"

"It is gone, and I cannot heal, I am afraid."

I wanted to ask more, but a loud grinding sound came from in front of us. An iron gate was closing. We ran through the opening, but not before it caught the back of my shoe, missing my heel by centimeters. Drake helped me untie my shoe when I was too afraid to move it. I couldn't help but remember the last time he'd done this. When the box had fallen on my foot at the food bank. That memory seemed like it was from another life. Once my shoe was free, I took off the other one to balance out my gait.

Again, we were met with another tunnel, only this time, I realized as I painstakingly hobbled along, it wasn't trying to murder us. We let the silence hang between us for a while as we walked. I still didn't know if I was ready to talk to Drake like we were best friends again. And what my mom said about Mara had my mind in knots.

"I heard you speaking your mother's name in your sleep."

"What?" I turned away from the hypnotic wall. "Oh yeah, I . . . I saw her. Like really saw her."

"I have heard of that."

"You have? What is it?"

"I do not know much, other than when a Fable dies, they are sent to another world created by the Council. The Council creates their life inside it but without magic and memories."

"But my mom remembered me."

"Yes, your mother was in the In-between. You cannot leave that world until you have found peace."

"Like a ghost?" He nodded. "I don't know how I feel about her not remembering me now, but I'm happy for her."

The light brightened as we came closer to the end of the tunnel.

"Did you find peace with your mother?"

"I did. I don't understand some things, but I will, one day. I'm going to move on and not live in the past so much."

"I am glad you have found what you wanted, Rylee."

"Me too."

Moments later we stood inside of a crystallized room. The only rock was on top of the ceiling. Wandering around, there wasn't another gate or passage to leave out from. This was our final destination.

"Help! Help me!" yelled a tall, hunched man hovered high in the air in a too-small cage.

Drake and I looked around for anything that would bring the cage down. There was no lever. No magical thing telling me what I could do to bring it down.

"What about your telekinesis?" Drake said. "You can use that."

I focused on the cage, and within a matter of seconds, it hovered to me. I expected it to be harder, seeing as the object was larger than I could ever carry, but with ease, the cage hovered down until it tapped the ground lightly.

Though his hair and beard were oily and dirty, I could still see the bits of red in it. Without a doubt, this was my birth father.

"I'll . . . I'll get you out. Just . . . relax, okay?" I didn't think of what my first words were going to be to him, but they weren't supposed to sound like some nervous little kitten. So much for a good first impression.

Regardless of my nervousness, he smiled. "I knew you would get me out."

I studied the lock that held the cage shut. The moment had finally come. When I held my locket to the lock, it transformed into the key, and the cage opened, every emotion flooding through me when I realized Mara's words were true. Standing in front of me now was a man I'd never met but who didn't look too much like me. He had one green eye and one blue eye. He had broad shoulders and thick eyebrows. And his nose. I had his small nose.

"Why, hello, Rylee." Michael held out his hand for me to shake, and I did. I could feel the calluses on his hands as if he'd worked in hard labor most of his life.

"Hello, Michael. I have so many questions."

His voice was low and husky. "I don't doubt that. Where's Mara?"

"Well, we ran into some trouble back home, and she had to stay behind and stop it." He studied me like he didn't believe me. "But she said she'd be here soon."

Suddenly, Drake's hand rested on my shoulder. "May I have a word with you?"

I followed him. "That was kind of rude," I huffed.

"Something does not feel right. This man, I have seen him somewhere that is not good." Drake glared back at Michael. "That is the man—" The ground shook beneath our feet, and Drake's tone changed. "The Council knows we have deceived them!"

"We have to get out of here!" Michael yelled.

I just found out that I had another father. I had so many questions. So many things I wanted to know. Now I was supposed to let him go and never know anything. But even feeling this way, it wasn't just about what *I* wanted anymore. I needed to know what *he* wanted.

"I can't make you stay. Even though I want to."

"I don't think this'll be the last time we see each other." He nodded toward Drake. "Plus, you got him. He seems good. But my people need me. I have to stop this war. Mara will come to check on you. So, I'm going to do what I do, and that's all thanks to you. You always remember that."

I had no idea whether the other portal was even still open even after being here for Lord knows how long. I turned to tell him what I thought, when Mara made her way through the tunnel that had almost killed us.

I ran to hug her. "Thank goodness you're here, but how did you make it through?"

"I got the Hex taken care of before your portal closed."

I jerked out of the way as rocks fell like a hailstorm.

"We have to get out of here, but I can't open a portal if the other one is still active."

"That portal closed when I went through," Mara said.

"But wait, if I open a portal for you guys to your world, how do Drake and I get back to ours?"

"You have to say, 'My work here is finished.' And it will take you back home."

"All right, well let's get this started. Where is it exactly that I'm taking you guys?"

"It's called the Grimm Ruins."

I opened the locket, telling it where to go. With the loud rumbling, I saw Mara's mouth moving but couldn't hear what she was saying.

"What did you say?" I asked.

She had a regretful look on her face as she nodded to Michael but spoke to me. "There's something I should have told you sooner."

"What?"

"You remember those people I told you about that would fight for Michael?"

"Yeah."

"Well, there's a world of people that needs him. If he doesn't go back, these people will be thrown into the Omega. Every time he comes back here, cloaked or not, he's at risk of being discovered. You have to decide. Either Michael stays here with you or he goes back to his people."

I turned my attention to Michael. "I need to know one thing before you go. Why didn't you want to be part of my life?"

"Your mother never wanted me to."

Large chunks of foundation gave way as a heaviness pulled at my heart. My mom hadn't wanted my own father to know me. I couldn't be selfish, though. Others' lives were more important than my closure.

I opened the portal for Michael and Mara.

"Keep him safe, Mara."

She turned back. "You can count on that." She and Michael jumped through the portal, and I ran back to Drake.

"All right, let's get out of here."

"I must tell you about Michael."

"Not now!" I took a deep breath. "My work here is finished." But nothing happened. "My work here is finished," I repeated. Why wasn't it working? A large part of the ceiling crashed onto the platform, which broke away and fell into the abyss.

28

An icy breeze whipped across my face. It had to be the breeze of the fall. But when I opened my eyes, Drake and I were huddled together in the park down the street from my house. Five seconds ago, we were falling to our deaths, and now here we were safe and sound.

"I've never been so happy to be back home." I stood up from my crouched position. "I guess the spell worked after all."

"It did not. Will you please allow me now to share—"

A green light broke out in front of us. Out of the light came a young fairy in a teal gown, her wings fluttering behind her.

"Aurora?" Drake asked. "What are you doing here?"

My eyes followed Drake's as a dark-skinned woman hovered in front of us. She had high cheekbones and teal hair. My nose flared. This was Aurora. The leader of the Council no one had spoken highly of. The woman who was trying to take away everything I loved.

"Why the hell did you save me? So I'll just give you what

you want, is that it?" I snapped. "Or if not that, to throw us into a prison like you threw my birth father into."

"The Council has been perceived in many different ways over the millennia," Aurora said. "Take Drake for example. I think that it's rather unfair to make him into this creature. But once it is written by the ancestors, there isn't much we the Council can do. I tell you this hoping to change your negative thoughts of us. I have also come here to tell you that you have made a grave mistake when it comes to releasing Michael Bowden."

I scoffed. "So, you want to start a war then? But then again, if you want me and my dad's hearts, I can see that."

She shook her head. "Dear, you don't understand."

"What couldn't I possibly understand."

"Michael is a warlock. He is also the leader of the Hunters Grimm, a group of humans who hunt and kill Fables they believe to be a danger to humankind."

I laughed hysterically. She had no idea what she was talking about. Sure, I didn't know him, but the man she'd just described didn't sound anything like the battered man I'd just seen. Mara would never let someone like that out.

"You're wrong. You're just trying to manipulate me. Mara warned me about you."

Drake sighed next to me. "This is what I was trying to tell you. He was the man I foresaw in the seer's vision."

"Maybe you saw it wrong."

He shook his head. "I do believe there is something else we should consider. My sister. There was the spell she gave you to take us from the cave that did not work. Aurora had to rescue us. And must I mention all of the time she was away *looking* for Nikolas?"

"If you knew all of this, why didn't you say it all earlier?" I snapped.

"I did not think of them as ways of betrayal at the time, but now that things are beginning to fall into place, these things make sense."

"Stop!" All of this couldn't be right. Something wasn't adding up. "If all of this is true, what you're saying about Michael . . . Then that means . . ." I couldn't let the words leave my mouth because I knew what this meant. It meant that Mara had lied to me about everything. My fist clenched. "But then that means Mara's the seer friend. Nikolas's seer. And if that's the case, why let Drake see the vision?"

Drake turned to me. "I do not believe my sister thought I would tell anyone. A mistake on her part."

I thought of the story Mara had told me about Michael and herself, then about the vision Drake had seen. I fell to my knees but didn't cry. My body burned with such excruciating pain, I screamed, and flames burst around me.

"What have I done?"

"Rylee, calm down," Aurora commanded. "That gift is very powerful. Just breathe."

Breathe in. Breathe out.

My flames died away after a moment, but tears replaced them. "Mara kept telling me I was stopping a war when I was helping start one."

Drake attempted to comfort me. "This is not your fault."

"Hell if it isn't!" I cried. "He looked me dead in the eyes when he said what he's about to do is thanks to me. So don't you dare tell me this isn't *my* fault." I stood, ready to go home.

"Where are you going?" Aurora asked.

"Home. I . . . I just . . . I can't." I stopped but didn't turn back to face them. "Do you know what it feels like to think you're doing something right? Doing something you can hold your head up high and be proud of? And then you find out that it's all a lie. I'm not saving anyone. I'm killing them. I never did this to be a hero. It started out to be for my mom, but then it changed."

The scent of cinnamon warmed me like a blanket. If only for a small moment. Drake. "You feel as if you have been used. We can fix this, but let us see what else Aurora knows, shall we?"

It was hard to decipher the feelings wrestling for attention inside me right now. The woman I thought as my sister had lied and betrayed me for weeks. Had held a secret agenda for who knew how long. I didn't know how much I wanted to know, how much more I could handle, but I needed to know everything.

"Aurora, tell us what you know." I still wasn't sure if I wanted to hear what she had to say.

"Of course. First, you must know that I am the one who sent the Hex. I thought they were going to Mara, so my apologies. And second, everything I'm about to tell you about her is everything I learned from reading her mind once I found her."

"Okay, well I forgive you for almost killing me because you just saved me," I joked.

Aurora just raised an eyebrow and continued. "Mara was part of the Council for a little while. We learned one of the reasons was to gather information for Michael. When he was sent away, she remained with us to keep an eye on him. We were informed that someone had tried to get in contact with Michael. Little did we know, it was Mara."

"But how can they do that? I thought it was a whole other world."

"We are still working out all the kinks. Nevertheless, Mara knew she had to get Michael out because he has another plan that even Mara doesn't know about."

"It sounds like Michael knows how to abuse Fables as well as kill them."

"Why do you say that?" Drake asked.

I told him the story Mara had told me about meeting Michael. "And if that's true, which I believe it is, then why wouldn't he trust her? If he doesn't trust her, he's just using her."

"So, you side with my sister now?"

"No!" I growled. "I'm just saying no one should be mistreated." Aurora cleared her throat. "Oh, sorry, go on."

"Anyway, Mara came up with a plan to save Michael. First, she had to get the locket from its maker. When she learned she couldn't force him to use it, she killed him, but not before learning that *you*, Rylee, were a descendant of the locket maker. The only issue was that you couldn't use it until you had complete access to your magic."

My heart stopped. Yet again I'd been fooled. "It's what they both wanted. That day on the bridge, he got inside my head with that damn comment, and . . ." I screamed, the excruciating burning returning. "I thought I was doing something good." *Breathe in. Breathe out.* All this time, Nikolas and Mara were on the same side. Nikolas acted as my motivation. My reason for getting stronger faster. And I'd played into everything Mara wanted for me. I took in a deep, seething breath. "Where does Mara come into play in this?"

"Her job was to get the locket and make sure that it was given to you."

"Why couldn't my mom or Michael have done this locket thing? They were descendants, too, weren't they?"

"Yes, but your mother declined the responsibility years ago. And Michael was not worthy to possess it. That, and he was locked away. You can do the same if you wish."

I stared down at my locket. The thing I'd worked so hard

on. "No, I've done so much to get it. But since you were able to get into Mara's head, was everything she told me a lie?"

Aurora sighed. "She had to tell truths in her lies. All those conversations she'd had with your mother and things she told Liliana were true. She couldn't, of course, let her know that she was up to anything. She only lied about *what* she was planning."

"My mom, I think—before she went away forever—was trying to tell me that the letter she'd left me was a fake."

"It was. Once you had the locket and everything was in place, Mara had to lay low. I'm sure she told you a lie of what she told Liliana. So when the time was right, she would come back and teach you magic."

"That, and keep me alive by not telling me all about the locket to keep the Hex from killing me so I could do her dirty work." I paused to think. "Okay, I understand my part, Mara's, and even Nikolas's, but why my dad?"

Aurora stared at a lonely swing set. "Michael was cursed by another witch years ago, and it was killing him, but if he were to turn back into a human, then he would live. Michael sent Nikolas to take your father's heart."

"But *why* his heart?"

"Michael believed that Lucas took you from him. So, this would be payback." Aurora paused. "I know the other reason why Michael is after you. It's the only thing about Michael's plan that Mara actually knows."

"What?"

"There is something inside your heart that can be good and bad. That is what he's after." I opened my mouth to speak, but she stopped me. "I will tell you more once this is all over. But as you know now, Michael is starting a war, and what's inside you can make him unstoppable and he can win."

I huffed. "Tell me how you guys could just let someone take the one item that could save Michael."

Aurora sighed. "Mara put a spell on the locket that hid its properties from us, and she was only able to do that because she had to kill the maker of the locket, a Council member. Their blood linked them, and the spell was broken after that. We use blood tracing for important items such as that locket, but the use of dark magic can do many things that endanger us all."

"But wouldn't that locket have been trackable in some other way or something because it was so important?"

"It was," Aurora began. "With Mara's magic connected to it, we knew she would find someone—at the time we didn't know it to be you—and open it and make a portal that would lead us to her and we would have found her quickly. So we thought. Being that we didn't know who really had the locket and it was cloaked because *you* were wearing it, it gave Mara just a little more time to let Michael out."

"You guys really should have had a better handle on this," I snapped, then breathed in deeply to compose myself. "So, let me see if I can put some of this story together. Because of Mara's crime for killing the Council member and taking the locket, you guys went after her. She gave the locket to my mom to give to me. Then Mara disappeared only to reappear when my mom died. Which is odd."

"What do you mean?" Drake asked.

"Mara told me that it was my mom's dying wish to save Michael, which now I know is a lie. Drake, even you told me they were close. She came to tell my mom she was going to die. But I never saw her at my mom's funeral. If someone were that close to someone, wouldn't they have come to the funeral to say their goodbyes?"

Suddenly my phone rang, and Mara's name flashed across the screen.

"What do you want?" I snarled.

She laughed. "I'm just here with your daddy dearest. Why don't you come join us? Don't keep us waiting." I looked at Drake then, and we both knew; she wasn't talking about Michael.

29

"Dad! Dad!" I nearly broke down the door running into my house. Magic coursed through my veins like wildfire. The silence worried me. My brain went into panic mode. Had she already killed him and left him for me to find?

"Dad, please answer me!" Drake and I ran from room to room. As we passed the bathroom, a muffled noise came from my room.

Terror struck me when I ran in the room. Mara had bound my dad's wrists with a towel, wrapping them around his wheelchair. Another towel was wrapped around his mouth. Mara stood behind him, holding a silver handgun to his head. Panic crawled in my veins as Drake and I stepped farther in.

Mara grinned. "I started to think you didn't care about your old man."

"Daddy . . . Are you . . . are you okay?" My dad tried not to look as terrified as I felt.

He nodded as Mara trained the gun against his temple. Lightning split to my fingers as I held one of my hands behind me. The first chance I had, I would zap that gun away. Now knowing the truth, I couldn't plead with her, but I couldn't let her kill the man I loved either. I just had to get close enough.

"You don't have to do this." I shifted my body just a hair, but not enough for her to notice. "You can change."

She laughed but didn't lose her handle on the gun. "After everything I've done to you and your family, you're trying to save me. I don't want to be saved."

Drake placed himself beside me. "Release Lucas. We can figure everything out."

Mara let the hammer of the gun slide back on her finger. My heart thudded, and ice washed over me.

"Why?" I asked. "Why do this to the woman you claimed to love?"

"That's your problem. You never listen. You always ask the question but never pay attention to the answers."

"It was you." It was Drake who'd spoken. "I'd found those words peculiar the moment you spoke them."

"What are you talking about?" I asked.

"Mara had said that Liliana may have died because someone betrayed her. And Mara also told us Liliana protected your heart because Liliana had wronged someone."

It was as if someone had ripped out my heart again. All I saw was red as I glared at the woman who'd killed my mother.

"Why?" I wanted to release the electricity building up within me. To watch her body convulse until she wasn't breathing. But if I did that, my dad would die, so I tried to hold it back. "I want to know why," I demanded through gritted teeth.

She didn't ease up on her grip of the gun. "She was the only mother I knew. But Michael told me she'd been playing him for years just to lock him away." She smirked then. "So, as Lucas here knows, I came to tell Liliana she was going to die."

Those eyes. Before my mom sped off the bridge, her eyes. "*You* had Nikolas hypnotize her."

"Once she heard those words of yours, they would all be dead. But of course, I knew you would live, Rylee."

I wanted to rip out her throat. I had to focus—to stay calm to keep my dad alive. "But how did you know I would say those exact words to her?"

She snarled. "Because they were the same words my father said to me when he abandoned me. Those are the words of someone who's had enough." Mara held the gun steady, her finger on the trigger. "Now, I'm not anything if not nice. So, I'll give you two a moment."

Mara took the towel from my dad's mouth. Defeat dulled his eyes.

"Daddy." I let that one pleading word linger as I gazed into his depthless eyes. Because he knew the truth, even if *I* didn't want to admit it. "I'm sorry about all of this. We'll find a way to—"

"All I want . . . is for you to . . . not blame yourself . . . for this . . ." he rasped. "And make it right. Promise me." Tears streamed down both our cheeks. "Promise me!"

"I promise," I cried. "I love you forever and always."

"I lo—"

Blood seeped from the corner of my dad's mouth, and in Mara's hand was the heart of the only man I had ever loved. My knees gave underneath me as I screamed, his blood dripping onto the floor. He was dead. The only man who gave everything to me even though I wasn't his own. I had believed Mara to be savable, until this moment when she took away everything.

"Thought I was going to use a gun?" Mara laughed.

"You did not have to do this." Drake eased closer to his sister. His skin crawled with those all-too-familiar white veins.

I stared at where my dad's head tilted to the side. His brown eyes wide and lifeless. The only man I'd ever loved was gone. My best friend. A hollowness crept in the pit of my stomach. It was like someone clawing at my chest to rip my heart out as well. I didn't want to go on without him. I wanted to lie here and die away. I glared at Mara then. No, she wouldn't get that satisfaction from me. I would avenge his death.

She killed my family, so I was going to kill her. No one would stop me. It was time for her to breathe her last breath. It was time to make this right.

The house shook with a vengeance. Lights flickered on and off, and waves filled my body as if my magic was kicking into overdrive. I didn't care if I hurt myself or any damn one around me. Drake stopped arguing with his sister and tried to comfort me. I didn't want him near me. He'd lied to me too. As the ground shook harder, my thoughts grew darker. I didn't deserve to be the last one alive, and Mara didn't deserve to survive after what she'd done. Praying we all would die, I screamed and released an explosion of magic. Drake and I crashed into the wall facing the back of the hallway. Mara crashed into my headboard, shattering it into a million pieces.

My ears rang as I crawled from the rubble of the hallway. Back in the room, Mara lay motionless on the floor, but I was smart enough by now to know she wasn't dead. A huge gash marred the bridge of her nose, under her right eye, and her left arm looked as if it were bent backward. Seeing this made me smile. But this wasn't all I was going to do. With my telekinesis, I threw her into the hallway, then I let her body dangle in the air as I thought of what I wanted to do. I wanted to squeeze the air from her lungs. Watching the life drain from her eyes as it had my dad's.

"Do not do this!" It seemed Drake knew to stand back. "I understand she has wronged you, but there is a better way to proceed with this."

I freed Mara. I wanted to feel her brittle bones beneath my fingers as I crushed her windpipe. I applied a small amount of pressure to torture her, to let her feel the realization of her death.

"This will change you forever." With no regard for his safety anymore, Drake passed through the damage I'd caused. "You see what it has done to me."

Mara managed to let out a forced half laugh, and I threw her against the wall. She attempted to crawl her way up it. "Nikolas was . . . right. You're more like . . . Michael than . . . you think." She laughed maniacally. "I see that . . . same hatred in . . ." She coughed. "Your eyes. No one will stop . . . you now."

I didn't know how I did it, but I jammed my fist into her chest, taking her heart and squeezing it. Her heart felt like glass in my hand. I wanted her to crumple from the inside like she had made me. I squeezed her heart again. Mara screamed in pain as her eyes turned black, and black veins shot up her body. Blood seeped through her shirt.

"Rylee, you must stop! You are too strong. You are killing her."

"Good!" I screamed.

"You do not need to become my sister. She does not need to die."

"Yes, she does!"

Blood poured from the side of her mouth; I only thought of my dad's last words. *Make this right.*

"Rylee! You know in your heart your father would not want this." Tears cooled my flushed cheeks as I released my grip on her heart. "He would not have wanted you to ruin your life for someone who was not worth it."

Drake gently took the wrist that I had jammed in her heart. And without a second thought, I ripped my hand out. As Mara teleported away, I fell to my knees, screaming and sobbing into the floor. Drake cradled me, telling me everything was going to be all right. But it wasn't.

Everything I loved was gone.

30

There was a reason I sat in the waiting room of Farrah Alastair's office on the morning of my dad's funeral. With Drake by my side. I needed answers. Although she wasn't going to have all of them, it was better than nothing. Drake had done the best he could to help me in the last week, as his emotions came and went. I didn't know how I could have made it through without him.

"Rylee, you can come in now." Farrah was already sitting in her chair by the time I stepped inside. "I'm so sorry for your loss."

Three hundred thirty-five. That was how many people had told me that since my dad's death. Drake had someone help mend the hole in my dad's chest so people wouldn't ask any questions. When people asked how he died, Drake and I couldn't tell them the real reason. Drake had come up with telling them that my dad died from a heart attack. Every time I heard it or said it, my heart shattered. Because the truth was, Mara killed him. It was why I sat here now.

"Thank you," I said, knotting my fingers.

"Today's your dad's funeral. So, why are you here with me?"

I promised my dad that I wouldn't blame myself for what happened to him, but I had let Mara into our lives. I could keep one promise, though; I would make this right.

"If I never would have let her into my life, he would still be here." I bit the inside of my cheek to keep my tears at bay. "If I hadn't had trusted so easily. If I would have just dealt with my grief like a normal person. If I'd just spent more time with him, other than running off and doing something I shouldn't have, he'd still be alive."

"That's a lot of ifs." After writing something down in her notebook, Farrah looked back up again, her features soft and loving as always. Something I desperately needed right now. "So, do you believe your dad's death wasn't an accident?"

I had to be careful. "Mara cut my mom's brakes. So, we went off the bridge . . ." I laughed almost hysterically. "You want to know the messed-up part? She told me I had a gift, and it would help people when she was just using me to get my birth father out of prison. That's right, my mom slept with another man and had me. But my mom was trying to get my birth father caught. So, Mara found out what my mom did and killed her."

Farrah's voice took me out of my revelation. "Do the police know about this?"

"Yes." I thought of the Council. "I came here today to understand. To understand how someone could be so heartless." I stared down at my fingers. "You know, if it wasn't for Drake, I don't think I would have been able to make it through any of this."

"Who's Drake?"

Momentarily, I forgot their relationship. "He's Mara's brother. We went through some things, but I think that made us stronger as friends. He was the only good thing that came from all this sadness."

Farrah wrote more down in her notebook before she spoke again. "In dealing with any kind of grief, we try to find the silver lining anyway we can. Whether it be in drugs, alcohol, or relationships. This gift you were given was a way for you to deal with your grief. It gave you hope that if you believed in it and were made better by it, it would help you through all of this. You wanted Mara's help because you wanted to believe what you were doing was for the right reasons."

I chuckled. "You sound just like Drake."

"He must be very smart then."

"You have no idea."

Farrah took her pen and notebook and set them on the coffee table between us.

"It's clear you still carry some blame for your family's deaths. But it isn't your fault."

My chest warmed thinking of my mom. "I know that now. I guess it just hurts to know there was nothing I could have done. But then I still feel to blame because I let Mara into my life."

"Whether you knew something bad was going to happen or not, it was going to happen with or without you letting her into your life. She knew what she was going to do."

I thought back to what my mom had said about me holding onto guilt because I didn't want to deal with the pain, and as always, she was right. "Mara will get what she deserves." And though I was angry and hurt, I didn't mean it bitterly at all.

She picked up her notebook and pen again. "There's something I've been thinking about for a while now. You told me a while back, you didn't think your grandmother was all there. What did you mean by that?"

That was a random question, but I answered. "She would always tell me I was special and that I would make a difference in the world one day."

Farrah's eyes questioned me. "But why would you find that odd?"

Why *had* I found that odd? What had she done that seemed so weird? My eyes wandered around the room as if it would give me an answer. But then, on Farrah's desk, I noticed a small compact mirror. The mirror.

"One night," I started, "I went to visit my grandmother at the hospital. I'd been complaining about my mom being gone again. Grandma Ana told me they were away so much for my best interest at heart. But then, she handed me a mirror. In the mirror was an image of me fighting someone. All I could make out was a silhouette of a man, but I couldn't see what he looked like. To stop him, I had to kill him. Grandma Ana told me she'd seen this many times. That's why she kept telling me I was special."

Farrah tilted her head. "You saw an image in a mirror?"

My heart raced and my palms grew clammy. Dammit! I'd said too much.

"You told me a few weeks ago you were having dreams about water and hearing screaming voices; were they happening before or after the accident?"

I couldn't answer her questions, so I ran out to the waiting room. "Drake. Drake." I whispered his name so quietly, I wasn't shocked he couldn't hear me until the third time I called for him.

He stared up from his magazine. "Yes."

"Tell me again what happens if a Fable exposes a human to the Fable world."

"They would wipe both the human's and Fable's memories. Then exile the Fable and strip them of their magic. Why?"

I bit my lip. "Okay, didn't know that last part. But I think I said too much to Farrah, and I'm afraid that she's going to start asking more questions. And then she might start putting it together that I'm not exactly human."

Drake came with me back into her office.

As I closed the door behind me, Farrah spoke. "Some things are starting to make sense. You kept saying if you'd only understood those dreams, you could have saved your family. So, I think somehow, you saw your family's deaths before they happened. And that's why—"

"You don't know what you're talking about." I turned to Drake. "I know this is asking a lot from you, but I need you to hypnotize her into forgetting me."

Drake studied Farrah. "I will do this for you."

He sauntered toward her, but then he turned back. "You may wait for me outside if you wish."

I went for the door, not ready to see him this way. Not yet.

31

It was just past noon as half of the people from the funeral came to the house. Déjà vu caught me watching everything unfold. Someone had given me a blue tulip during the funeral. My dad's favorite flower. I stared at it now as my numbness replaced itself with anger. Only three months ago I was here. Hearing the same damn people tell me they were sorry. The same damn food. And some even looked to be wearing the same damn clothes. Mara had caused all of this. She'd ripped a family apart and laughed at it like it was nothing.

My head throbbed at my temples. I had to get away from this. From everyone. My first response was to go to my room, but I remembered what happened when I stood at the threshold of my bedroom. Drake had cleaned up the mess. And with help from his parents, who now knew everything, he helped pay to get the wall fixed. But no amount of money or cleaning could ever take away what happened.

I could envision the blood pouring from his mouth as he bled out on the floor. And as the sunlight peeked in through the curtains, I could see where the blood had been. Where

Drake had worn away the hardwood with bleach. It was still soft there, and the color served as a scar of a memory. My throat tightened, and I ran from the room. I wanted to curl into a ball and cry. I thought of the bathroom floor but knew people would use it. That left only my dad's room.

I expected to see him sitting on the edge of the bed looking out to the backyard, but the only remnants left of him were his unmade bed and his wheelchair. I gripped one of the rubberized handles, listening to the sound of it squeak. Tears fell one after the next.

"This wasn't suppose to happen. We were good. We were going to make things work again." I threw the wheelchair against the window and fell onto the mattress, burying my face in my hands. "Why!"

I crawled into his bed, pulling the covers over my head, and cried. He wasn't coming back. No one was coming back.

Thirty minutes or so later, a light knock came on the door, and then it creaked open.

"I brought you some food," Drake said.

"I don't want any food," I groaned.

The bed dipped at the end of the side I was curled up on. Drake's hand rubbed my legs. "When was the last time you ate?"

I threw the cover from over my head and sat up. "I don't want food. I want him!"

There was heartbreak in his eyes for me. I couldn't let this happen. I let him stay because I was lonely and needed comfort. But I couldn't, for the sake of keeping this wonderful man alive, let him be with me anymore.

"We will get through this together."

Damn him. He couldn't see what being around me did to the people I cared about. I had to make him leave. To never come back. I'd already lost so many. What was one more?

"Why are you still here?"

He didn't seem hurt by my words as he spoke. "Because I care."

"Well stop it! I should've told you to leave, but as always, I was selfish."

Drake moved closer. "You are not selfish. There is nothing wrong with not wanting to be alone. But why are you so adamant to push me away?"

"Why can't you see what happens to the people I care about? The closer we get, the more likely someone's just going to use you against me." Tears flooded down my cheeks. "Then you're dead."

His face was just inches from mine as he wiped a tear from my eye.

"You may say anything you wish, but I will not leave you. You need me as I need you. I understand that you are scared, but do not push away the people who want to be here for you."

And without thinking, I hugged him. It took a bit, but he awkwardly returned the embrace. "You're all I have left," I sobbed into his chest.

He drew my head from his chest, wiping at another falling tear. "And *you* are all *I* have left."

He pulled away, then stood from the bed.

"Can you send everyone home please?" I tried not to let my voice crack on my last words. "I need to be alone for a while."

"Of course. I will come back by later to check on you." And then he was gone.

The afternoon had become the evening. I'd cried myself to sleep when Drake left. Before getting out of bed, I checked my phone. The same picture from last Christmas morning was on my lock and home screens. Looking at it now and knowing the truth, my heart hurt thinking of what my dad must have been feeling at that moment. To have known he was never going to be able to give the woman he loved what she wanted. I had to find another image. Sliding through the pictures, I found a picture of Drake. The one I had marked with a heart as my favorite was a picture of Drake as we were leaving the food bank. The day I knew I would make him my best friend.

It was nine o'clock according to my phone, and I figured I should try to eat something. Containers of food filled the refrigerator. I suspected Drake had done it before he left. I picked out a green bean casserole and threw it into the microwave. I made coffee while the food was cooking.

I saw my dad's Odyssey through the window. My tears had long since dried up, but that didn't stop the aching in my heart. Maybe Chuck would want it. I *prayed* he would want it. The microwave dinged as I put in the last bit of water into the coffee maker.

"I'm sorry I couldn't be there," said a low voice.

My heart stopped. I hadn't heard the woman's voice enough to know who she was. I turned around slowly with my hands in the air.

"Aurora?" I asked, squinting into the darkness.

The kitchen light flashed on. After my eyes adjusted, Aurora stood on the threshold. Her hair was bright pink and matched her pink strapless dress.

"I'm sorry for coming by so late. And my condolences."

My racing heart slowed as I went to the microwave to grab my food, then set it on the table.

I asked my question numbingly, but I really wanted to hear the answer. "Thank you. But there's something I don't get about all of this, *how* was Mara able to take out my dad's heart? Only soullesses could do that."

She sighed. "Once in Mara's mind, I saw everything she did. So when she was on the bridge and took Nikolas's powers, it granted her access to take hearts for a time."

I brought the coffee and its fixings to the table as I thought of what she'd said. But I couldn't reply. She had black coffee while I loaded mine with sugar and creamer.

After taking a bite of my now-cold food, I looked up at her. "So what brings you here?"

She smiled from behind her coffee cup. "I'm not going to hurt you. That, and you haven't done anything wrong."

I forced my eyes to my food as I stabbed at the overcooked green beans. "I know. But I've heard you like to do things behind the scenes."

She put down her coffee. "It's sad to see what Mara's filled your head with." Bile rose in my throat, burning like acid at the mention of Mara. But Aurora just waved her hand as if it didn't matter. "Speaking of her, I came here to talk about her."

My nose flared as I dropped my fork into my bowl. "You wanted to have a casual conversation about the monster who killed my family? And I swear if you say Lucas isn't my dad, I will kick you out."

"There is nothing casual about Mara and the unspeakable things she has done. No, I came here to tell you since Michael is cloaked by Mara's spell, we can't find him. So, we have to focus on Mara."

My shoulders relaxed. "And what makes you think Mara will even come out of hiding?"

"To her, you have already served your purpose."

My blood boiled again. "Are you telling me you want to use me as bait to lure her out?"

Aurora's mouth dropped. "We would never be so thoughtless. For many years now, the Council and I have been working on a prison world we're calling the Omega."

I stirred my casserole, not really wanting to have this conversation. "Yeah, Drake and Mara mentioned something about it."

"Well, now that it is finished, we wanted to come up with a way to put the worst offenders there directly if need be. Normally a Fable waits in one of the cages like Michael was in." Hearing his name sent chills down my spine. "They go on trial and then are sent to the Omega. But because of Mara's treason, she will go there, then to trial, then back again."

"Kind of like giving her a taste of what she's in for?"

"She can't escape from there. You see, we have created a spell that will put Mara into the Omega, but we need something very special to make it happen."

"What is it?"

"We need *you* and your locket. Do you remember me telling you there is something good and bad inside of your heart?"

"Yes, which you still haven't told me about."

"And which I still will tell you later. Now after many failed attempts, we learned that what is inside your heart is the key. Figuratively and literally. It should open the portal."

"What do you mean 'should'?"

Aurora fidgeted with a loose string on her dress sleeve. "Though your heart is strong, you alone cannot open this portal regardless of what is inside your heart. It will kill you, but if you link yourself to a stronger Fable, then you would survive. The portal takes your soul, but if you were connected to a soulless, you could interfere with it."

"How?"

"When you link with a soulless, you give them everything that makes you a Fable. Soul and all. They would have to release your magic onto the locket, opening it, but still holding onto your soul. You will be human for a short while so the portal will not affect you."

It sounded extreme, but if it worked, then I had to give it a try. "Okay, so what, do you find one off the street?"

She shook her head. "Unfortunately, it doesn't work that way. To connect to a soulless like this, you must have an actual *connection* with them. A trust that this soulless will not take more than necessary."

My eyes grew wide. "You mean Drake, don't you?" She was quiet. "What is it?"

"There is another flaw."

"What kind of flaw?" I asked through gritted teeth.

"The Omega also takes away a Fable's magic when they enter. You would survive because you would be human. But those Fables who are around it, their power will be stripped from them. Drake's and Mara's powers will be taken. Only Mara will go to the Omega, of course."

"Will he die?" Aurora didn't look at me or speak. "If you want me to consider this, you better tell me something."

"Normally when a Fable dies, they are sent to a world we have created for them. With new memories and lives."

"Like the world my mom is in?" She nodded. "But why do that?"

"I believe everyone should be given a second chance." Aurora's eyes grew somber. "But with soulless, it's different. Because they have no soul, magic keeps them alive. Without that magic, Drake will die. And he will not come back as a human."

"But how can he die if he has my soul?"

"Drake isn't created to have a soul. He's only a vessel holding it. One of the portal's abilities is to be able to tell when something isn't what it should be. So, it will strip him of your soul, giving it back to you once the portal closes while taking his magic. Killing him."

I shook my head. "There has to be another way. I'm not going to let Drake die just to put one person away even if that's what my dad wanted. And why would you be okay with just letting someone die?" Aurora stared at her hand as it shook. "Are you okay?"

"Right now, there isn't a way to save him, but we are working on it. I must get back." She stood, waving her hands. A portal appeared like a distortion in the room. "I will try to find another way to save Drake. But I know you'll do what's right and follow your heart."

My heart was telling me not to say anything. To find another way. Because there was always another way. I just had no idea what it was.

32

Four days had come and gone, and I'd been avoiding Drake. It hurt so much to do it, but I didn't have a second option. It was the only thing that would keep him alive. I toyed with the compact mirror as I sat in the park swing where I'd learned that Mara had betrayed me.

Three days ago, after Aurora left, this mirror had been sitting on my bay window with a message from Mara. I couldn't bring myself to look at it. To see what else she had planned. What Michael had planned. As the days had passed, I found myself lonely, cold, and missing my best friend. So here I was waiting for Drake.

"Hello, Rylee." Drake took his place in the swing next to me. "I am glad you called."

I swung myself, looking at the dirt. "Thanks for giving me some time." I handed him the mirror. "Your sister left this for me a few days ago. I've just been too afraid to open it, honestly."

He studied the mirror and then handed it back to me. "I am sincerely sorry for what my sister did to you."

I dug my heels into the dirt. "You didn't make her this way."

He chuckled. "That, she would blame my mother for. When in fact my mother tried to be there for her."

I suddenly realized something. "She was punishing you."

"What do you mean?" he asked as he continued to swing.

"You told me that Nathan and Selena loved you. Then one day Mara told you they were sending you away. I never thought that made sense. But now it does. Mara knew that you would get out of there soon and go back to them. Having their love. And she would have nothing because she knows deep down that Michael's just using her like she used me. That's why she's so good at it. So, she saved you from the asylum but took you from the people who loved you."

Drake was quiet, but his face didn't show any emotion. "This does not surprise me. But I would take months of not seeing my family to being where I was."

I knew to leave it at that.

"But what I don't get is why tell me that story about her and Michael? That gave away everything. Smoke and gun."

"Maybe she wanted you to sympathize with her, and she knew that story would draw you."

I shook my head. "No, there has to be something more." I glared at the mirror again. "Maybe this thing has the answers."

"Would you like *me* to open it?"

I handed it to him. Mara's face appeared in the mirror covered by dark yellow smoke.

"Well, hello again, Rylee. The chase is almost over. Only I'll be the one to win. You see this lovely thing here?" The image zoomed out, and Mara stood behind a mansion of some kind. In her hand, she held what looked like a bomb, but as she rotated it, the sun reflected off the edges, making a rainbow effect.

"Rainbow crystal!" I yelped.

"Yes, and that is the Manor!" Drake exclaimed, closing the mirror. "She is going to kill the Council. We must warn them."

"Open it up again. We need to know what she's doing."

Drake did as I asked, and we waited until it got back to where we'd left off.

"In one week, if you don't give me what's in that new pumping heart of yours, something bad is going to happen to a lot of people. And I know you, Rylee. You couldn't even handle the guilt of your mother. What makes you think that you can handle the deaths of hundreds? Oh, and one more thing, if you let the Council in on my plans, I'll kill them. But that's not all." Mara stepped away from the mirror, and a red-haired boy with a side buzz cut and a scar above his left eye came into focus. I had to be seeing things. Those chubby cheeks and blue eyes. This boy was at least fifteen. But regardless of his age, I recognized my little brother. It was Damian.

"If I smell even an ounce more than just your and Drake's magic, Damian here, and the Council, will all die. Let us meet where you first saw the truth."

Drake snapped the mirror shut. "I thought you said your brother was dead?"

My head spun, and my stomach churned. "He was . . . I mean . . . I saw . . ." He couldn't be alive. And why was he older? "Mara brought him back to life."

"Either that, or he was never dead."

Suddenly, Drake's tattoo glowed beneath his black shirt.

"What does that mean?" I asked, trying not to think of what Mara had just said.

"I must harvest. But you are welcome to stay here if you wish."

I needed to think of something else, anything else, right

now. "No, I need to go. And if we're ever going to get anywhere in our friendship, I have to know the real you."

I had no idea what to expect as Drake and I made it into town. The shops and street bustled with people as they did almost every day even in mid-November. Drake told me he was looking for the *right one*, whatever that meant.

"Can you bring someone back from the dead?" I asked as we continued to walk.

"It requires a lot of dark magic and a sacrifice, but it can be done. Your brother is not going to remember you, unfortunately. Because of the potion she used to age him."

"Then why bring him back? Why age him? To torture me? It makes no sense."

"I know you do not wish to do this." Drake crossed the street before he continued, "but we must tell the Council."

I stopped in the middle of the crosswalk. "No! You heard her. If I tell them, they die and so does Damian." A car honked at me, so I moved on.

"So, you will give her your heart then and let you become the key to their war?"

"I don't have it all figured out, but he is my family. He's *my* responsibility. So, we will not tell Aurora. Do you understand me?"

"As you wish."

We walked another mile down the bustling side street until we made it to the gas station. As we wandered inside, Drake made his way to the front desk.

He stopped and turned to me with something like anxiety in his voice. "You do not have to watch this."

"I *want* to know all about you."

Drake and I stood in front of the cash register where a

young woman, with dark-brown hair and big hazel eyes, cut her eyes to us from her magazine, popping her gum.

"What pump?" she asked lazily.

Again came the buzzing sound I'd heard before. He was using one of his abilities. Drake whispered. "Please make your way to the back room. And please do not speak."

Her eyes went wide as she stood.

We all made our way into the back room. My heart hammered a mile a minute. The back room felt like it were miles away, not feet. I would have been lying to myself if I said I wasn't the least bit terrified of what I was about to see. Nikolas momentarily flashed in my mind, but something inside me told me I was going to be okay. Maybe because, in my heart, I knew Drake would never hurt me. By seeing him in his truest nature, I would understand him.

Drake had the woman, whose name tag read Chloe, sit in the boss's chair. Drake told her to show him her wrist. Rolling it over, for the first time I could make out the Roman numeral one hundred etched on her skin, bright white like Drake's veins. I wanted to ask what the numbers meant, but it was best not to break his concentration.

Drake focused his attention on Chloe, who was still hypnotized. I couldn't help but wonder why he hadn't paralyzed her.

His voice was low and just as hypnotic as it was the day he'd saved me from the barn. "Everything is going to be all right. You went to lunch and chose a bar, which is where you partook in the consumption of a lot of alcohol. And when you wake, you will believe you passed out."

Chloe just nodded. Drake could have told her any story. He could have done anything to her. He didn't even need to give her this comfort. And it was there, at that moment, that I realized how different Drake truly was from Nikolas. Nikolas took what he wanted, however much he wanted, and left. But Drake, sweet thoughtful Drake, gave comfort. Once again came the buzzing sound, and I watched the white essence leave her body, I wasn't terrified for her life. The smoke filled the air and went into the mouth of Drake's skull tattoo. A hint of sage permeated the air. And then his tattoo took on a dark blue tinge as if freezing from the inside. If it were painful, Drake showed no emotion toward it. But as the numbers decreased, I knew Drake wouldn't take her life. Because he cared.

Once he finished, Chloe looked as if she were sleeping.

He held out his hand for me. "We better leave."

"What about Chloe?"

"She will wake soon, not remembering anything."

Minutes had passed as Drake and I walked back. We were just past the park when Drake chose to speak.

"I have asked this question many times, but this time I need to know your true answer. Do you still perceive me as the monster that has haunted you?"

"I never thought you were like him. I was just angry that you lied to me. But I see now that you are nothing like him. Can I ask, though, why you didn't paralyze her instead?"

His eyes met mine as we waited at the crosswalk. Sadness swam in them. "I must be honest with you. I was like Nikolas before meeting you. But when learning what Nikolas had done to you, seeing the horror in your eyes, I never desired for someone to feel that helpless by my hands again. You showed me the error of my devilish ways without knowing it. That is one of the reasons I try to keep you from going down the path I had chosen for myself."

"So, there were more . . . victims . . ." I swallowed a lump in my throat. "After you were ten?"

The stick man lit green for us to go, and Drake focused on the crowd ahead. I didn't need to see his face to know how he was feeling. "Many more. Some old. Some young.

All because I was trying to feel something. Find something."

"And you found that in me." I didn't ask it as if it were a question because I could see he did. "I want to know everything there is to know about your soulless self. Scary or not."

I could almost hear the plea in his question. Almost. "And you promise not to run away?"

I nudged him, almost making him knock into the guy next to him. "It's kind of too late for that, don't you think?"

"Fair enough." He released a long sigh before continuing. "Every Fable and human possess a mark of the Roman numeral for one hundred. This can be seen by the soulless. Once the Roman numeral reaches below fifty, the one we are taking from will die. And as the essence absorbs into the tattoo, there is a strong burning, freezing sensation coursing through our bodies."

I couldn't help but wonder what my number was after what Nikolas did to me. "Can you see my number?" I asked, rolling up my sleeve.

It only took him a few seconds to examine it. "Your number is seventy."

"Great, so I'm only seventy percent alive." I groaned. "So, those words that you guys use, what do they mean?"

"Over time we have established our own language known as Lessvenic. If we chose to paralyze our victim, we must say *paraseum*." The word sent sudden chills down my spine. "I can stop if you wish."

"No, I'm fine."

"Well, to hypnotize them, the word we chose was *hypnmouitum*. To do both, we say *souparhypnum*. And lastly, to take said soul, we must say *essoultaka*. Once we have absorbed the human's or Fable's essence, we begin to feel the emotions of the said host, along with their memories. The memories fade after a few hours, but the emotions remain until the need to harvest comes again."

"So how did the teleporting ability come into play?"

"The word is *Telvenitum*. It has been said that the Council did not want to risk someone finding out in the beginning that we were created. It allowed us to stay in the shadows. For my sake, it allows my story I tell my . . . victims . . . to be more believable."

I wished he wouldn't call them that, but I didn't have a choice in that part of his life.

"What memory did you see from Chloe?" I asked.

He stared ahead again. "It was rather heartbreaking. So much so that I do not wish to repeat it."

"Do you only see sad memories?"

"I am a miserable Fable-natured creature, so yes, I do."

"There's something that I don't understand, though. Why do I only hear the word for being paralyzed but buzzing for the others?"

He thought. "It has been said that some special Fables can actually hear our language."

I grinned. "Well, guess that makes me special."

He smiled in return. "I have known this since the moment I met you."

We walked most of the way home in silence, but my brain wouldn't shut up. Should I tell him? What other option did I have? Mara had to be sent away forever for what she did. I hated her for killing my family. She deserved not to be here on this earth, and I guess in a twisted way that's what I would get. But was Drake's death worth that? His life, his friendship, meant more to me than locking her away.

"Something is occupying your mind, I see," Drake said as we walked into his driveway.

"It's nothing I can't handle."

"And you handling it alone means it will be dangerous, and you do not wish for me to get hurt."

I huffed. "Dammit, I hate it when you do that." I sighed because I wasn't mad at him. "I'm sorry. I just don't think it's worth it."

"What is?" He sat on the bottom step while I still picked at the top of the banister.

"Aurora came by a few days ago. She told me we could lock away Mara. That there's a way to put her directly into the Omega."

"Good! She will not be able to harm anyone else. But why do you not seem overjoyed by this news?"

I couldn't look him in the eyes and tell him he would die if he helped. It would show how selfish I'd been to think of it. I turned and began to walk away.

"Wait!" He appeared in front of me. "Will you please tell me?"

"If I do this, I need you to help me."

"You know I would."

The longer I dragged this out, the more my heart shattered. "I know, and that's the problem."

"I do not understand."

"We would have to link together. You would take my magic and soul. When you got the portal open, it would know that you're not meant to have a soul and take it and your magic. And it'd . . ."

"I will die," he finished. "Then we will go in the morning to London to see Aurora and find another way."

"But there isn't one. And if we go, Aurora will read our minds and know what Mara's planning."

"You leave that to me."

33

rake called his parents, asking them for money to make a trip home. They were excited to do it too. Drake told them that he couldn't explain everything. He asked them if they could get him a potion that made it so Aurora couldn't read our minds. They had it sent to us within the hour. For most of the way there, I chose to sleep until around six that next morning when the morning cart rolled past us. I could have teleported to the Manor, but I wanted to see where Drake had lived. Where I thought I would want to live, to start over.

Rolling open the curtain, we were below cloud level now, and I could see the top of Big Ben. I stared at Drake, who was reading an anatomy book.

"Do you ever miss it?" I asked, staring back at the window. "Home, I mean. She took you away from it."

Drake closed the book and set it on his tray. "I want to tell you yes, but all my life, all I have ever known is misery. Living my life with someone else's emotions. My parents are kind people, and I wish at times I could return those feelings, but that is not the case."

I turned away from the window, hoping to see something in his eyes. "You've said many times you want to feel things, so you harvest. And then you spend time with me. But what makes the emotions I give you any different from the ones thousands of other people have given you?"

It was at least five minutes before Drake could even look at me, let alone speak. "When I harvest a soul, my emotions feel as if putting a Band-Aid over a bullet hole. But after meeting you, it is as if you were stitching up the hole entirely." He paused. "But I think I have a problem."

"What do you mean?"

"Those three days after I left for London, and these last four days I was not with you. My emotions reverted. So, I harvested, and the cycle started all over until I saw you again. Then my connection to you restarted my emotions as if I had never left. I do not know why this need is so strong."

I didn't know what to say. I was a literal drug for him.

"It's okay. I know you're not hanging out with me just for that."

"Of course not. I just wanted to be honest with you as you asked."

My smile wavered, but I hoped he didn't notice. "Thanks." Suddenly I thought of something. "Hey, when you went home, why didn't you go see your parents?"

He sighed. "At the time I did not think they wanted to see me."

I couldn't stop thinking about what Drake told me as we were about to land. I couldn't imagine how painful it had to have been for him. To have come so far and have to start all over. But I'd never seen anything change. I stared at him as he continued to read. I wondered if he would have ever been friends with me if I hadn't made him feel this way. I didn't think I wasn't cute or anything special. I was just never his type. But then I remembered why we'd connected—because of our parents' neglect. Because of our pain.

"How long did you and Selena stay here after . . . your dad left?"

He set down his book again. "About six years. My mother had taken a job at the local pub as a waitress. There she met Nathan."

"How did Selena and Nathan meet?"

"My mother met Nathan at the pub at night but worked as a nurse at the veterinarian clinic during the day. After a few weeks of dating, Nathan told her she did not have to work two jobs so she could spend time with me. That he would pay her to let some of his friends get treated. He was a werewolf, and she knew about it. And he knew she was a witch. My mother was never one for handouts, but she said she missed spending time with me. It also helped her learn all about werewolves, but if it was not for your mother, Nathan would not be alive today."

"What happened?"

"His pack was attacked by the Hunters Grimm. He was left for dead, but Liliana found him and brought him to my mother. I do not know about my mother's relationship with yours, I am afraid."

"Wow, I'm glad it worked out for them then. So now I know why you guys are knights in shining armor for me." I chuckled.

"That we are," he said with a smile.

We touched down at the London airport, which was like every other airport. After getting our bags, Drake hailed a cab. I had no idea where the Manor was. Or if it even had an address. But Drake told the man something, and the man said it would be about a forty-five-minute drive. For at least fifteen minutes of the drive, I stared out the window at the tiny shops. Cobblestone roads blurred by as the car sped on.

Beautiful Victorian homes followed us through the streets. Big Ben stood tall. And going over the bridge, the lights lit our way to other more sophisticated buildings.

"It is rather beautiful, I must confess," Drake said.

"It really is," I confessed.

"Many Fables are not allowed at the Manor, but we have an appointment with Aurora."

"How did you get one?"

"I told her it was information about my sister."

My eyes widened. "Please tell me you didn't."

He shook his head. "I only mentioned the fight."

I took a deep breath as I looked at the driver, then back at Drake. "So, where does he think he's taking us?"

"A private school."

"When we get there, what do we do?"

"You will see."

We stood in front of a black rustic gate. Drake called for a man named Arthur. In a matter of seconds, a heavyset man who wore a toupee and smelled like he smoked too many cigars stood in front of us.

"State your business," the stuffy man asked.

Aurora appeared out the front doors. "They are with me, Arthur. Do let them in."

Aurora greeted us and asked if we would follow her. I was overtaken by the spaciousness of the inside. My hand glided up the spiral staircase. Old portraits covered the walls. The wallpaper itself had to be from the mid-eighteenth century and looked like it would easily peel away if I touched it. I expected to see paintings of people who used to work in the Council, but pictures of Colombian art dating back to the 1900s hung in their place.

Strolling down the short hallway and passing by doors, goosebumps crawled up my arms in the eerie silence, making me uneasy. Maybe it was because I felt trapped, but I tried to pull on one of the doorknobs, and it was locked.

"Aurora, why is it so quiet here, and why are all the doors locked?" I asked.

Aurora stopped, then turned to face us.

"Every member of the Council bears a mark. The mark determines what access each member is allowed to have. Many things are done at the Manor. We can't risk everyone knowing what we do, so once the door is closed, a silent spell is activated. When a member enters a room, they use their mark to lock the door. The only one who can open the door again is the person who locked it."

That uneasy feeling still wrestled in the pit of my stomach until we reached the end of the hall. I couldn't stop myself from wondering why they needed to be so secretive. We stopped in front of a small wooden door. Aurora exposed her sleeve to show a mark of a silhouette lion's head with a circle around it. She pressed the mark against the door, and the wood glowed a dark emerald.

Walking into the room, I expected to see an office with bookshelves, a desk, and maybe one computer monitor. The room did share the same hardwood that matched the downstairs foyer, but the wallpaper was a baby blue.

Being a lab, though, I thought more of computers and monitors, but all I saw were glass orbs suspended in midair. A few men and women in lab coats stood around other orbs. As we walked past them, a young girl who couldn't have been more than ten talked in one of the globes, carrying on a normal conversation.

"What is this?" I asked as we made our way to the far back of the room where Aurora's desk was.

Aurora sat in her chair. "This is the rehabilitation room."

"Why is your office in here?"

"Seeing someone get better motivates me. And when they don't, it motivates me even more." She folded her hands over her desk, leaning closer. "What brings you here?"

"It does not require you to be involved," Drake assured her.

"Why can't you get involved? I mean you're the leader after all."

She turned her attention to me. "I was cursed to the Manor years ago. A story for another day. If I'm gone for too long, my heart begins to disintegrate. That is why my visits are short." I remembered back to her last visit when her hands had started to shake.

My heart broke for her. I couldn't see someone cursing her. She was only doing what the ancestors had written. But what hurt even more was knowing that I was standing here lying to her.

"As much as I want to open this portal, I can't and won't risk Drake's life just to lock away one person. No matter how bad she is."

"Did Mara ever tell any of you exactly how Jeremiah died?" she asked.

Jeremiah. That was her father. "She burned him alive." I looked at Drake to gauge his reaction. Nothing. So I went back to Aurora. "But wait, if you knew all this time, why didn't you punish her for it?"

"As I have said before, I believe in second chances. I kept an eye on her until Michael made her believe that *we* were the true enemies."

"How does telling us this keep Drake alive?"

Aurora's eyes darkened. "Drake, may I have a moment with Rylee?"

Why couldn't Drake know what Aurora had planned? Drake stood and left the room.

"Okay, that was weird. What's so important that he can't know?"

"I didn't think you would want him to."

I eyed her. "Okay. Explain then."

"In our research, we learned that Drake will die no matter what *we* try to do. But *you can't* die. If he truly means that much to you, *you* can save him." She looked down, then up again. "But in doing it, you and Drake can never be apart."

"If it could save him, then that would just have to be the case, wouldn't it?" I thought of what Drake had told me on the plane. "What can I do?"

"You know that your heart is strong. So, you must give half your heart to Drake, and he can live. If you are apart for too long, Drake will die. I know it sounds rather melodramatic, but he would share part of you then." She reached into her pocket before handing me a piece of paper. "These are the instructions. Recite them out loud when you know your heart is truly ready."

I wanted to ask her when I would know that, but I unfolded the paper instead.

To share one's heart, the host must say, "*Two halves of one whole.*"

"But you said that I wouldn't be strong enough myself and had to be human. And the portal would know we'd deceived it."

Aurora's face fell. "You must still go through with the plans as we discussed. Once the portal is closed, you have only a few moments to transfer half of your heart into his." Aurora opened a portal for us. "It is your choice, Rylee."

It was a choice I couldn't make. All I could do now was go home. Be this savior everyone kept thinking I was.

34

I tossed and turned throughout the night with nightmares of all the possibilities of today's events. None ended without someone dying. Me included. I had woken up Drake at some point in the night from crying. I asked him to lie with me in hopes of stopping the nightmares. He climbed into bed, lying on top of the covers. As the night dawned on the morning, I was going to make sure my nightmares didn't come true.

Staring at the ceiling, I thought about how I would lock Mara away. But if I couldn't, I would have to give her what she wanted or everyone would die, and that blood would be on my hands as much as Mara's.

After taking a shower, I went to the kitchen. The smell of bacon comforted me, reminding me of my dad. Today was for him. For my mom and Damian. I still couldn't believe he was alive. Drake messed with the stove. Would this be the last time I saw him? Would I wake up tomorrow and he wouldn't? Still thinking of the nightmares, I took a deep breath to keep myself from crying. I wanted at least to enjoy my last meal with him because I knew the truth. I wouldn't win.

Drake looked up when he noticed me standing in the doorway. "Lucas told me how much you enjoy your coffee." He took nearly burnt biscuits out of the oven. "I am not very confident in my culinary skills."

I grabbed one of the biscuits. "It's the thought that counts."

Drake lathered butter on his biscuit as he spoke. "I would like you to know, I hold no ill will for what you are going to do to my sister. It is time she pays for her crimes."

"I appreciate you saying that." I took a piece of bacon.

My heart sank. He was my family now—all I had left. I wasn't going to lose him. I looked down at my bacon, not wanting to see the look on his face.

"Please don't go with me," I whispered.

His disappointment was almost as thick as the amount of butter he put on his biscuit. "Why?"

Moisture built in my eyes as they met his. "You are the only family I have left. And I . . . You need to live your own life now. Your family knows the truth, so you can go back to London."

Drake reached across the table to touch my arm. "I vowed to protect you, and that is what I will do. I will fight no matter the cost."

I pulled away from him. "No! I won't let you die." A hot tear streamed down my face. "You've already done enough."

"Stop pushing me away. I want to fight beside you. And before you start to think it, I am fighting with you not because I think you are helpless, but because I see you as courageous."

"I don't know what I would do if you died." I couldn't look at him.

"The only way for that to happen is if my sister had

another knife. Aurora told me that the cave full of crystals was destroyed after Michael had gotten out, and the one I used on Nikolas burst into flames. There is none left."

"But she pretty much told me she could get her hands on some anytime she wants."

"Do you truly believe my sister would risk getting caught for some crystal?" He placed his hand back on my arm. "I promise you everything will be all right."

"But how do you know?"

"Because you are Rylee Jenkins."

I smiled.

"Well, I guess that'll have to be enough." I paused. "There's something else I wanted to tell you. One of the reasons I didn't teleport to the Manor was because I wanted to see London. I want to leave here. I graduate in December, and you can go to school in your hometown. Being here now and knowing everything is just too much. And maybe Aurora can teach me more about myself. We can move to London if you want. You can live your life and I can live mine. But I think we need a fresh start. Don't you agree?"

"That I do. I was able to graduate early as well. But if that is what you wish, that is what we will do."

When my family died on this bridge, I thought that would be the last time I would come here. But here I was now, for the second time since, and something had changed. What had happened wasn't my fault, but that didn't make the pain hurt any less. We were on high alert for Mara, waiting for her to pop out of nowhere. We had one shot before I had to risk the last thing that mattered to me.

"Where the hell is she?" I asked.

"I was afraid you weren't going to get it," Mara said, stepping out from the trees.

"It wasn't that hard to figure out. Now, where is my brother?"

"Oh, little Damian is right where he needs to be. As long as you give me what I want."

"You'll get what you want. But I just have two questions. The Council?"

"Not dead."

"Good, then one last question. Why tell me the story about you and Michael? It wasn't a lie. I could have turned you in."

Mara laughed. "You always need the answers, don't you? Well, it's simple. I knew my end. You forget, I am also a seer. I know that you're going to win and I'm going to rot in some dark hole for maybe the rest of my life. But I had to help Michael before my reign ended, and that's exactly what I've done."

Mara threw her hands in front of herself, using force to throw us into the railing.

"But I promise you I won't be easy. And *he* can help if he wants to." She gestured to Drake. "But be careful. Wouldn't want anyone to die."

My magic hummed in my veins, and I built a force field around me. The only thing around us were trees and rocks. So, my first choice was a small tree to the left of me. With my mind focused, the tree broke away from the ground and flew toward Mara. She flicked it away as if it were a fly.

"Oh, come on. I taught you better than that."

A dark electric orb rested in Mara's hand. She glowered at me, bouncing the orb between both hands. After a second, she threw it at me. I ducked, missing it by inches, but it smashed my shield to bits. I had to think of something else to get her. She knew every spell I did and more. Then I realized something that Mara had never done. I'd never seen her combine spells, which gave me an idea and hope. Lightning flourished in one hand and flames ignited in the other. I focused my mind on my telekinesis and fused the two elements into a ball.

"Wow, I'm impressed you managed to learn Sphere Magic."

"Oh, you ain't seen nothing yet." I threw the orb as far and as fast as I could. She stopped the orb as I'd expected, but then I took a deep breath and teleported behind her, my lightning ready to go.

"What the—" Mara convulsed on the ground. This was my shot. Drake appeared at my side in a matter of seconds, his body and eyes glowing white. This was it. Mara would be gone forever.

Suddenly both Drake and I flew back across the way. Our bodies collided with the guardrail.

Mara rose with not even a scratch on her. "You're not as smart as you think."

Mara lifted her hand, throwing me into the trees. Blackness shadowed my vision as I gathered myself. I was no match for her. I couldn't let her win. If she couldn't go where Aurora wanted, she could go somewhere else. I rose from the trees and made my way out.

I threw as many flames as I could at her, but she blocked it all and conjured her dark orb. Electricity danced inside of it. I readied myself to stop her, but she appeared behind me, throwing it into my back, sending Lord knows how many volts throughout my body. White spots clouded my vision.

"Are you ready to give me what I want?" she snarled, pulling me up by the hair. Drake ran to stop her, but she held up her hand. "Now, brother, let's not be chivalrous and die."

She formed another dark orb, but the pulse radiating from it wasn't as strong. So, she was going to interrogate me, not kill me, yet. Good to know. She jammed it deep inside me. I screamed out in pain. I couldn't think; it was as if the electricity were rewiring my brain. She pulled the orb from my chest, and the pain dulled, giving my mind space to think again.

"Now, it's time to get the last piece to this mysterious puzzle." Mara's fist rammed into my chest, causing all breath to leave me. "I didn't need Nikolas alive, after all. Not when I could just take his power from him."

"Go to . . . hell," I rasped. I found a small amount of strength inside me to grab her wrist and shock her.

She screamed, jerking her hand from my chest. "You know I don't get it. Why you?" she snarled. "What makes you so special?"

Mara kept her grip on Drake as I tried to regain my thoughts. If I didn't get the upper hand soon, Drake and I would both die. Then I saw the water puddle.

Electricity trailed around my fingers as I dipped them in the water next to her. She jolted, giving me enough time to teleport away.

"I should have done this so long ago," I said from behind her, but when I reached for my locket, it wasn't there.

Mara choked out a laugh. "Always too eager to go." An invisible force shoved me and Drake away from her. I wasn't sure what I would do since I didn't have my locket. I didn't have my extensive power.

"You must find the locket!" Drake yelled. "I will distract her."

"But—"

He turned back to me, fear burning in his eyes. "It must be this way." Drake reappeared near Mara, and his body turned white. "Your time is up. Give up before it is too late."

I ran back to where I'd been thrown by Mara. The sun hit perfectly, shining on the locket just right. When I turned around to tell Drake I'd found it, Mara held a white crystal knife to his chest.

"It's you who is too late, little brother." She laughed. "This knife belonged to our father. He kept it just in case he needed it for you. If you die, Rylee can't open that portal." And with one quick motion, she lodged the knife into his chest.

Drake's body fell lifelessly to the ground. I screamed, throwing Mara hard into the guardrail. My legs nearly buckled. He couldn't die. The heat from his skin burned me as I cradled him in my arms. He seemed so peaceful as if the flames were consuming him from the inside.

"Dammit! This can't be how it ends. I need you. I can't do this without you. There has to be . . . a way . . ." His skin grew hot. I cringed as blisters pebbled on my arms. I had to save him. "I can't . . . can't . . . do this . . ."

I pulled his head to my chest, and with that small gesture, I knew what I could do. I laid Drake gently on the ground. Regardless of what would come after this moment, I at least knew he would be alive.

I jammed my hand into my chest.

"Two halves of one whole."

My heart split in two like Aurora said it would. I reached into his chest to feel for his heart, but it was as if there was a shield around it. I tried keeping his heart in and putting mine with it, but that didn't work. His temperature continued to rise. Had Aurora lied to me too? With no hope left I placed my heart back inside of me. Tears streamed down my face. I waited, but the heat continued to radiate from his body. Only moments remained, then he would be gone forever.

I took him in my arms one last time.

"Goodbye, my wise owl."

I laid Drake's head gently on the ground as I opened my locket. Aurora would have to get Mara to the Omega her own way. Once the locket was open and the portal was ready, I told it to go to the Manor. Mara had awoken to the sound of the portal *swooshing*.

"No! Nooooo!" And before she was thrown into the portal, she threw a dark orb to me. I was too exhausted to try to block it. All at once, Mara was swept away into the portal. Drake's body glowed, and my eyes fluttered closed as the orb struck me down.

35

"Be careful. Boss doesn't want him hurt." A deep, booming laugh stirred me awake. "He's got plans for the boy."

As my blurred vision focused, it only seemed to see the marred and splintered remains of the metal and wood from the chaos Mara and I had caused. But in the daze of gazing, a gray-haired, frail-skinned man stood over Drake's dead body.

"Who are you?" I asked, disoriented.

His gray eyes ripped at me. "It's about time you got up," he snarled in a thick Russian accent. "Thought that spell would keep you out forever."

My eyes shot open as my body jolted up like a spring. When I fell back down from exhaustion, my eyes landed on Drake. His skin was as pale as a ghost. Petrified, I watched the mysterious man come to me, wondering why they were here and what they wanted with Drake's body. Inches from me, the man stopped, folding his arms behind his back.

I climbed to my feet, but in going to grab him, my hand

hit an invisible wall. My eyes catching on the sand nearest my feet. I attempted to kick at it, but it did nothing. A malevolent smirk drew across his face as he laughed.

"My name is Toby."

"What did you do to me?"

"Xavier did. Can't have you stopping us."

The man named Xavier picked up Drake as if he were as light as a feather. I beat at the wall, screaming for him to put Drake down.

Xavier ignored me, but Toby turned back. "I should congratulate you, though. You made things a bit easier for us." Toby's grin nearly ripped his cheeks apart.

"I don't know what you're talking about." Even though I did.

He tutted at me. "I'm surprised Aurora hasn't told you. Such a pity."

Toby leaned in closer to me, yanking my locket from around my neck. "Now, we're going to take Drake and this locket here and be on our way."

"He's dead. So what could you possibly want with him and my locket?" I clutched at the missing space around my neck.

"Oh, he's not dead, dear."

Toby turned back toward Xavier, Drake limp in Xavier's arms. Anger wrestled in my veins. I wouldn't let them take him away. When I looked down, my mouth fell open in surprise. The sand circle that had bound me was broken.

"Let him go!" I screamed.

Holding my hands in front of me, I planned to pull him forward so I could grab Drake. But suddenly, both men fell to their knees, screaming in agony, Drake's body tumbling from Xavier's arms to the ground. I hadn't realized what was happening until I saw their blood-soaked chests.

I was ripping out their hearts.

As much as I wanted them away from Drake, I didn't want to kill them. I had to make them think otherwise. I had to make the fury in my eyes believable. I had to make my words raw. I had to squeeze their chests just a bit tighter.

"Drop the locket and walk away. And never come near my family again. Or so help me, I will rip your hearts out and send them to Michael himself!"

They hesitated, making me add more pressure to their chest. The chilling crunch of their rib cages almost made me hesitate. I only prayed they'd stop before something bad did happen. I'd come too far to stop now.

"Fine! Let go of us!" Toby screamed.

When I did, they ran through the portal and everything fell silent.

Aurora appeared moments after Xavier and Toby left, but Drake was who I cared about at that moment. His skin so cold as if he were made of ice, but the reassurance was hearing him breathe. I watched as his chest rose and fell as Aurora hovered inches from me. How was he alive?

"Aurora, I'm sorry. I failed you. I couldn't get Mara where you wanted."

She held up her hand to stop me. But she didn't look annoyed. "I prepared my people for anything. We were waiting for her in case this didn't go as planned. But we *do* have her. And people will be watching her around the clock until her trial. It's not ideal, but things happen. You tried. That is what matters." She stared down at Drake. "What all happened?"

I still held Drake's head to my chest as I looked at her. I told her everything. How Mara killed Drake and I tried to save him, but it didn't work. And how Toby and his friend tried to take Drake and my locket.

"We'll head back to the Manor."

Drake stirred. I thought I'd never see his sparkling blue eyes again. I also never thought of what his first words would be to me when he awoke, so when I heard them, my heart swelled with something new and beautiful.

"Hello, my phoenix." He smiled.

Aurora helped Drake to his feet. "We must get you to the Orb so you can heal. Remember, all you must do is turn soulless and then the machine will take care of the rest."

Drake nodded as Aurora opened a portal to the rehabilitation room, and we all stepped through.

Aurora had stepped away after we came through the portal, showing Drake and the seemingly new doctor what to do with the machine. Her brow furrowed as she spoke with the doctor, but my mind wandered after a while. Mara was gone. It was over for now. But then I thought about Damian and where he was. That he wasn't dead.

Footsteps came from behind me. Turning around, Aurora was making her way to me.

"Would you follow me please?" she asked, turning away without waiting for my response.

Nothing was said, which made the eerily quiet hallway more daunting. Three men in white lab coats walked past us.

"You must have many questions for me," Aurora said over her shoulder.

I ran to catch up to her. "Yes, but let's get the obvious one out of the way. I think it's time for you to tell me about what's so special about my heart."

"You are a strong witch—that I'm sure you can see—but there is something inside you that makes you even stronger. There is an essence inside of you known as the Suffering."

"Okay, not the best name for a gift, so why do I have it?"

"Every thousand years, the Elders choose one child they

foresee as worthy to possess it. Because of the power that is inside, it can do great harm or great good."

"Why didn't my mom ever tell me about it?"

"As you have learned now, your mother was going after Michael to stop him and his organization. She had to let you and your father believe that she didn't want you in her life because she'd said it was better you hate her than be dead."

"If she wanted us to think that, why didn't she just leave us?"

"So she could still keep an eye on you. When your mother learned of you, she felt something inside her. She went to see a seer. This seer showed her of what you would possess as you got older and what *could* happen if it fell into Michael's hands. So your mother went after Michael to stop him but stayed near you to watch over you."

Hearing this now made me want to cry. All this time I'd thought my mom had hated me. That she'd only cared for other people. When really all she wanted was to protect me. I thought back to one of the last things she'd said that I could remember. That everything she did was because she loved me. And it made sense now. She'd given her life to prove that.

"All this time, when my mom was leaving for charity trips, she was helping you guys?" I said, finally understanding it all.

"Yes, your mother worked as a Fable Hunter, the human equivalence of a bounty hunter. But she was different from Michael, of course. She hunted down criminals and brought them back to us to stand trial."

"Okay, so what does this have to do with my . . . what's it called again?"

"Essence," she repeated. "Liliana believed that Michael would one day go after it because he knows how strong it is. Michael hates Fables, but he still uses our tools."

"Because he's a Fable too. That doesn't make sense."

"You're right, it doesn't."

"So, you figured out that he's after my essence after seeing into Mara's mind?"

"Liliana put a protection spell on Lucas's and your heart just in case."

All this time my mom had loved me. I had been good enough. Good enough that she gave everything she had to save me.

"Aurora, what exactly does my essence do?"

"It can cause unimaginable pain. A feeling worse than death if not controlled." The image of Toby's and Xavier's blood-soaked shirts came to mind. "But," she went on, "you can also take away the pain."

"What do you mean?"

"Have you ever felt as if you wanted to take away someone's pain, and then suddenly something changed about that person? Or have you ever known anyone who should be sad about something but isn't? That they feel as though something just took it away?"

I thought long and hard about her question. I remembered the old man from the food bank. How I wanted that exact thing for him. And he smiled and thanked me. And then how my dad had told me it was like someone took his pain away when he was driving me to first meet Farrah. Then Drake.

"That's why I felt sadder for those people? Because I was taking their pain?"

"Right." Suddenly, a brunette woman in a lab coat ran up to Aurora and whispered something in her ear. "Will you excuse me for a minute?"

"Sure."

Aurora left me in the hallway staring at the pictures on the wall for at least five minutes before she returned.

"I do apologize for that," she said, coming toward me.

"It's fine. So what's up?"

She still didn't look at me. "There's something I must ask you, and I need you to be completely honest with me."

"Okay, what is it?"

"One of my technical team was looking into Drake's blood work to make sure everything was okay, and she found something . . . Have you ever noticed Drake seeming like he's . . ." She turned her focus back to the room again.

"He's what? Tell me what's happening to him."

"It's clear to see you care for Drake. But maybe you shouldn't."

My eyes widened. "What are you talking about? You're all about second chances. Why doesn't he get one?"

"He only survived because of you," she snapped.

"I don't know what that means."

She sighed. Taking a moment to compose herself. "Has he ever told you anything about him needing to be around you?"

A huge lump caught in my throat. "What does that have to do with him surviving?"

"Please answer the question."

"Yes," I huffed. "He told me that I make him feel things. Then he told me when he went to London for a few days, it was like that all went away. Saying that he *needed* to be around me. But I don't see how this has anything to do with why he survived."

She sighed. "There's something else you must know about your essence." She paused. "It makes you immortal because dying is the most unimaginable pain." She didn't turn to the room this time but didn't look at me either. "Drake is siphoning your essence. Like he would take a soul from a victim. He didn't need your heart because he had your essence, well part of it. That is how he was able to survive."

She had to be joking. Drake would never do something so malevolent. "He wouldn't do that."

Her tone softened. "If I'm being honest, I don't think he knows he's doing it."

I exhaled in relief. "So, my essence is healing him?"

"Yes, but it won't stay that way."

"What do you mean?"

"First it will be your essence, then it will be your magic, and lastly it'll be your soul. Which will in the end kill you."

My heart skipped a beat. This wasn't right. There was no way any of this was true. I had to think of something else. Like I was immortal. Sure, I had some good luck because Drake was always there to save me, but there was no way I couldn't die.

"I was stabbed by that crystal." This reminder was more for myself. "I died and saw my mom."

"Did you see the crystal when you awoke?"

"No, Drake said it just disappeared."

"That is because it absorbed into your bloodstream to create an immunity. Think of why you lived that day on the bridge. That day you set your barn on fire. You may not have had full access to your magic, but the essence was still inside of you to protect you. It was a coincidence that Drake was there for most of your incidents, but it was your essence that truly saved you."

Everything she'd said made complete sense. Several times, with or without Drake, I should have died.

I was immortal.

Drake was my best friend. I had to find a way to keep him with me. But also to keep me alive. How could I make him not so dependent on my essence? "How long would it be until he took everything from me?"

Aurora walked with me more down the hallway. "A few months or even a few years. You have to decide now if staying with Drake is worth that risk."

After everything we'd been through, everything we'd learned about each other, I couldn't imagine not having my over-analytical best friend by my side.

"It is. But will you help me find another way to help him?"

Her eyes softened. "My family did this to him. It is the least I can do."

"Then I will stay with him. There has to be another way this can work for both of us."

Someone's footsteps echoed behind me. "Rylee, if I help you, you have to tell him the truth."

I couldn't, but to save both of our lives, I lied.

"I will, just not right this moment." Drake came into view then. "Drake!" I screamed, running to hug him. He winced and I pulled away, blushing. "Sorry."

He smiled. It was so beautiful, so alive. "It is all right. So what did I miss?"

I told him everything but what he was doing to me. Not yet. I hated to keep this from him, but it wasn't doing any harm right now.

"Do you remember me telling you I felt as if I possessed this need to be around you? As if you were healing me in some way?" I nodded. My heart hurt because he had no idea what his words meant. "You are healing me."

Aurora added, "Sadly, you can never fully heal him because that is who Drake is. But it can help his suffering."

I tried to give Drake a believable smile. "I'm so happy." I turned my focus back to Aurora to avoid dwelling on my lie to Drake. "Do you know what happened to my brother, Damian? Is he really alive?"

"Yes. He's with Michael. But I fear that Michael will

corrupt him. You must save him. And that is a question I have. You had to make a portal for them to leave. Do you remember where?"

I couldn't come up with anything. And then I remembered seeing Mara saying something, but I couldn't understand what it was. "I'm sorry, but I don't. I think she erased the location from my mind."

She sighed. "Well, it won't be as easy as we anticipated to get to Michael, but you can do it." There was a hidden meaning lingering in her tone. "I must know if you are truly ready for this. You know everything now and he knows that. What do you want to do?"

I stared at Drake. We'd barely made it out of any of this. Michael would continue to rip everything from me if I didn't stop him, but this had been my fault. Regardless of if I knew who I was letting out of that cage, I had to send him back.

I took in a deep, sharp breath. "I'll go after Michael."

Aurora looked at Drake. "I have an idea. Now both of you, please hear me out before you get upset. Rylee, you said Toby wanted to take Drake when you were at the bridge. We need to let him do it again." Something like acknowledgment settled in her eyes. From the corner of my eyes, Drake's body tensed. Fear branded his eyes. I wanted to know why, but Aurora went on. "You can tell us what's going on, and you, Rylee, can go and get him."

My cheeks flushed. I knew what she was doing. "You're the one who warned us of how dangerous he was. So why the hell would I send Drake after him?"

Drake was the one to answer. "You know this way will work. I promise you I will come back alive. We have to do this. Aurora will protect me."

I looked at Drake. Here in front of me stood another person I cared for, and I was to let them go for the greater good. I needed him here now more than ever. But I couldn't say any of this to him. I didn't want him to find a way to make this his fault and stay.

"We will not let anything happen," Aurora said. I hugged Drake as if he were already gone. "But until that time comes, sweet Rylee, enjoy some parts of life."

"He's not going now?" I asked, relief flooding my words.

"No. Michael holds no threat right now. I will contact you when the time is right." Aurora waved her hands, and a portal appeared.

"Thank yo—" As I pulled away from Drake, my watch caught his sleeve, causing it to rise. Showing his cuff bracelet. But now a slither of white crystal wrapped around it. He'd made it so I couldn't see it this entire time. Though it hurt to know this, I needed to know what that bracelet did. If anyone knew what this was, Aurora would.

"Aurora, do you know anything about this bracelet?"

Drake rotated his wrist so she could see it. Ever so slightly, her eyes widened. But her response said something else.

"It's nothing to worry about." She was clearly lying. I wanted to call her on it, but before I could, someone came into the room. "Rylee, there's two people who would like to meet you before you go."

As I turned, a short skinny woman with snowy blonde hair walked alongside a much taller man with dark-brown hair.

"Hello, Rylee." The man held out his hand for me. "My name is Nathan. Thank you for what you have done for my family."

I couldn't help but stare into his hypnotic golden eyes as I answered, "You're . . . you're welcome."

The woman came next, but she wrapped her arms around me and pulled me close. "Thank you for bringing back my boy."

Again, I didn't know what to say. I wasn't expecting it. "You're welcome . . . too."

Drake brought me in for a sideways hug. "Mother, please do not scare away the one good thing in my life." We all laughed, even Drake. And something about this felt right. Like it was truly the start of something new.

Acknowledgments

As some of you may know, this book has taken me many years to bring to life. And now I am so glad it is! There are many people who have been on this journey. So, my endless thanks go to:

To my editor, Cayce Berryman. I have been through a few editors, but none were like you. I can't even begin to write the words on how grateful I am to have found you. You helped bring "soul" to my story. I can't wait to do this ride again. Thank you so much for all your hard work.

To my two best and oldest friends, Chelsie Lyle, and Candace Shinall. You guys were there from the very beginning when it was just a Twilight knockoff, now it became so much more. Even some of the names and people of this book came from you guys. But most of all, I want to thank you guys so much for supporting me.

To my fans. I know I may not have many of you, but I want to thank you for wanting to come on this journey with me. And what a ride it will be! And I also want to thank my unnamed family and friends. Thank you so much for your support too.

And last but certainly not least, I want to thank my mother-in-love Diane and loving husband Jonathan. Because without both of you, this could have never even happened. To Diane, who was always asking how it was going. To if "I talked to my editor yet?" Thank you for taking the time to care. I love you. To Jonathan, most of this story would never have been thought of if not for you. Thank you for your whiteboard lessons and hours on hours of help and ideas. And thank you most of all for putting up with me for the last seven years it took to write this. You made this story possible. I love you.

About the Author

Ally Marie was born in Georgia where she spent most of her younger years writing and singing. It wasn't until college, moving to Tennessee, did she realize writing was her truest calling. Which is where she lives now with her husband, five dogs, and bird. She thinks of them as her saving grace. If she isn't spending time with her fur babies, family or writing, she can be found with either a book or game controller in her hands. *Destiny of a Fable* is her debut novel.

Ally Marie on social media:
www.instagram.com/am_indie_author
www.facebook.com/allymarieindieauthor
www.tiktok.com/@allymarie0924
www.allymarieindieauthor.weebly.com